A MARK OF THE DIVINE

RUSS BROWN

Copyright © 2011 Russ Brown
All rights reserved.

ISBN: 1461086728
ISBN-13: 9781461086727

ACKNOWLEDGEMENTS

This book is dedicated to all those millions of people who are suffering from lack of employment or underemployment and loss of housing not because they were irresponsible but because of circumstances beyond their control. Don't give up.

I want to express my gratitude to my wife Connie who has supported me all the way on this project and to our six children and their spouses, our thirteen grandchildren and their spouses and our ten great grandchildren. Love You.

My many thanks for the tireless hours expended in making corrections and providing other inputs to bring about the finish of this book that was contributed by my Chief Editor, John R. Kelley. John is a graduate of the University of Iowa, resident of Boone, Iowa, former math teacher, school principal and superintendent, loving husband to his wife and long time partner Netty, grandfather and last but not least, an avid fisherman. John also was fortunate enough to be included in a small fiction writing class while attending the University of Iowa that was taught by American novelist and Academy Award-winning screenwriter John Irving.

A Mark of the Divine

Also my thanks go out to Marie Risner of New Leipzig, N.D. for her contributions in providing some very unique and perspective inputs related to our current situation. Marie works on a ranch in western N.D., and her fresh and delightful approach to life was reflected in her suggestions of how to make A Mark of the Divine a entertaining read.

EPISODE ONE
DISCOVERY AND PREPARATION

CHAPTER ONE
The years of 2012 & 2013

The weather bordered on close to perfect. Luc made a quick observance of the sky. Not a cloud could be seen and there was a true brilliance to its blue color. *The color reminds me of the new dress my daughter will be wearing to her big school event tonight, celebrating her class' graduation. How is it possible, that little Sally will be a seventh grader next year? Time really is a very precious element.*

Lieutenant Colonel Luc McCannon pressed his microphone button "Command Center Air Traffic Control, this is F/A-18 Hornet three zero zero zebra, descending from 3600 feet to low level strafing altitude." "Zero zero zebra you are cleared to strafing altitude."Luc had made several of these runs northwest of Las Vegas, over the sparse Amargosa Desert and flying parallel to Highway 95. He always got a little chuckle as he passed vehicles traveling on the highway. There was usually a shocked look on their faces of the drivers as they looked out the window and did a double take when they saw him in his jet at about telephone wire height bulleting by them. He was close enough for them to get a good visual of his helmeted head in the cockpit.

But today it was Luc's turn to be shocked. *What am I seeing?* Suddenly Luc observed what appeared to be a trench directly under his aircraft. The content of the trench appeared to be water or some other liquid which was giving off a soft glow. The crevice ran in a straight line for several miles. Then it quit just as fast as it had started. *Why haven't I ever seen this trench before when I have made this run?*

Luc immediately pulled the Hornet up and rolled over in a loop bringing the jet back to the beginning of about where he thought the narrow trench started. As he passed over the start of the trench he locked in the coordinates. Passing the end of the trench, a quick press of a switch and the LED registered thirty-three miles from start to finish. *Thirty- three miles long, why did the number thirty-three seem to carry some significance to him and what was that soft golden glow emanating from the trench? The trench almost appeared to be some kind of living organism as it pulsated with that strange light.*

"Command Center, this is F/A – 18 Hornet three zero zero zebra, patch me through to Major Anderson". Almost instantaneously, Anderson's voice came through his ear phones. Luc gave a description of the trench and the coordinates, suggesting someone should drive out and make an 'on-the-ground' inspection. After answering a couple of questions, Major Anderson agreed with Luc, "I'll have a part of our security team on their way within the hour."

Two hours later a team descended upon the southeast end of the trench. Just three hours after that, a baffling document with pictures was handed to the Base Commander, General Josh Jenkins, who in turn placed a phone call to the Pentagon. The information quickly spread to Homeland Security and from there it was passed on to the White House. It didn't take long before a leak to the Press happened, followed by 'breaking news' broadcasts filling the airwaves with this very strange story.

Within twenty-four hours from the time Lieutenant Luc had spotted the trench, which truly was in the absolute middle of nowhere, a steady flow of people started to appear at the site. Included in this parade of the curious were government personnel from what seemed like every state and federal department in existence, plus geologists, theologians, academics, and many other on-lookers including the media.

The trench was quickly dubbed by the press as THE Line in the Sand. What that really meant, obviously no one knew for sure at this point, but it was rapidly becoming a main talking point with media broadcasting networks and talk shows. It seemed to be a prominent topic of conversation wherever two or more people were gathered throughout the United States and around the world. Speculation was rampant as people voiced their opinions while trying to make sense of this new phenomenon.

The trench measured exactly thirty-three miles long and in that entire length, it didn't waver one-tenth of one degree. It was as if someone had a laid a thirty-three mile straight-edge ruler on the desert floor and marked off the distance. Another startling and mysterious fact had to do with the other dimensions of this remarkable trench. Measuring exactly thirty-three inches wide and thirty-three inches deep these dimensions didn't change even a thirty-second of an inch over the entire thirty-three miles. Add to this, the amazing discovery of finding out when a strong wind was blowing the

A Mark of the Divine

sand across the desert, there appeared to be an invisible shield covering the trench. No sand entered the trench so as result of this miracle, the dimensions of the trench did not change.

All of these facts concerning The Line in the Sand plus the soft golden glow which continually emanated from the trench spurred the growing fascination, speculation and arguments over the meaning of this almost eerie wonder of wonders in the Armargosa Desert.

Some had even tried kicking sand into the trench, but the sand would simply migrate off and not enter the trench. Many people came to the conclusion that whatever the intended meaning or whatever it symbolized, THE Line in the Sand, could not have possibly been produced through the efforts of human beings. Therefore the conclusion by most seemed to be that it signified a meaning of some sort which was being communicated to mankind. Therein lay the crux of the speculation. What was this meaning? Was it some kind of urgent message that needed a response?

For Christians, the trench carried an explosive message with a meaning providing a very clear directive. After the sighting Luc, a devout Christian himself, could not get the picture of that trench out of his mind. He was even having dreams about it at night. In his own mind Luc came to the conclusion that God must be getting a little more than just upset with the way things were progressing in the United States and around the world. Luc concluded that God had drawn His own line in the sand.

Luc concluded this was His way of sending a message to the people of the world and really getting their attention. To Luc's way of thinking the world was on a slippery slope to hell. The moral base of America seemed to be deteriorating quite rapidly and without a strong moral base everything else we did would always be on very shaky ground at best. If that was the case, he thought God put that trench out there to see if the people were smart enough to not only interpret its meaning, but to also act on that meaning. In Luc's mind, this was a potent message to His people to shape up!

Based on the results of this past November's election, Luc predicted to himself that we would become a completely socialistic Country within a couple of years. In his opinion, this might also account for the timing of the trench's appearance.

The time when Luc could take early retirement from the Air Force wasn't far off, and it was something he would have to consider soon. As a single dad and raising a young daughter he had to prioritize his own thinking and direction in such a way that he could give his daughter as much guidance as possible.

CHAPTER TWO

Greeting Robert as he arrived at their appointed place to meet, Ben said, "You look a little troubled today brother." As identical twins, Ben and Robert were not surprised at the glances from other patrons in the restaurant. In fact it was phenomenal how 'identical' they truly were. Since grade school, the similarity was very obvious to their parents, teachers and close friends. Both boys, physical and mentally, were totally in sync with each other.

Robert and Ben were six foot two, had broad shoulders, and were very athletic and very athletic looking. Their sandy brown hair and sky blue eyes along with their high cheek bones, straight noses and rather square jaws gave them that 'Marlboro Man' look. All they needed to complete the rugged cowboy image was to be sporting cowboy hats. Of course as part-time ranchers in western North Dakota, they naturally owned cowboy hats. Larger demands than their Ranch, were the commitments they each made to the individual and extremely successful law professions they pursued with extreme vigor.

Tragedy struck the O'Neil family in December when the boys were in sixth grade. In a split second, their lives changed forever. Jim and Nancy O'Neil were returning to their home in McCook, Nebraska, when they ran onto an invisible patch of ice. Jim apparently had barely touched his brakes; however that was enough to cause their car to spin out of control. It collided head-on with an eighteen-wheeler going in the opposite direction.

Pastor Jake and Jane Johansen, life-long friends of the O'Neils, took the boys into their home and became their guardians until they both enlisted in the Army after high school graduation. They were very lucky to have their early lives in such capable hands after their parents were killed. Jake and Jane finished what the boys parents had started, molding them like clay into very fine young men. Sadly, the same year the boys went into the Army, Pastor Jake and his wife Jane were also killed in a car accident! Fate had dealt the boys a pretty hard blow with the loss of two sets of parents before they reached the age of twenty.

After basic training they were granted internships at their Army base's Judge Advocate General's office. The unusual decision to assign such duty to untrained lawyers was based on their high academic achievements in high school and their profound interest in law. Their military bearing and appearance may have also weighed heavily in their favor. At the beginning of the Gulf War Ben and Robert were assigned to Iraq. They were frequently engaged in combat missions and their leadership abilities became well known. They were both awarded the Silver Star for their tenacity, bravery and concern for their fellow man.

Following their stint in the service, Ben and Robert continued their march toward careers in law. Armed with grants, veteran's pay for school and part-time jobs in hand, Ben and Robert went their separate ways for the first time in their young but already high-achievement lives. Ben attended Law School at the University of Michigan and Robert attended School at Kansas State University and majored in Law.

For almost twenty years following their graduations, both men distinguished themselves on many fronts: Robert, as a federal appellate judge and Ben as a highly recognized Corporate attorney. Robert lived out at their Ranch in western North Dakota and Ben lived in Wisconsin. Although they lived quite a distance apart, they made a pact many years ago to meet once every other month. It was a ritual they both enjoyed. They would always meet at different places, one picking the spot one time and the other the next.

Robert was hosting this month's get-together and waited for Ben in a far corner booth in the little Italian restaurant. When he saw Ben approaching, a big smile crossed his face and the frown disappeared. "You looked pretty serious or in very deep thought when I came in," Ben commented as he slid into the booth. "For the moment, let's just say that I was deep in thought", Robert said.

Robert was the married brother and Ben the single one. Ben's wife of less than a year had passed away tragically and quite swiftly after being diagnosed with cancer. It had devastated Ben to the point where, other than an occasional low key date, he seemed numb to the idea of even considering a serious relationship.

Like clones because of their identical good looks, these two rugged and extremely handsome men continued to draw plenty of stares when they were together. Today was no exception, as many of the restaurant patrons had a hard time avoiding a stare at the two of them, but Ben and Robert took it in stride and were generally quite oblivious to their surroundings.

A Mark of the Divine

"Ben said, "Who is this mysterious visitor that we are supposed to meet with today?" "Sorry," Robert said, "to be so closed lipped about this, but those were my instructions. You will be finding out the answers ......" Robert was stopped in mid sentence as a woman in a baseball cap pulled low over her forehead, wearing dark glasses, jeans and a non-descript plaid wool shirt, slipped into the booth next to Ben.

"Hello Robert, Ben." There was a complete silence for a few seconds, as even Robert was momentarily unable to identify the lady who had so suddenly joined them, and then a grin appeared on his face as recognition hit home. Ben was still in the dark. "General Elizabeth Taylor, what a pleasure!" Roberts's voice had dropped close to a whisper as Elizabeth put her finger to her lips to signal Robert to keep his voice low. Ben did a double take and then reached over gave her a hug saying, "I can't believe it," Ben said. Elizabeth responded, "I know you must have a whole plane load of questions, so I'll dispense with a lot of the chit chat. But I'll give you a brief update on my personal life and I'd appreciate it if you guys would do the same."

Except for an occasional email or a short phone call from Elizabeth over the last many years, Robert and Ben had had minimal contact with her. Robert and Ben had led a recue mission that successfully brought Elizabeth back to their headquarters after her jet had been shot down. During her convalescence, all three of them had become very good friends. At the time, now Brigadier General Taylor was a Lieutenant in the air force and considered to be one of the top pilots involved in the Gulf war.

Over the next half-hour a quick run down of all their personal lives were discussed. Then very abruptly, Elizabeth turned the conversation to the business at hand. "Ben, Robert, so you know, I haven't dressed in this kind of attire since I graduated from high school and was accepted into the Air Force Academy. It is extremely important that we are not identified with each other and I will tell you why."

"I am one of thirty people who make up a 'think tank' that continually assess the stability of our Country and it's relationships with other Countries around the world. We have no name and no outside identity. Not even any of our Countries Presidents have been privy to our existence. When we determine need for a certain direction, we do what I am doing with you right now. We make a contact, lay out our desires and then fade back into oblivion. I wish I could tell you who the other twenty-nine people are, you would be very impressed, but unfortunately that is not possible. Let it suffice to say that they come from wide variety of disciplines and are considered to be among the best in their fields."

Ben interrupted saying, "If you represent the military Elizabeth, then the quality of your group must be exceptional and that probably is an understatement." "Thank you Ben."

Elizabeth continued, "This, I am sure will really catch you off guard, but our group is making a huge request of you. Your selection came after weeks upon weeks of deliberation as to who might have the knowledge, the tenacity and courage to move our request to reality. We are asking that you give very serious consideration to leaving your chosen and very successful careers and head down a completely different path." Ben was just taking a drink of water and at Elizabeth's remark he choked and spewed water all over the table. Then he said, "At the ripe old age of thirty-nine, don't you think we're a little young to retire, even though we probably could financially?!" Her reply was a simple, "No."

Elizabeth's statement set the tone for the rest of their get-together. They stayed glued to their seats, engaged in a very intensive and concentrated conversation, hardly aware of their surroundings, for five straight hours. Finally after agreeing they had pretty much consumed all their ideas, Robert and Ben decided some time was needed to contemplate and assimilate everything they had talked about. Elizabeth passed a slip a paper with a telephone number on it, "Ben, Robert, please call me within forty-eight hours with your decision, after that time period this phone number will not exist." She then slipped out of the booth and disappeared.

"I am sure glad I didn't miss out on this meeting today!" Ben chided his brother. Another two hours was spent coming to a conclusion; than they parted company with an initial agreement and a preliminary plan of action in place. Procrastination was a word that had never been in either's vocabulary since day one, so initiating immediate action was doing what came naturally.

As Ben and Robert left the restaurant, they embraced, slapped each other on the back and separated. The trigger that launched their total life changing direction as purposed by Elizabeth was the phenomenon the press had so quickly dubbed 'THE Line in the Sand'. In fact it also prompted the brothers to recognize in themselves the realization they could no longer just verbalize the dire situation which had been developing for quite some time in the United States. It was time for them to take action.

CHAPTER THREE

Ben and Robert gave themselves a month to tie up loose ends and shut down their practices. At that point, they would be free to move forward with a hundred percent effort on their new quest.

Then for five straight months they labored doggedly and vigorously, shaping their new mission and the Corporation that would be the mantle piece for their bold and daring endeavor. They had decided to name their new Corporation, A Mark of the Divine. In the history of the United States, nothing had ever been tried that even came close to paralleling this daring and gigantic effort. Their stunning game plan would no doubt cause ripples of enthusiasm throughout the land as they pushed forward. At the same time it would generate hate and contempt in many sectors. But both Robert and Ben felt an inner thrust catapulting them in this new direction. They were confident and determined to develop a successful plan of action.

As they began to shape their plan, Robert said, "Our first efforts need to define the 'who', 'what', 'why', 'when' and 'where' of our direction. Who will be targeted and what will be provided by A Mark of the Divine, need to be addressed first and the answer to these particular questions will be our 'launch pad'." "That also is in line with the parameters suggested by General Elizabeth and her group."

"Alright," Ben stated, "first off we are providing an alternative direction to those people whose current situations require intervention. These alternatives will include villages which are a safe haven from religious persecution with freedom to worship and pray. This in itself will be a big motivator for a lot of people. These safe havens will also be sanctuaries from terrorist confrontations and abuses. Children will be freed from the exposure to the gangs which are terrifying them in so many schools and on the streets. This will be another motivator for parents to relocate. Adequate lodging will be a big motivator that will be high on the list, due to the financial devastation of so many who have lost their homes or are in jeopardy of this happening and have a desperate need for adequate housing of their own.

An alternative to the current form of public education will be a must. Many are fed up with the public schools and the kind of education their children are receiving. Excellent educational opportunities thru exemplary home schooling, complimented with highly selected Internet support, will motivate many to seek residence in one of the villages.

Then of course there are a tremendous number of people who have honestly and with persistent determination been trying to find job opportunities and have failed. They have failed through no fault of their own but because of the economic situation and the hiring freeze by so many companies. These folks will be very motivated to seek a new way of life and an environment that will be conducive to creating a decent way of life for themselves and their families.

"Alright," Robert said, that's a pretty good start on the 'who' and the 'what' this mission entails. "The 'why' we are doing this, in addition to those items already mentioned, relates to the devastating employment numbers, a melt down of the housing market and an accelerated tax mania on the part of the Federal Government. All of this is destroying the entrepreneurial spirit of America while at the same time moving more and more people into poverty." "That's a good short definition of the 'why', Ben stated.

"The 'when' would have to be defined as our plan being fully operational as soon as is humanly possible," Ben said. "Because there is no precedent for what we are doing, establishing time lines will be hard, but still I think we should set up target dates for certain things to be accomplished." "Agreed," Robert said, "plus we have to keep in mind what the General said as it relates to the urgency of the mission."

"The 'where' we have defined as the Great Plains States and many adjoining states who want to join in this effort," Ben said. Villages will be established on farms and ranches spread from the Canadian border in the north to the Mexican border in the south."

"There is another gigantic aspect of our mission which the two of us must address," said Robert. Assuming events continue in the direction they are currently going, and we get closer and closer to becoming a completely Socialist Country, a huge need for counter measures to that direction emerges. In order for that to be achieved, it will probably require a catalyst for action by the governors in the Great Plains and surrounding states to form a coalition. We will likely be that catalyst. Eventually this coalition will most likely determine that their only alternative is to break from the United States and form a separate Country," Robert declared. Ben sucked in a gulp of air and squared his shoulders a little before exclaiming, "Sounds like we are going to have to lengthen out our days a bit big brother."

CHAPTER FOUR

Five months from the time when Ben and Robert began this life-changing mission, Ben was in Chicago standing off to the side as approximately 250 Rotarians and guests filed into their luncheon meeting room. They were greeted with this wonderful and meaningful song:

AMERICA THE BEAUTIFUL
Words by Katharine Lee Bates,
O beautiful for spacious skies,
For amber waves of grain,
For purple mountain majesties
Above the fruited plain!
America! America!
God shed his grace on thee
And crown thy good with brotherhood
From sea to shining sea!

O beautiful for pilgrim feet
Whose stern impassioned stress
A thoroughfare of freedom beat
Across the wilderness!

A Mark of the Divine

America! America!

God mend thine every flaw,
Confirm thy soul in self-control,
Thy liberty in law!

O beautiful for heroes proved
In liberating strife.
Who more than self their country loved
And mercy more than life!
America! America!
May God thy gold refine
Till all success be nobleness
And every gain divine!

O beautiful for patriot dream
That sees beyond the years
Thine alabaster cities gleam
Undimmed by human tears!

America! America!
God shed his grace on thee
and crown thy good with brotherhood
from sea to shining sea!

O beautiful for halcyon skies,
For amber waves of grain,
For purple mountain majesties
Above the fruited plain!
America! America!

Russ Brown

God shed his grace on thee
Till souls wax fair as earth and air
And music-hearted sea!

O beautiful for pilgrims feet,
Whose stem impassioned stress
A thoroughfare for freedom beat
Across the wilderness!
America! America!
God shed his grace on thee
Till paths be wrought through
wilds of thought by pilgrim foot and knee!

O beautiful for glory-tale
Of liberating strife
When once and twice, *for* man's avail
Men lavished precious life!
America! America!
God shed his grace on thee
Till selfish gain no longer stain
The banner of the free!

O beautiful for patriot dream
That sees beyond the years
Thine alabaster cities gleam
Undimmed by human tears!
America! America!
God shed his grace on thee
Till nobler men keep once again
Thy whiter jubilee!

A Mark of the Divine

After all were seated, Ben was introduced by the Rotarian National President, and he came to the podium. Ben thanked the President for inviting him to speak. He then began to explain his reason for attending the meeting.

"Recognizing that everybody is on a tight schedule, this will be a rather abbreviated presentation about a matter which I hope many of you will eventually consider embracing."

"Please enjoy your meal and if you don't mind in the essence of time, since many of you need to be at your place of work by around one o'clock, I'll make my presentation while you eat. As you entered the room just now you were greeted by a very famous and wonderful song 'America the Beautiful'. The words in this song, in many respects, underline what I want to talk about today."

"First let me further introduce myself and the mission that I represent. I, like you, am a professional. For many years, I was engaged as an independent attorney in corporate America. Approximately five months ago, I left my profession as did my twin brother who was a very prominent appeals court judge. We had both arrived at the decision to make an abrupt change in the direction of our professional lives. Our intent is to dedicate the rest of our working lives to a mission for which we both feel there is an urgent and necessary need to accomplish. We have determined that the time has arrived for us to stand on those principles we have lived by and totally believed in all of our adult lives. We know we can no longer just give lip service to an ever growing slate of national problems, but rather we had to move ourselves into an action mode which will work toward the correction of the consequences caused by all of these problems. I should also mention, lest you think we are acting solely on just our own beliefs, that we were originally recruited by an extremely prestigious 'think tank' group. Unfortunately, I am not at liberty to disclose any names. We were approached and asked if we would be willing to switch all our energy an resources to spearhead a monumental movement that would eventually more than offset the hole we as Americans had dug. Naturally, this was a rather earth shaking request, but we eventually accepted the challenge.

"About all I can do today is to give you the 'why' we are doing what we are doing. I think most of you can relate to and accept the idea of that old, wise and very profound statement which simply states *we can only serve one master*, and most of us recognize where that piece of wisdom comes from. Using this important principle as to how so many of us believe we are to conduct our lives, my brother and I formed a corporation to help anchor our mission. Although for all practical purposes the organization will function as a nonprofit corporation, it wasn't formed in that manner simply because we did not want to go through all the hoops of government compliance and interference." "The name of the corporation is A Mark of The Divine, Inc."

"As you might have guessed, THE Line in The Sand, that now extremely famous trench discovered awhile back in the Nevada desert, served as an important part of the springboard which only launched our decision to move forward. In fact it will probably always serve as an important stimulant to us. Its perceived message played a major role in our decision to form A Mark of the Divine. We are convinced, as are most leading theologians and Christians; this trench which appeared in the Amargosa Desert a few months ago is a reminder from God, a reminder that the teachings of His son, who was brutally murdered for the benefit of all mankind, are not being followed in this country.

As we know Jesus was thirty-three years old at the time of His crucifixion. We believe that is the significance of the dimensions of the trench, thirty-three miles long, thirty-three inches wide and thirty-three inches deep. We believe this trench has appeared as a call to action for His people here on earth. We also feel the timing of this appearance seemed to be very significant in the face of the strong movement in our Country to put down Christianity, Judaism and any other religion whose beliefs are centered on God. At no time in the history of America has this threat been more prevalent than it is today."

Ben held up a relatively large drawing and said, "This is our corporate emblem. You will notice above the cross in a separate writing is our corporate name. There are four major elements to our mission which have been matched to the four points of the Cross. At the top you see CHRISTIANITY, at the bottom you see FREEDOM, on the left point of the Cross you see LIMITED GOVERNMENT, and on the right point HONEST & STRONG LEADERSHIP. When you become a shareholder in A Mark of the Divine, you will receive a smaller version of this corporate symbol."

"The mission of the corporation, simply stated, is to provide a platform which will accommodate a huge base of what we refer to as 'everyday American Christians'. In addition, it also will include all Americans of faith who recognize our Christian and Jewish God. A Mark of the Divine will be made up of people from all faiths who recognize that it is our duty as human beings to respect life, to be honest, to be caring, hard working citizens of these United States and willing to stand up and fight for our religious freedom.

"As shareholders in A Mark of the Divine, you will have the opportunity to be provided a very profound alternative as far as a way of life, should this be your desire and or need. Shareholders who wish to move to one of the thousands of what we call Villages that will be constructed over the next years will have that opportunity. All of this will be explained in the information packet you will receive when the meeting is over."

"A Mark of the Divine also has to do with how we see America in terms of the Constitution, how we see America in terms of individual freedom, how we see America in terms of 'In God We Trust', how we see America in terms of unbiased education. These are some of the basic principles that will define the shareholders of A Mark of The Divine, Inc."

"We believe that as 'everyday Christians and other people of faith', we can no longer let the radical and powerful super minority, whom I might add are moving closer and closer to being the majority, dictate the direction of our Country via unethical, immoral and in many cases downright criminal tactics. We cannot stand by any longer and let the non-Christian and non-religious segments of our society who are anti-family, anti-freedom and anti-God, be the voice that rises above all others, dictating that our America should be one hundred and eighty degrees from our Constitution and religious values." Ben was a little surprised as the entire audience came to its feet and applauded loudly.

When things settled down Ben continued. "We cannot stand by any longer and let this group, including so many in the Halls of Congress, in the White House and throughout our justice systems, drive actions that thwart Christianity and other faith-based segments of society.

In our opinion, the checks and balances of our two party system have been relegated to the status of a wounded giant. We are no longer, as 'everyday American Christians and other people of 'faith' being adequately represented by anybody in our Government. True faith leadership in government has and is diminishing at an alarming rate."

"Just one more thought and then I'll have time to take a few questions. There are two huge segments of our society who we believe are ultimately responsible for a lot of the damage that has taken place in our Country. One of these segments is composed of people who for one reason or another are total 'followers' or are in the category of being influenced only by 'dazzle'. They are people who have no moral foundation or conviction. They are people who really do not understand what it is to have values and to stand up for those values. They are also people who are either politically lazy or just don't care and if they even bother to vote, they cast their ballots for all the wrong reasons. It is understandable given the character and values of so many in governmental offices, that people would become disgusted and discouraged enough to not care, but that should not be an excuse to not stand up for what is right."

"The other segment is made up of a group that has grown in leaps and bounds here in the United States in the past few years. These people are those who hate us as Americans and particularly Christian Americans, and whom they call infidels. You may be aware of this quote, and it seems very appropriate at this time. Benjamin Franklin said: '**Only a virtuous people are capable of freedom. As nations become more** corrupt and vicious, they have more need of masters.' When you think about these powerful words, it certainly gives one pause."

"A lot of people are easily and unwittingly lead down a path that has the tremendous potential of eventually destroying their lives or imprisoning them in 'no win' situations. These consequences might relate to a state of poverty or something even less desirable. "In other words folks, this Country has arrived at a point in time, where we are either going to trade in our beliefs for everything that goes against our whole being, or we are going to make the determination to stand firm in what we believe and act on those beliefs."

Ben's last statement brought about a big round of applause. "Okay, I realize this is a pretty sketchy presentation of what A Mark of the Divine is about. However, as you leave today, you will be handed our Corporate Packet that among other things contains a DVD which will explain and answer most of your questions. We hope you will give serious consideration to becoming shareholders and join us in standing tall for our moral beliefs and our Constitutional rights, I will be taking applications following our meeting."

"I can take two questions now. Yes, the gentleman with that nice checkered tie (that brought a little chuckle from the group), I think your name tag says Tom?" "Thank you. Yes, my name is Tom and incidentally, I love this tie." Again this brought a laugh from the group and helped lighten things up a bit.

"My question is, what is the procedure for involvement and what commitment does it entail as far as it pertains to the mission of the Corporation?"

A Mark of the Divine

"That's getting right to the heart of the matter Tom, thanks for that question. This is all explained in the DVD you will be getting, but let me summarize.

1. You become a partner in our corporation by buying a minimum of one share at $25.00. Your involvement needn't go any further than just being a shareholder and thus a partner in our endeavor. Being a shareholder you will want to keep yourself abreast of the activities taking place within the Corporation and hopefully, you will encourage others who are like-minded to join our group. By late winter or early spring we will be in a position to launch a new and exciting direction for the shareholders that is totally unprecedented in the history of our Country.

2. Naturally, we would hope that you would get involved in making presentations to folks, just as I am doing with you today. I should mention that although we just launched this program less than a month ago, we already have over two hundred thousand members. We are not doing any advertising; all recruitment is by personal presentation and word of mouth. My brother Robert calls our process, mouth to mouth resuscitation.

We will be communicating with our shareholder partners by email and by regular mail. All extremely sensitive material will be sent by regular mail. Unfortunately our group will attract extremists who would like nothing better than to terminate this movement and will use any method they can to destroy us.

As I mentioned, you will get a much more complete answer to Tom's question in the DVD you will be receiving. Alright, one more quick question."

Ben nodded to the lady holding up her hand off to his right, noticing that her name tag said Amber. In a short moment of mental distraction, he was taken by the fact that her name and the color of her hair were certainly a match. A thought struck him from somewhere that the word amber is the symbolic color for the spiritual energy of God. He hoped that the time lapse which took place before answering her was so short she didn't think he was staring at her. "What is your question Amber?" She had noticed the delay in Ben's acknowledgement and for some reason it caused a low voltage jolt to her system. "I guess my question would be a follow-up to your answer to the previous question. What kind of personal danger to us as partners would you anticipate might be present?"

"That is a difficult question to accurately answer. Let me frame it this way. First, I think if you are a Christian or a Jew and you stand firm on your values, whether you become a partner in A Mark of the Divine or not, as time moves on your life will not be anything like it has been in America in the past. What I am trying to say is that life in America is going to become more and more dangerous as time goes on, regardless of what we do. We feel, given the deterioration in America, compared to how we once knew it, there is just cause to be very concerned about our future as Christians and also for the Jewish and other people of faith. I am sure that many of you have already experienced firsthand the persecution of those who hold to their religious beliefs.

A Mark of the Divine

The chances are becoming very high that sometime in the future, and perhaps not so far in the future, all people who are willing to stand up for God will most likely be subjected to some form of religious terrorism. We are assuming we will continue to see radical factions of such groups as atheists, Muslims, plus hate groups and many other secular segments of our society continue to grow in strength and in their hatred of Christians, Jews and any other people of faith. Also we think that this hatred will be fed like kindling on a fire from an influential segment of federal government and our federal justice system."

"Second, if you become a partner in A Mark of the Divine by becoming a shareholder, the degree of personal danger will most likely elevate in proportion to how active you are within our movement. Your risk could parallel your level of activity. I really wish I could express a more positive response to your question Amber, but that's my honest opinion and it really hits at the basis for A Mark of The Divine, Inc."

Thank you so much for your patience and attentiveness. I hope many of you will join us in our mission to fully establish and positively identify what we hope will be the strongest and most unwavering population in terms of moral and Constitutional belief in the United States. I will be sticking around here for awhile if there are any of you who would like to visit with me and have the time to do so. God bless you." As one, the entire group was immediately on its feet and giving a thunderous applause.

Ben spent two more hours visiting with a number of the attendees, fielding their questions and discussing the direction of A Mark of The Divine. As it turned out, Amber was among those who stayed and was a big part of the very spirited discussion.

As Ben stepped outside, he stopped and inhaled deeply. He wished he had time to go for a run. He was really energized and needed to peel off some of that energy with a good physical workout of some kind. Just as Ben started to move he was spun around and fell over a pot of flowers near where he had been standing. He felt a severe pain like his shoulder was on fire. Ben had apparently passed out because when he regained consciousness, he discovered he was in a hospital. As he was examining the bandages on his shoulder the doctor came into this room. "Glad to see you are awake and looking fairly alert. "Dr. Healer," he said as he introduced himself, "and it isn't necessary to make any brilliant remarks about my name. " "Glad you said that, since I was just about ready to spout something quite apropos," Ben said with a grin. "You were one lucky dude, Mr. O'Neil, if that bullet had wandered another inch to the right we wouldn't be talking."

"Thanks for patching me up Doc, I guess the good Lord still wants to keep me around and has some more work for me to do. Which reminds me, at some time in the future Doc, you might want to seriously consider becoming a shareholder in our Corporation, A Mark of the Divine. I see that my briefcase was brought in with me. If you like, just reach in there and take one of the folders which also contains a DVD explaining our purpose and our direction. When you get the time, take a look at the information. It could be something that might be of interest to you." "I will do that Ben. I have heard rumors of your corporation and some of the amazing things that you have planned." "The only negative I see at this point", the doc said with a grin, "is that as I look at you, this doesn't seem to be a very safe direction you are asking me to take!"

In spite of the 'incident' with Ben, A Mark of the Divine was now launched and over the following weeks sign ups were off the charts, and recruitment of people to put on meetings was growing exponentially at an unbelievable rate.

Meanwhile, other events were also moving at an astonishing rate. The federal justice system which was now loaded with liberal judges was continuing to hand down decision after decision which kept peeling away freedoms belonging to States as well as individuals.

CHAPTER FIVE

Ben's thoughts were interrupted as he glanced out the window and saw a large herd of antelope grazing on some pasture land far to the east. His eyes automatically searched the horizon for the Sentinel, the lone antelope off by himself ready to sound the alarm if danger approached. *Mother Nature, Ben* thought to himself, works *in mysterious and wonderful ways.*

Sandy came whipping into the room, "Ben, Robert just called and he'll be flying into the ranch by late afternoon. Everything had been going extremely well and he's bringing in one of the people who is working for us full-time putting on seminars. She said she had met you at the seminar where you got shot. Robert said her name is Amber, and he felt she was already an extremely valuable asset to the Corporation and our efforts. We'll put her in one of the guest cabins. It's going to be nice to have another female here for awhile," Sandy said.

Ben got up from the desk where he had been working and rotated his arm. Sandy noticed him flexing his arm and said, "How are you doing? Do you think we should do some more therapy on the arm?" "No thanks Sandy. You have worked your magic extremely well. I think I am at about ninety-eight percent healed. By the way aren't you glad you finally have a physical mark which identifies me when compared to Robert? Now you don't have to worry about who you are sleeping with," Ben said with a big grin on his face, as he side-stepped a pan that was flying at him.

Ben's thoughts turned to the wonderful relationship the three of them had. Robert's wife Sandy was a blessing in so many ways. They all were so compatible and their children adored their Uncle Ben. On top of everything else Sandy was a very capable nurse and had really helped get his health back after he had been shot. Ben knew he had been lucky since the Doc had told him how close the bullet came to ending his life. Until recently he hadn't known the investigation had determined there had been two shots fired at him and the second shot must have just missed him as he stumbled over the flower pot and fell. The fact that he had just started to move when the bullet struck him probably saved his life.

Ben wandered out to the big deck that wrapped around Roberts and Sandy's house, it was a gorgeous day. He plopped down in one of the chairs to relax while enjoying the weather and the cool breeze. His thoughts turned to the ranch they had bought together a few years ago and all the work they had put into it since then. Now Robert, Sandy and the kids had a nice big log house that served them well. Ben and Robert had built four small guest houses which were also made of log, one of which Ben occupied. He felt he really didn't need anything any bigger since he was single and traveled a lot.

On their 'things to do' list was a plan to build four more guest cabins in the very near future. Now that The Mark of The Divine Corporation was in full gear, it seemed they were continually receiving guests. Also they had converted one of the guest houses into their Corporate Offices, and it looked like they would definitely have to expand that office space. That would leave only two for guests.

Ben thought of what Sandy said about Robert bringing in a guest who was now working for the Corporation full-time as a presenter. He remembered meeting her at the Rotary meeting in Denver and he recalled the little jolt he felt when he first talked to her. Smiling, he realized he had not been affected like that by a woman for many years. It was shortly after she and the others had left the question and answer session when disaster struck, and he was hit by a bullet that found its mark.

Ben had put on hundreds of meetings and met literally thousands of people as he criss-crossed the United States. *Amazing,* he thought *that she should be so clearly etched in his mind from just one encounter.*

The O'Neill's ranch, nestled up against the Theodore Roosevelt National Park in the Badlands of western North Dakota, was proving to have been a great investment. Prior to the time the purchase was made, several states were scoured trying to find what Ben and Robert thought would be the right kind of ranch property for them to purchase. At that time there was no thought nor did they ever visualize they would be doing what they were now completely involved with. In hind sight, Ben couldn't help wondering if there was some divine guidance involved back when they made their decision to purchase the property. Their cow-calf operation had grown steadily and been very profitable. They always felt fortunate and blessed to have Big Joe Walker as their ranch foreman. He was worth his weight in gold.

A Mark of the Divine

Apparently I have been sitting out here and daydreaming for a lot longer than I realized, Ben thought to himself as he heard the hum of the little Cesena's engine. He saw Robert bring the plane in over the top of the trees and neatly set it down on their small grass runway.

Ben and Robert gave each other a big bear hug. Robert turned to his passenger and said, "Ben this is Amber, our guest for a long weekend." "I certainly remember Amber," Ben said. Another little jolt of electricity seemed to pass through Amber as they shook hands and greeted each other. Robert said "Come on let's head up to the house so you can meet Sandy and the kids. Then Ben will show you to your guest house where you can freshen up before supper.

As they made their way to the big log house at the other end of the ample yard, Amber was very impressed with the neatness of everything. It seemed to make the statement that this was a very big and successful operation. Ben said, "Amber, if you don't mind my asking, how did it come about Amber that you left what I assume was a successful career and decided to join our efforts full-time?"

"After I left the Rotary meeting where you made the presentation on A Mark of the Divine, and then read about your being shot, I decided there wasn't anything more important in my life than to, in some small way, help magnify your efforts."

Ben recognized what a powerful statement Amber just voiced and was quite taken by her comment. "Let me just say that we are extremely grateful Amber, for your unselfish and exemplary commitment and thank you so much for joining us." Amber's cheeks colored slightly from Ben's comments.

CHAPTER SIX

The evening's dinner had been devoured; the conversation had been light and peppered with laughter. Sandy and Amber instantly hit it off and were in the process of putting the kitchen back in order. Afterward, they joined the guys in the great room where they were engaged in a discussion about the ranch operations.

As Amber and Sandy settled on a couch next to the men, Amber said "Could I ask a little more about how all this got started?" Robert responded, "About two-and-a-half years ago a document was produced by one hundred twenty-five Christian religious leaders across the U.S. It was called the Manhattan Declaration: A Call of Christianity."

"The underlying theme was to urge all Christians to remain unwavering in their Christian convictions and in the face of all the cultural and political obstructions being advanced against their beliefs."

"You know, when you think about it, that is really a strong statement," Amber said. "I wonder how many people have thought about the implications of remaining unwavering in their Christian convictions when adversity knocks on their door? Especially if physical harm might come into play; few people living in the United States have ever been faced with the scenario of either compromising their faith or facing physical harm or abuse. Do you think that type of scenario would substantially reduce the number of those who call themselves Christians? I would expect this kind of scenario is going to test a lot of people's faith." "You have that right Amber," Ben said, "and I would hate to venture a guess as far as your question is concerned."

"Sorry to interrupt, Robert," said Amber. Robert replied "No problem, your point is very well taken. Anyway, Ben, Sandy and I looked at this document like it was a breath of fresh air. We thought it was a tremendous and courageous act for Christian leaders from many denominations to link arms so to speak against all that was happening."

"To give you an idea of how solid and powerful this document was, here is what was stated in part: 'We will not comply with any edict that purports to compel our institutions to participate in abortions, embryo-destructive research, assisted suicide and euthanasia, or any other anti-life act. Nor will we bend to any rule purporting to force us to bless immoral sexual partnerships, to treat them as marriages or the equivalent, or refrain from proclaiming the truth as we know it about morality and immorality and marriage and the family.'"

At last a Christian-based movement was actually drawing their own line in the sand and standing up to the Federal Government as well as all factions or segments of society whose goals were to water down or completely snuff out Christianity. Sandy and I spent hours discussing this," Robert said, "and it really was another spark that started our fire smoldering."

"That is an amazing story, and what a statement it makes about the three of you. I truly am honored to be a part of your team," Amber stated with a real note of pride in her voice. "Thank you for those kind words and I am sure I can speak for all three of us in saying that the feeling is mutual," Ben said.

Sandy spoke up and asked Amber if she would tell a little bit about herself. "From the little bit I have heard about you, it certainly sounds like you have had a very interesting career."

Amber said, somewhat embarrassed, "I'll try to give you a brief summary of my work and keep it from being boring! As it pertains to my profound interest in A Mark of the Divine, I think it was born out of the 'pro-bono' work, as you lawyers call it, that I have gotten involved with over the last couple of years."

"As you know, I have been in the business consulting business for most of my working career. Somehow, and I am still not sure how, I seemed to get pulled into doing work for single women who either had children to care for or were just living alone, but were in deep trouble financially with no apparent way of avoiding living on the streets. Sandy asked, "Aren't there shelters that women who get into this kind of a jam can go to?" Amber responded "The big problem is that because of the sustained devastation of the economy, the numbers of people seeking beds in the shelters has risen astronomically. This in turn is causing a situation where the number of people seeking shelter is far outnumbering the available beds in the shelters. The situation is getting really scary and especially so for single women, either alone or with children."

"Mostly, I am talking about women who have no living relatives or if they do have relatives, those people are in no shape to help. These are women who were struggling to make ends meet even when they had some kind of job that at least gave them some income. Then all of a sudden, they find they are laid off and are immediately broke. Of course given the employment situation, replacing a lost job is continuing to get worse all the time."

"There are a number of various charities that are desperately trying to at least aid in these situations. However, they too are so overwhelmed with requests while at the same time seeing their incoming dollars steadily declining, that in far to many cases there just isn't any help."

"That has to be a horrendous situation, how do you deal with it?" Ben asked. "Not very well I am afraid. I did develop a list of charities that I would call soliciting help for some women and both I and some friends actually have taken women into our homes on a temporary basis just to keep them off the streets," Amber said.

"I can't imagine myself being put into the kind of situation where all of sudden I had no money, no relatives, and nowhere to turn and had to gather a few meager items and live out in the street. It totally blows my mind," Sandy said.

"Now you understand some of my motivation to become an integral part of A Mark of the Divine. We have to succeed in this mission!" Amber said. "Sorry, I didn't mean to put such a damper on a wonderful evening, but what is happening to our beloved Country is killing me. I just can't comprehend how we could have gone from where we were just a few short years ago, to where we are today."

They all sat in silence for a few minutes digesting what Amber had said. Robert finally spoke up and said, "Amber you have, in just a few short sentences, defined the urgency of our mission. It is indeed mind-boggling when it comes to understanding the devastating consequences of so many missteps that have been taking over the recent years."

CHAPTER SEVEN

Amber's thoughts set the stage for the rest of the conversation that evening. Robert said, "You know when you try to imagine how you would respond to certain events in your life that could take place, think about this; as Americans most of us have never been put in a position where we actually had to fight either physically or verbally in order to keep our right to practice our faith." Robert paused for affect.

Sandy finally spoke up, "That certainly brings up an interesting question and one that is starting to become quite applicable in our Country. How many people, if they are put into this kind of situation, would deny their faith to avoid verbal or physical conflict or abuse?" Once again a rather stunning question had been asked that begged for a correct answer.

Ben said, "As we have been told, part of the population we are preparing for will be joining the Villages for this very reason, religious persecution. Again it is hard to comprehend that we are talking about people having to flee religious persecution here in the United States. Like so many things, this has happened gradually. Starting with laws being passed that banned prayer in public places and then banning the traditional national prayer day. From there, laws have been enacted that started to strip religious symbolism from public places, then the word 'God', being expunged from government documents.

Oh yes, we mustn't forget the 'politically correct' greetings at many retail store as they didn't want to offend non-believers by using the word Christmas, because obliviously that refers to Christ. Most of us have a false sense of security that religious persecution couldn't possible happen here in the United States, but not only is it possible, it is happening! This is much like losing your home, most who have had this happen would haves said, 'that's not going to happen'. Do you think there is any parallel to this and the sudden appearance of The Line in the Sand?"

Amber said, "I guess I kind of got us going down this path of thought and although it is very depressing, it doesn't mean that what is happening all around us can be ignored. Complacency coupled with ignorance has brought down dynasties in the past and it is knocking at our doorsteps."

Robert responded, "I guess that brings us right back to A Mark of the Divine and answers a lot of the 'why' we are engaged in this monumental task."

CHAPTER EIGHT

They were sitting in the great room having a conversation. The TV volume had been turned down, but they did hear the famous and very well-liked news broadcaster Eric Smith announce that he had some very important things to report. They stopped their discussion to listen.

Smith said, "In the last two to three years, government has intruded into the lives of Americans more so than at any time in the history of our relatively young Nation. We are at the point where more and more people are becoming dependent on our Federal Government. It appears that this dependence is exactly the intention of the majority of our leadership in Congress and the White House. Their actions have resulted in a continued creep toward Socialism which is in itself anti-Christian because it replaces God with people."

"Yikes, that's laying it right on the line," Sandy said.

"As dependency spreads, more and more people loose their independence and their freedom, which again is what we believe their over-all plan envisions. Taxes and debt have or will soon drive most all of us except the very rich into a situation of having few options but to perform a kowtow to the wishes of the Federal government."

"As Americans, most of us believed this could never happen. For the most part we stood by and watched as purposely reckless and irresponsible spending drove us into a debt situation that has for all practical purposes bankrupted our Nation. The Chinese, not Americans, now own a great deal of America."

"Somehow, and this is really is hard to fathom, the 'old guard' that has done this to all of us, was voted back into power in this last election. It is hard to comprehend how this could have happened. It is believed that there were and are just too many people who really aren't paying attention. Many don't care or are just too lazy to try and find out what is really happening. They have adopted a 'whatever' attitude."

"I certainly agree with Eric's analysis," Sandy said. "This public announcement means that somehow we have to push forward even faster. Our timelines will need to advance as much as is humanly possible since the needs of so many shareholders will be accelerating while their way of life deteriorates. The Corporation can offer an alternative direction these people can take which will eventually lead them to a much more positive way of life. It offers them the chance to survive and then move forward and better themselves."

Ben said, "I had a long phone conversation with one of the leaders of a highly respected theological Christian think tank yesterday. He told me that the group's leaders feel that the suppression of Christianity in America is being accelerated to a much higher level than anything we have seen in the past. He also said they felt this eventual heightening of anti-Christianity both by the Government and by the secular population, which also includes much of the main stream media, will also parallel the continued suppression of Capitalism and the many freedoms Americans have taken for granted for many decades."

"They also anticipate that the on-going disregard of the Constitution will become much more prevalent. His parting words to me were, 'Brace your shareholders in A Mark of the Divine Corporation to start preparing for much worse conditions then what we have now, even though most feel it can't get worse. We don't know how fast this deterioration will continue to take place but we firmly believe it is going to accelerate."

"That is really scary," Amber said, "it's like reading a novel about the evil King and Queen of the United States and their Generals. Remember the words of that song that came out awhile ago, "They are the Hammer and We are the Nails?'"

"When they say deterioration, are they speaking about both our Christian freedom and our individual freedoms as citizens? Those freedoms we have fought so hard for and shed so much blood for over the many decades?" Amber asked. "Both," Robert responded. "George Washington is quoted as saying: *'Of all the dispositions and habits which lead to political prosperity, Religion and Morality are indispensable supports'.* I believe what he was saying is that you must have religion and morality as the foundation for good political and corporate leadership or corruption and decay are inevitable. So if you lose religious freedom you are bound to lose freedom of citizenship because corruption will have turned the leadership away from God."

A Mark of the Divine

Sandy declared, "I don't know about you guys but that scares me like nothing ever has!" "What are we going to do?" Amber asked. "This is why I wanted all of us to get back here at this time. It is really necessary we start to revise our timetables as Sandy suggested," Robert replied. "A Mark of the Divine," Sandy muttered almost as much to herself as to anyone, "is suddenly starting to have even more meaning and reason for its existence. God must have put that trench out there in the desert as a warning that we better heed what is happening in the world and particularly in America."

"It's like when someone draws a line in the sand," Amber said, "someone is being given an ultimatum. The meaning is that a particular activity or activities will not be supported or accepted." She thought *the figure thirty-three that defines every dimension of the trench is a heavy reminder that we are getting away from the teachings of Jesus Christ, who was brutally crucified on a cross at the age of thirty-three, so it would be possible for all who believed to gain heaven. "*

CHAPTER NINE

Robert called Ben on the two-way radio, "Sandy and I have some errands that need to be run in Dickinson, and there is a show the kids wanted to see, so I think we'll head in this afternoon. Is there anything either of you need in town?" Amber said she was okay as did Ben. "We'll take the four-wheeler while you're gone, and I'll show Amber around the ranch." Ben said.

Ben gave Amber a tour of the Ranch property, and she had a chance to also see some of the Badlands in the Theodore Roosevelt Park. They had packed a picnic lunch. About halfway through the tour, Ben pulled the four-wheeler into a hollowed-out cave. The cave gave them good protection from the north wind that had picked up and was feeling a bit chilly. In fact, it felt downright comfortable. As they lunched on the sandwiches Ben had made and brought along, he gave Amber a little history of the area.

The sun was just setting when they pulled back into the farmstead. They gave each other friendly little hug at the door of Amber's cabin, and then she went inside. As her door closed, Ben turned away and started for his cabin. Just as he turned, a bullet smashed into the log siding above his head. He dove for the ground, knowing exactly what had happened. He crawled around the side of Amber's cabin and then ran stooped over to the backside of his cabin. He planned to go through the back window and get his gun, because he knew he had left that window open.

As he approached the window he saw that the screen had been removed. He stopped short and pressed himself against the side of the cabin. *What to do now? Most likely* somebody was in his cabin waiting to ambush him when he came through the front door. How could he have left his guard down so completely? Guess he knew the answer to that.

As Ben pondered his next move, he heard his name called in a high whisper. It was coming from the back of Amber's cabin. When he made a mad dash for the back of her cabin, no shots rang out. Amber, who had heard the shot, was leaning out her back window holding a rifle. He'd forgotten there was a rifle in each of the cabins. She handed it to him along with a box of bullets. "You're an angel," Ben said.

Then he remembered something else. "Amber, right below the mantel where the rifle was is a small drawer. In there are two flares and some matches. Bring those to me, but don't turn on any lights.

He didn't think that Robert and Sandy were back yet as he didn't remember seeing their SUV parked up by the house, so he figured they would be showing up at anytime. How was he going to alert them to the danger? He wasn't sure how many intruders were out there or exactly where they were. The night was dead still, and he was thankful for that as he'd be able to hear the slightest sound. Just then as he was thinking about how to alert Ben and Sandy, he heard the sound of a vehicle approaching on the ranch road. It had to be Robert. He immediately set off one of the flares. As the flare arched high in the sky Ben did a quick scan of the area that he could see, but nothing appeared out of order.

Robert slammed on the brakes as soon as he saw the flare. "Something is wrong. Kids get down on the floor. Sandy grab our rifles from under the seat." He switched off the lights. There was enough moonlight that he could still see the road. He grabbed his cell phone and hit the speed dial button for the sheriff.

"Sandy, kids, as soon as that flare goes out, we'll make a dash for the garage. The door will be open by the time we get there. When I drive into the garage, everybody get out immediately. Kids you stay low going through the house and go down to the shelter. Your mom and I will go up in the cubicle." *Ben had probably heard the car and fired the flare to alert him*. Robert flicked the microphone switch and said, "Ben" and nothing else. This was a way he could let Ben know where they were and that he understood the warning.

Ben breathed a sigh of relief that Robert, Sandy and the kids were okay and he thought to himself, *this is really starting to annoy me. Okay, the guy who is in my cabin waiting to take me out has to be dealt with now*. Ben raced back behind his cabin. He peered into the open window every so slowly, but he couldn't see anything. *Somehow I have to be smart enough to flush him out. I think that if I fire a flare through the window, it will pass through the open bedroom door and hit the door going to the outside. As quick as I fire I need to be through the window and into the sitting room, and disable the intruder while he is still trying to figure what happened. Then I can grab the fire extinguisher and put the fire out before the cabin burns down. Sounds like a piece of cake he chided himself, now do it.*

Taking a deep breath, he did as he had planned and the execution went exactly as he had visualized. He then grabbed his two-way off the shelf and let Robert know what had happened. Robert said, "Sandy and I have seen only two people, and we put them down. I think we are clear."

"We seem to be under siege," Ben said to Robert. "Apparently we are getting to some folks on the other end of the spectrum who are not liking what we were are doing," Robert said.

Making light of a serious situation was a trademark of the brothers, and it definitely helped relieve tension that might hamper their ability to function at one hundred percent. "I think the sheriff should be showing up at any moment. Let's get these guys hog tied so they are nice and ready for him when he arrives," Ben said.

CHAPTER TEN

The summer disappeared and fall was on its way out. October quickly slipped into November, and old man winter would be knocking on the door anytime. Robert, Ben and Amber all went into a two-minute drill to finish up the recruitment meetings they had scheduled before Thanksgiving. There were many days of meetings scheduled across the U.S. that still had to be accomplished. Sandy continued to streamline the corporate administrative duties in their absence. She kept things in order at the Ranch and was totally immersed in home schooling on top of everything else.

The first phase or the Discovery and Preparation Stage was nearing completion and the results were astounding, even to them. They had all agreed to meet back at the Ranch three days before Thanksgiving, so they could take a little break and regroup.

Following a whirlwind of meeting activities, Ben, Amber and Robert all arrived back at the Ranch as planned. Now as they were seated in the big family room engaged in general conversation Sandy said, "I am so glad we were all thinking along the same lines when we asked Amber to join us as permanent staff for the Corporation. You are an absolute gem, super friend and a lifesaver in all the work that you have been doing and what you have accomplished." *I think I agree whole heartedly with Sandy's assessment but I also think my definition of her assets might be a bit broader,* Ben thought to himself. "Thank you Sandy," Amber said, "it is so good to be back at the Ranch and have all of us together again. This is going to be the best Thanksgiving ever, and that's because we are all together."

"You know," Sandy said, "this may come as a shock to you, but based on the average daily sign up that is taking place at the present time, we are going enroll our three millionth member before the end of this month." That brought a gasp from everybody as they hadn't realized what the multiplying factor was doing to their numbers. "Every time one of them held a membership meeting, they were signing up an average of ten members, who agreed to volunteer time and put on membership meetings. The multiplying factor is phenomenal," Sandy said. "This is really astounding," Robert gasped. "Based on that information, I think we should start diluting our membership meeting efforts and start conducting shareholder/developer meetings at least by January sometime."

Just then the phone rang and Ben picked it up. "O'Neil Ranch, Ben speaking." "Ben please don't say my name." Ben knew immediately that it was General Elizabeth. "Robert, Sandy, Amber and I are the only ones in the room; would it be alright for me to put this call on speaker?" "That would be fine. Hello Robert, Sandy and Amber. Ladies, I am sorry we have never had the chance to meet. For your information,

I am the contact person Ben and Robert have mentioned." "I'll make this very brief. Our group is very impressed with what you have accomplished in such short period of time. Although we are not visible, rest assured that we are monitoring your efforts constantly and are running some interference for you in many different ways."

"Now for the reason I called. Inflation will be starting to ramp up at a startling rate in the near future. This is going to cause more misery and disaster within the general population. Costs of food, particularly, will start to cause some panic situations as income holds flat or decreases. Once the people figure out what is happening there will be a run on grocery stores. Panic will be begin to spread. We wanted to make you aware of this only because it is going to put more pressure on your mission, accelerating the need and the desire for a faster and heavier migration to the villages. We would suggest that you start to substantially reduce your shareholder information meetings and swing your efforts toward a swift acceleration of developers. I will be back to you in the future. Keep up the fantastic job you are doing. Goodbye."

"Dang it," Ben said, "I sure would have liked to have had the chance to ask her some questions." "Why do you suppose she didn't want her name mentioned?"

Sandy asked. "I expect that she must have been calling from someplace where she wasn't sure about the security of the phone line she was on," Robert said. "This sounds kind of spooky," Amber said. "Well one thing is for sure," Ben said, "things are not getting any easier as we move the mission forward."

Early preparations for Thanksgiving Dinner that evening had already started. In fact the first scents of the baking turkey were starting to seep through the house. Ben yelled to the ladies in the kitchen, "Is dinner ready yet?" "Almost," was the reply followed by some other words which were **not** in the Thanksgiving spirit.

"Big Joe, come on in," Sandy said, when she heard Joe Walker, the ranch foreman, knocking on the door. After he entered the kitchen, Sandy pointed to the interior of the house saying, "The guys are hanging out in the family room." Joe said with a grin, "I am wondering if it would be alright if I just hung out in here. It sure does smell good," Joe was really much more like a family member than an employee and he was loved by all the O'Neil's.

CHAPTER ELEVEN

Sandy and Amber had joined the fellows while they waited for the Thanksgiving turkey to finish cooking. Ben said, "I have something very important to share with you that happened to me on my last meeting before returning to the Ranch, and I hope when I finish, you will be in agreement with the direction I took."

"Something quite profound happened. This was by far the largest audience I had had the privilege of talking to. As it turned out it was an annual joint luncheon of service clubs in Spokane, Washington, which takes place annually before Thanksgiving. There were approximately five hundred people in attendance. I had finished my presentation and was beginning to take a few questions. Here is how things played out at that point." "Yes," Ben said, "I believe your name tag says Marie. What is your question Marie?" She was sitting at one of the tables that were fairly close to the front. Since it was such a large audience, there were roving microphones, so that the entire audience could hear the questions being asked.

"Before, I ask my question Mr. O'Neil, I would just like to mention that I actually live in the little town of New Leipzig,

A Mark of the Divine

N.D., less than a hundred miles from your ranch and I am here in Spokane visiting my brother, who invited me to be his guest at this meeting." Ben interjected at this point, "I am very familiar with New Leipzig and the surrounding area. In fact I have very good friends who own the Tail Feather Ranch, not very far out of your town. Hunting pheasants along the Cannonball River that runs through their ranch is a wonderful treat." Ben noticed the smiles on many of the faces in the audience and said, "Sorry for carrying on a personal conversation on your time!" But Ben could tell the audience had enjoyed the little chit chat.

"I hope that you won't think me to forward or assuming, because of the question I would like to ask. What I am wondering is if it would be possible for you to consider a little broader definition of those who might be eligible to join one of the Villages, rather than limiting it to just those who at least in name are called Christians or Jews? If you would, please allow me to explain. My experience is quite parallel and I believe very representative of hundreds of thousands of people who are honest, hardworking, caring and moral American citizens but who do not associate themselves with any particular religion."

"Mr. O'Neil, this is a little hard for me to discuss in front of so many people. However, I feel there are so many of us who for a lot of different reasons, do not belong to a particular church or denomination. Perhaps you might say we are unidentifiable in our beliefs of a divine presence in our lives because of this. Many of us are unchurched, yet we cope with and practice our beliefs on a more personal basis." Marie's voice became a little emotional and those sitting close to her could see tears starting to gather in her eyes as she finished her statement. "We are people who, when it comes to being defined by a religion or denomination, are nameless. However, we are good people who would be the first to step forward to help another individual in need or literally give the shirt off our backs to someone else. Many of us are also among those who are hurting real bad from the negative effects of the economy and would cherish the opportunity to join one of the villages. Thank you for any consideration you are willing to give this possibility."

Then Marie sat down, and for a least a whole minute that seemed like five or ten, not a sound could be heard in that big auditorium. Ben was caught completely off guard and it took him a few seconds to gather his thoughts.

"Marie, thanks for your wonderful question and comments. What Marie has just asked in essence is I believe, how broadly do we at Mark of the Divine define Christianity? Frankly, I am hard put to say why we have not identified this segment of society or why it has not been brought up before. Man has historically had the ability to drive a wedge between people and their God, because of the way in which they have acted. This, in turn, has caused many people to remove themselves from these formal settings of religious identification. This is a shameful fact.

Marie, you are a very brave person and please believe in your heart that as of today you are solely responsible for giving the thousands of people you represent, a second chance to recoup their lives. This is what Christianity is all about. We will be glad to accept you and anyone else of your ilk as a member of our Village." With that, Ben stepped down from platform walked over to Marie and gave her a great big hug. The audience was instantly on its feet with an arousing applause and there was no absence of tears as this meeting came to a startling and unanticipated end.

Amber came over and gave Ben a hug. She said, "You truly are a wonderful person Ben O'Neil, and I am in complete agreement with the direction you took. Robert and Sandy also commented in the affirmative and so a new dimension was added to the definition of eligibility in A Mark of the Divine.

CHAPTER TWELVE

Still feeling like that stuffed turkey they had eaten yesterday, Ben and Robert sat in the den talking about their progress and how they should approach this next four weeks before Christmas. Ben commented in a very humble tone, "I think that our reaching our three millionth member before this week is out, as Sandy reported, is truly astounding, and I am actually flabbergasted." Robert brought his glass of wine up and said, "Well done, brother," and they toasted the good news. "There is one more item that I think…" Robert's sentence wasn't finished as an alarm sounded in the house.

Sandy and Amber dashed into the play area and hustled the kids into the shelter that was built below the house. Ben grabbed the fire extinguisher and doused the fire in the fireplace. All the lights were shut off. Someone or something had crossed the outside perimeter of the ranch. Grabbing their high-powered rifles and night vision goggles, without a word, both men headed for the little cubicle on top of the house.

"Sandy, Amber can you hear me okay?" Robert whispered into his mike. Both came back with affirmative answers.

"Okay, I have an open line to the Sheriff and he is on standby until we can identify the cause for the alarm being set off," Robert said. They continually swept the area trying to pick up any movement they could. Suddenly Ben whispered into his mike, "There are three in a military crawl at 150 degrees about 200 yards out from the garage. I'll keep an eye on them Robert, and you keep scanning the area to make sure there aren't any more coming in from another direction. Also give the sheriff a report and have him get out here pronto."

After about five more minutes of surveillance, Robert said, "I haven't spotted any more activity." "Okay," Ben said. He flipped a switch on the wall and keyed a microphone that was connected to a loud speaker system. His amplified voice, loud and clear, commanded , "Listen very carefully; we will give you exactly 10 seconds to throw your firearms out in front of you and beyond that do not move a muscle."

The placement of the speakers throughout the entire ranch was state-of-the-art. They were perfectly camouflaged. When Ben's voice came over the speakers, the perpetrators must have thought that he was right behind them. Ben shut off the microphone and said to Robert, "When I reach the count of five, if they haven't thrown their weapons, we'll lay down a line of fire about two feet in front of them. If they get up and start to retreat, hit them in the legs."

As the count reached three, their weapons were thrown out in front of them. Ben activated the microphone again. "Now slowly crawl backwards three feet away from your weapons and lay flat on your bellies with your arms and legs outstretched." Robert went back on line with the sheriff and gave him the location of the perps and then activated some of the lights that were spread throughout that area.

CHAPTER THIRTEEN

The chatter around the breakfast table the next morning was in full gear, mostly discussing the events of the previous evening. "Let's hope the sheriff can convince those guys to spill the beans on who they are working for," Amber said, " this is starting to get spooky". Everybody chimed in with "Amen!"

"I guess they, whoever 'they' are, really do not have a clue how far along we have progressed with our program and how totally ineffectual it would be at this point to take us out," Robert said. "Well, I wouldn't say it would be ineffectual if they managed to kill you," Sandy mumbled. "I was referring to the fact that at this point, killing me or Ben or both of us would not stop the movement, it has already progressed too far," Robert said.

After further discussion the subject matter was changed to something much more positive and that seemed to move the children's mood onto a much brighter level.

"We are making marvelous progress," Robert said. "By spring I am projecting when we can start construction on housing, our Corporate shareholders will number in the ten's of millions and there will be literally several thousand shareholder/contactors in the fold, supporting the development of the Villages that will dot the Plains from Canada to Mexico."

"Ben and Amber, I have been doing a lot of thinking about how the three of us should proceed as we make this last meeting blitz before Christmas," Robert said. "Because we need to take heed about what General Elizabeth told us, this will be our last set of meetings with potential shareholders. If you are okay with this direction, I am thinking that I will only stay out one week, then return back here with Sandy and the kids and help out with the corporate work before returning to the field for a week."

"As much as I love our time at the Ranch," Amber said, "I know it is critical for us to hold as many informational meeting as we possibly can, as we have already have been told, time is running out." "Amen to that Amber, "Ben said "and I think you are right on, time is not on our side." "However, Ben and Amber, I am going to suggest you travel together and hold your meetings in the same town at the same time. That shouldn't cause much of a problem but in view of what has happened, I think it would a lot safer for Amber." Amber started to object, but Ben jumped in and said that he totally agreed with Robert on this one.

CHAPTER FOURTEEN

Ben came rambling into the ranch house the next morning and plopped his suitcase in the hallway. "Good morning Sandy, Robert, kids." Then looked at Jimmy and said, "Did you save anything for me or did you eat it all? Just because you are growing an inch a day, doesn't mean you can't leave a little breakfast for your favorite uncle." "You know what?" Jimmy said, "You are my favorite uncle. Do you know why you're my favorite uncle?" "No Jimmy, why am I your favorite uncle?" "Because you are the only uncle I have," and then laughing he bounced away from Ben's intended swat on the butt.

"Has Amber been up here yet?" Ben asked. "We'll have to be underway shortly." Nobody had seen Amber. Ben walked over to her cabin only to find that Amber was not in the cabin and was nowhere in sight. *Hmm, she must have gone for a walk, but it's funny because she knew we were planning on leaving about this time.* Her bag was packed and sitting near the door.

Ben jogged back up to the ranch house. He said, "Robert, I am going to take the jeep and scout the immediate area for Amber. Her bag is packed but she is not in her cabin. I'll also checked the barn before I go out on the trail." Sandy said,

"Oh my God, I have a bad feeling about this. She knew you were planning on leaving about now, so I can't imagine she would just be out for a long walk. "I am going to saddle up a horse. I'll check the eastern area of the Ranch." "I'll take the four-wheeler and head south and then work west," Robert said. "Ben, why don't you head up north and then work your way back west, and we'll meet up at the loading pen. Sandy, Ben, be sure and take your two-way's with you so we can constantly be in touch."

Two hours later, Ben and Robert met up and then headed back to the Ranch house, they arrived just as Sandy came galloping up the trail from the east. They had found no sign of Amber at all. Ben ran into the house and called the sheriff, alerting him to the situation. "I fear that she has been kidnapped, and I am thinking this is related to last night's attack," Ben told Sheriff Buck.

"You are probably right about that Ben," Sheriff Buck said, "I'll turn up the heat on those guys you captured at your Ranch last night, they may very well be able to shed some light on this. I'll be back to you as soon as I can. If I find out anything I'll radio you immediately, and you stay in touch with me." "Will do," Ben said.

Ben, Sandy and Robert were in deep discussion, trying to figure out what might have happened and what their next step should be. "I am thinking she was up early this morning, packed and then decided that it was early enough that she had time to go for a walk," Ben said. "Alright, I think that is a good assumption," Sandy said, "do you have any other guesses as to which way she might have gone?" "My best guess is the only area we haven't checked out. She might have taken that old cow trail that meanders to the northwest," Ben said. "I think that might be a good guess, as that is the easiest trail to follow and is fairly scenic," Robert pointed out.

"Okay," Ben said, "I am going to set out on horseback and take that trail. I will try to find her footprints or anything that might suggest there was trouble." "Alright, I'll take Sandy's horse and search the area out to the southwest one more time. It seems to me that might be the most logical way for intruders to enter the Ranch," Robert said. I'll stay at the Ranch in case a call comes in from the sheriff," Sandy said.

The ground was hard, and the light snow that had previously covered the path had been blown away. It was frustrating Ben that he couldn't pick up any prints as he carefully studied the ground. He got about a quarter mile down the trail before he spotted what had to be Amber's shoe prints. They were clear enough that they had to have been made this morning. He pulled out his two-way and let Robert and Sandy know that he had picked up her foot prints. They were clear enough that they had to have been made this morning. Robert immediately turned his horse and headed towards where Ben was waiting for him.

They followed the trail for about another mile but didn't see anything suspicious until they were nearing the fence line separating the National Park from their land. They stopped to examine the path when two more prints appeared coming from the National Park and it looked like a scuffle had ensued. "They've got Amber," Ben said. "Yep, brazen aren't they? Came in right over the fence from the Park," Robert said. "Were they just lucky or had they somehow learned that this is the only section on the perimeter of the Ranch where we hadn't yet put in security?"

A Mark of the Divine

Ben was immediately on the two-way talking to Sandy. "Sandy, call the sheriff and tell him where we are and what we have found. We can't be more than a couple of hours behind these guys," Ben said. "Ask the sheriff if he will send out his helicopter and ask the pilot to watch for us. We are going into the park and follow their trail. Also ask the Sheriff if he can set up some patrols along the south side of the park."

Ben and Robert were just coming over a ridge when Robert halted his horse and backed it up. At the same time, he signaled Ben, who was behind him, to get down. After Robert and Ben dismounted, they crept up to the top of the ridge and looked down. "I think those are the culprits," Robert said. Ben ran back to the horse and grabbed the binoculars out of the saddle bag. As he adjusted the lenses, he said, "There are two men down there, in front of what appears to be small cave. I don't see Amber." Ben handed Robert the binoculars. As Robert watched he said, "I think they are in the process of building a fire. Get Sandy on the two-way and have her relay this information to Buck. I am guessing that they have Amber tied up in that cave, and they are building a fire to signal a helicopter that might be coming in to pick them up. We have to cut them off."

"Ten to one they don't have any permit to be in the park in the first place, but sheriff Buck can check that out to see if any permits were issued this morning. Before we can do anything we have to be sure these are the guys that kidnapped Amber," Ben said.

"Alright, why don't we do this Ben. You circle out around to the right. I'll go left, and let's get in a little closer. Since we only have the one rifle, I'll get myself into a position where

I can get a clear shot off at both the helicopter and them, if necessary."

Ben had good cover as he crept up to within twenty yards of the two men. From what he was able to hear, he quickly determined that in fact they did have Amber tied up in the cave. He crawled back so he was out of earshot and called both Sandy and Robert to let them know he that he was sure Amber was a captive of the two men. He said he did not know what condition Amber was in. "I just got off the radio with the sheriff," Sandy's voice came over the two-way; "he said he was about fifteen minutes out from your location and was also keeping an eye out for another helicopter flying in the area but had seen nothing yet."

Why the heck didn't I take a rifle with me when I left the house, Ben thought. *How was all this going to play out? There were just too many scenarios as to how this whole thing could come down. I am really concerned about Amber's safety.*

Ben got Robert on the two-way again and expressed his thoughts. Robert said, "Ben I definitely see your concern for Amber's safety. But now that we know for sure these are the kidnappers, I think we should waste no time. I can get good shots from where I am. Ben had no doubts that if Robert had a clear field of fire, he could disable the kidnappers before they could react. Both he and Robert had received medals for expert marksmanship during their stint in the Service.

Could you tell what kind of weapons they have?" ask Robert. "No, I couldn't get a clear visual, but they looked liked semi-automatic rifles," said Ben. "The other unknowns are what kind of fire power and personnel will be on the 'pick up' helicopter, if there is one, and what the sheriff has with him for deputies and weapons."

"Alright Ben, those are good points. I am going to have Sandy see if we can get patched through to the sheriff in their helicopter." It seemed like an eternity before Robert got back to him. "I had about three minutes of back-and-forth with the sheriff, and he finally agreed that we should proceed. He said he only had the pilot and himself aboard. He is going to set down about mile out, on top of one of the buttes, so he can get a good sighting of any other copter flying into the area."

Ben said, "Give me two minutes to get back to my earlier position Robert and then fire away. As soon as they are down I will go in and get Amber. Then I will get those two guys into the cave, douse the fire and make it look like it isn't the place they planned for the landing." "It's a go," Replied Robert.

A radio message was received on top of the butte, "Sheriff, this is Robert again, mission accomplished. The two kidnappers are wounded pretty badly but not dead. If you can pick them up and get them to the hospital, they should make it." "I'll get back to you in a couple of minutes Robert, said Sheriff Buck. Let us get this bird off the ground and take a good look to be sure that another copter isn't in sight. Then we'll be right on over."

Ben had untied Amber and they embraced for a minute as Amber couldn't hold back the tears. "Amber we have to get out of the cave and take cover away from this area," said Ben. I'll pull those two bandits into the cave for right now. Then we'll go over the ridge and find some cover where we can wait for the sheriff to get here before anyone else shows up.

When the sheriff had picked up the two wounded outlaws and was headed for the hospital, he saw a helicopter flying in a direct line to the site they had recently departed. "That has to be the accomplices," the sheriff said. He pulled his binoculars and was able to note the copter's identification markings. Next he radioed the Highway Patrol and brought them up to speed. They were going to contact the FBI and dispatch an aircraft immediately. They thought they should be able to pin down the alien copter in short order. "Okay," said Sheriff Buck, "I'll lay back and see where he goes once he is unable to make contact with his buddies on the ground. Than I'll let you know."

CHAPTER FIFTEEN

A few days later, Ben and Robert were sitting in Sheriff Buck's office with two other officers, a local highway patrolman and a member of the FBI Counter Terrorism Team.

"Ben, your intuition and heads up call to take out those two jokers was right-on," the sheriff said, "and Robert, I have spoken to the judge. You have been absolved of any wrongdoing." "That is sure good to know," Robert said.

The FBI guest said, "Thanks to you both. You did your Country proud. The helicopter led us to an isolated ranch in northwestern South Dakota, and fortunately our pilot merely reported the coordinates of the ranch and went back to his base. It turned out there was a nest of terrorists living and training there with their primary goal of taking out anything and anybody that symbolized or represented Christianity.

We have determined that their organization, which is quite far flung, was also instrumental in a number of Church bombings in the last few months. Although this was but just one terrorist nest, it nevertheless was a big bust, thanks to you guys."

A Mark of the Divine

When Robert and Ben got back to the Ranch, they were pretty much rung out. After bringing Sandy and Amber up to speed, everybody decided to turn in. Ben asked Amber, "Okay with you if we leave here about six tomorrow?" We have a strenuous workout ahead of us if we are going to get back on schedule with our meetings." I'll be packed and ready to go," Amber said, "and I promise not to go for a walk before we leave." Since they were leaving so early, everybody said their good-bye's before turning in for the night. "We'll see you all the week before Christmas," Ben and Amber said, as hugs were given all the way around. Robert and Ben talked briefly after Sandy and Amber had retired for the night.

"It's imperative Robert," Ben began, "that we start working full steam ahead on setting up rancher and farmer shareholders who will be developers, duplicating our efforts as far as developing villages for all those who wish to leave their current situation." "You're absolutely right. I'll start working on that project first thing tomorrow morning and see if I can't get the preliminary work out of the way before I head out on the meeting trail," Robert said. Let's set a date with the leaders in each State for our first meeting of shareholder/developers in January. Following that meeting we can really concentrate our efforts on a full-fledged assault on getting new shareholder/developers in the fold." "That sounds like a good plan of action for us to pursue," said Ben.

Robert stated, "With the explosion we have had in shareholder numbers and with what seems like breakneck speed being taken by the Federal Government to move us totally to Socialism, we are really going to be under the gun, figuratively and literally. It is just so hard to believe how fast our country seems to be collapsing financially and morally.

How could so many people have been solvent and working hard one day and in what must have seemed like it was almost instantaneous, they were being reduced to having no jobs, their houses going into foreclosure and wondering where and how they were going to survive?"

"Our timing for this mammoth project seems to be right on target, but you know what brother?" Ben said, "We're going to need a few miracles along the way." "No question about that, and we have already experienced a few of those."

CHAPTER SIXTEEN

"Jim, this is Robert O'Neil with A Mark of the Divine Corporation. Do you have a few minutes to talk?" "Hi Robert, it's nice to hear from you. Yes, as a matter of fact my wife and I were just saying last night that we should give you a call." "I am glad to hear that Jim. First off, I want to thank you again for being a shareholder in the Corporation and for your ongoing support over the last year. You have no idea how much your efforts have meant."

Second, I wanted to alert you to the fact that we feel, based on all that has taken place within our Federal Government, as well as the continuing direction a majority of the population apparently seem to want to take in terms of not only accepting but encouraging the move to Socialism, we need to activate our plans. We now have well over three million shareholders in A Mark of the Divine, Inc., and that number is growing at over twenty thousand daily.

I have contacted the lead person in each of the twelve States who are so far acting in concert with our movement, including yourself. You are the folks who will initiate and put into motion what will probably will be considered the most daring, provocative, and certainly the most exciting program ever conceived and launched in the history of the U.S."

"Two items Jim: in just a few days, you along with the other eleven, will be receiving a packet from us detailing our initial plans and suggestions; second, can you clear your calendar for a meeting of the twelve of you along with Ben and myself, for 10:00 A.M. on January 15th? We'll plan on meeting in Denver at the Metropolitan Inn, and I have reserved the Gold Room." "I sure can Robert, and will look forward to seeing you and Ben again. I will also be looking forward to have the chance to meet the other eleven guys, it should be a very interesting meeting to say the least."

Jim Peterson had been a long-time friend and was deeply respected by both Robert and Ben. As a rancher and also a state senator who had fought long and hard for limited government, low taxes and a balanced budget, his leadership was paramount in keeping his States' prosperity and high employment numbers where they were.

"Would you anticipate we'll be finished by evening?" "Yes Jim, we definitely should have everything wrapped up by 6:00 that evening. One more thing, our wives will be accompanying us and if it can work out, it would be great if Betty could also come to the meeting. Sandy has planned a separate meeting for all the wives who can attend."

"Okay Robert, I am pretty sure Betty can make it and we'll be looking forward with great anticipation to this get-together. See you on the 15th. A blessed Christmas to all of you Robert." "Thanks Jim and a very blessed Christmas to you and your family."

Sandy and Robert spent the next couple of days putting together a packet to send out to the twelve developers, so they had plenty of time to look over the information before their get-together.

"This afternoon," Robert said, "I'll cut down a Spruce tree that I have had my eye on. It will make a really nice Christmas tree. I will set it up tonight so you and the kids can get it decorated. I know they are really anxious to do that."

It was nice to take a break from their hectic schedule and to now concentrate on the Christmas holiday. The kids, of course, were really getting pumped up and had been drawing, coloring and cutting out paper ornaments for the tree. So when their Dad had said he'd have the tree up tonight, they could start to decorate it, they disappeared for the rest of the day to finish up their drawing, coloring and cutting.

CHAPTER SEVENTEEN

Christmas was just three days away. Ben, Amber and Robert were all back from their meeting blitz across several states. Robert, Ben and sometimes Sandy, had been in a planning mode all morning. They refined a plan of action for security on the west side of the Ranch and outlined other measures to secure the Ranch and the upcoming Village.

"Ben, I am concerned about Amber. We haven't seen hide nor hair of her this morning," Sandy said. "You're right," Ben said, as another internal alarm went off in his head. I'll go check on her right now," Ben said.

Five minutes later Ben and Amber came strolling into the kitchen. Amber had been on her way out the door when Ben came over to check on her. "Hi there, sleepy head," Sandy said. Amber was carrying a file folder and set it down on the table while greeting everyone. "As a matter of fact, I have been working all morning," Amber said, "and I have put together a suggestion that I would like you all to look at and see if it makes sense to you." She had everybody's attention. "Okay Amber," Ben said, "have at it."

A Mark of the Divine

"I know you have said that advertising A Mark of The Divine, Inc.., has not been something you were real interested in doing. However, I am going to ask you to consider my proposal. I'd like you to run this thirty second ad on perhaps a couple of TV stations, say Fox cable and ABC during prime time. There will be no speaking, just a real readable copy with a soft background rendition of America the Beautiful." Amber passed out a copy to each one.

NOTICE
TO
TERRORISTS LIVING IN AMERICA

We draw your attention to the fact that this Notice does not say American Terrorists but Terrorists living in America. We believe the words 'American Terrorists' are a conflict in terminology because we don't believe you can be an American and a Terrorist.

To those who have made several attempts to end the lives of our founders and mistakenly believe such acts of terrorism will accomplish your mission, we say to you:

A Mark of The Divine, Inc., is now the largest Corporation in the United States. More than 20,000 people a day are becoming shareholders. That number is expected to double following this ad. There are now over three million shareholders and the Corporation is still a very young. The shareholders aren't investing in this corporation for the purpose of receiving financial dividends or in anticipation of stock appreciation.

No, they are buying shares because of the principles which this corporation stands for and advocates.

So you see Terrorists, your mission to wipe us out or silence us is an impossible mission.

We the shareholders of A Mark of the Divine, Inc., are just good old Christian and other people of faith. We are American patriots who have finally been pushed too far by radicals like you. We will no longer remain silent and passive as we have in the past.

If you would like more information, visit our website
amarkofthedivine@america.com
*In God We Trus*t
PS: Have a very Blessed Christmas

"Good job Amber, that's impressive and right on the mark," Ben said, "what do you guys think?" "I like it also," Robert said and Sandy echoed their thoughts. "Great, then I'll go ahead and get it set up," Amber said. "It will sure be fun to see the response we get from this."

CHAPTER EIGHTEEN

On Christmas Eve Jimmy had crafted a plan for he and Maggie to be up at the crack of dawn the next morning, quietly sneak down the stairs and check out all the gifts under the tree. As the children huddled at the base of the tree with all the presents, Jimmy whispered to Maggie, "Do you think we could open just one of our presents?" "No way Jimmy," Maggie said, "but we could check out our stockings hanging by the fireplace to see what might be in them."

Robert and Sandy had woken and were kind of giggling to themselves as they imagined what was going through the kid's minds as they pondered on whether or not they dared to open just one present. "Okay," Sandy said, as she and Robert came into the room, "You can each open one present, then you need to get ready for church and don't forget whose birthday we are really celebrating."

As Christmas day unfolded at the O'Neil Ranch, in addition to Robert, Sandy, Jimmy, Maggie, Ben, and their Ranch foreman Big Joe, they had invited some friends to spend Christmas with them, and it also gave them a chance to tell about the new life they were embarking on. This was something they had not had the opportunity to do. Up to now, no one other than their family and Big Joe were privy to this massive change in direction that was starting to unfold in their lives.

Following Christmas dinner, as everybody was sitting around just chatting, Robert broached the subject. In outline form, he gave their guests a sampling of what the O'Neils were embarking on. For the next couple of hours there was a very lively debate but in the end there was no question that their guests were not only impressed but extremely supportive. Although they had been some of the first shareholders in the corporation, nobody up until now had been privy to the Village concept that would be making it's grand entry on the scene in the near future.

Later that evening after everybody had left and they were about to retire, Ben said, "We have just under three weeks to get ready for our meeting with the first group of shareholder/developers. So we should be getting that program put together along with all the other things we have to get done." "Amber and I will work on the women's program," Sandy said, "since we'll be holding that meeting at the same time you two are meeting with the men."

They all agreed to shut down their minds, if possible, and get some sleep after a wonderful Christmas day.

CHAPTER NINETEEN

Robert, Ben and the twelve farmer/ranchers were all seated at a big round table.

Introductions had been made along with opening remarks from Robert and Ben.

"Hopefully, all of you have had a chance to review the information contained in your packets we sent out," Robert said. All of the attendees acknowledged they did indeed have the chance to review the information.

Robert continued, "Since you have looked over the information, I think it would be most beneficial at this point to open our meeting up by going straight to a question and answer session. Chances are the questions you have will probably be the same as what a few others will want to ask. So, I think we can cover more ground doing this kind of format and working our way through to a successful conclusion." Everybody was in agreement that this direction made sense.

J..J. signaled that he had a question and Robert said, "J.J. from the State of Arizona, fire away." "Thanks Robert, my question relates to your business model that you have presented and specifically the economics and return on investment. I'd appreciate it if you could go through that one more time." Robert and Ben knew that all the farmers and ranchers present in the room were very wealthy individuals, so naturally their mind set would focus on this kind of thought process.

"J.J., I think it might be easiest to put the answer to your question in two parts. The first part is not related to economics, but rather it is more related to what is in your heart. As you know, we have a disastrous situation with many hard-working and honest people being reduced to little or nothing in terms of their financial situation. This is not because they are lazy or wanting a handout, in fact quite the opposite.

"This is a class of people that truly represents the soul of America. So how can a situation like this be dealt with and brought to a successful conclusion? We have developed a business plan which will allow investors such as you to continually invest, recoup and reinvest. At the same time your investment and efforts will provide millions of people with the necessities of life. Not in the form of charity, but in the form of reward or perhaps a better word would be <u>exchange,</u> for productive work. This whole process will preserve individual dignity and will reward ambition and determination."

"The second part of this equation is economics. As you are aware, our shareholder base is now approximately twenty million people and growing by the hour. It will probably reach close to fifty-five million by spring. The increase in shareholder growth has been so phenomenal that we have to continually revise our figures upward as to where we think this is going.

Our shareholders can be categorized into three groups. The first group consists of passive shareholders who will choose to sit out the economic meltdown and the unbelievable public display of anti-Christianity. This group will probably represent about ten percent of the total.

A second group is made up of those who are financially well off, but who will, for various reasons, move into the Mid American Beltway. That Beltway consists of the plains states we have identified in our movement plus the adjoining states that have asked to join us like your own state of Arizona. This group makes up 35 percent of the shareholders.

The largest group is the third group, with about half of the shareholders in A Mark of the Divine. This group has the following characteristics: They are hard working, conscientious, desperate, broke or nearly so and devastated by what is happening. They are terribly troubled by what is happening in terms of religious persecution. Those with children, are concerned and upset in many instances with the school system their children need to attend.

"The desire for what we are offering could easily outstrip us all in terms of finances unless we set up a method by which we are able to continually replenish our outgoing dollars. We will be walking a fine line as village developers, or as we commonly refer to you as shareholders/developers of A Mark of the Divine Corporation. You will be able to tap into Corporate funds as long as they are available in addition to using your own resources. So again, continually replenishing the financial investment output is going to be a necessity. No small part of this will come from the second group who will be the ones that will utilize a large number of people in this last group over a period of time. These people will hire people from the third group to build houses and will undoubtedly provide a lot of employment as they start up new businesses in the community.

At this time we are estimating that there will be approximately fifty to sixty million people who will eventually want to move into the Mid American Beltway and become a part of this movement. That's a pretty staggering figure and it's hard to get your arms around something like this. If we just use averages, this means it is going to equate to somewhere around 4 to 5 million people moving into each state to live in the villages that are established from Canada to Mexico." A little gasp went up from the group as they tried to absorb and quantify what Robert was saying.

"But let me get back to the rest of the answer to J.J.'s question about the specifics of economics and return on investment. I think to accomplish this I will use an example of a potential Village resident. Of the hundreds of jobs you will create over a period of time with this project, one of the more immediate jobs to fill will be carpenters.

In going through our database, we have identified a lot of carpenters. What we can't identify at this time is how many are out of work, depleted all their savings or are down to few choices of being able to move forward. However, before coming out here for this meeting, we identified one typical example, a carpenter who is on his last leg financially and is thinking that he and his wife and two daughters ages 14 and 15 may be out on the streets before this month is out.

The name of the man I am using in this example is John Waters. In a phone interview with him I told him about the project. He all but leaped through the phone in accepting our invitation to move into the Village and become employed immediately.

As I explained to Mr. Waters, what we plan to do in the first six months is to build one hundred houses and a general use or commons building. All the houses will be straight line houses, with no garages and two or three or four bedrooms, all on one floor. All houses will have a root cellar beneath the house which will be left totally unfinished except for very basic shelving. This will be used not only for canned goods but for miscellaneous storage and as an emergency shelter.

Also we will not be using any electricity in the houses; the heating system along with the appliances that will be furnished will run on propane. Up in our North Dakota Ranch we will not need air conditioning. Kerosene lanterns will be furnished for lighting. A small generator will be furnished to run one or more head bolt heaters for vehicles in the winter time. We are also going to furnish the houses with not only the necessary appliances but the basic furniture needs for the bedrooms, kitchen and living room. All houses will be pre-wired for electricity that will probably be brought in at a later date.

"As a side note, we plan on building into the floor a safe with a combination lock. The reason for this is that we are going to encourage the use of cash and discourage the use of credit/debit cards, charging or the use of any delayed payment tool. Therefore, we would have to anticipate that everybody will have a fair amount of cash at times, once these families begin to get their feet on the ground.

In addition to encouraging extremely frugal spending, we also want to encourage the ability to diminish, to the extent possible, any kind of paper trail. We all know what is

A Mark of the Divine

happening on the tax side of things with our Federal Government. Taxation has now reached an alarming level. Government spending is bordering on being criminal. I know we will be walking a fine line, but to whatever extent possible we will encourage the use of cash, barter, exchange or whatever other means we can to reduce the intolerable burden of taxation.

Eventually, all these beltway states will form a new county called Mid America. When all of this is accomplished then we know we won't be dealing with a monster like the IRS nor be subjected to the tax and spend mentality of our current Federal Government."

"Sorry for getting off on that side road gentlemen, but I thought it was an appropriate time to reveal this information." They all voiced a very enthusiastic affirmative. Getting back to construction, we will plan on using 2x6's on the outside walls so that we can over-insulate these houses and there will be triple-pain, tinted windows and a ceiling height of eight feet throughout the house.

We are estimating we can do all of this for a materials cost of twenty to thirty thousand depending on the number of bedrooms and bathrooms. This would include putting in individual septic tanks for each house and either individual or shared wells for water.

The availability of water will determine the spacing of wells. We are planning as general rule of the thumb for a population density that would allow one-fourth acre per house.

Prior to turning over the house to a resident, a relatively large area will be tilled for the planting of a garden.

"Also included in the above estimate is the grading and laying down of gravel roads and driveways. The construction and operational costs of a community building or buildings will be financed by a monthly fee assessed to each resident."

Now let me get back to my example of John Waters the carpenter. We have a guest cabin on our Ranch where John and his family can stay until he gets his house built. It will be pretty crowded for them, but realize that they are taking those first steps to totally rebuilding their lives and are ecstatic to have this opportunity. We'll help get his house built and will also hire some locals to help us get this project underway. A contract for the new house will be drawn up with John agreeing to a payoff time for the house of five years. He will have no money to put down, so payments on the house will be in the form of exchange for his labor."

"You can tell where I am going here. You will have to plan on a lot of investment without a return for about five years. But we believe that once these people have stepped back to almost the frontier days of America, regrouped and have the opportunity to literally revive their lives; things will start to move forward rapidly. With your help they will get back on their feet, start to utilize and expand their skills. Because of these actions we will eventually start to see a rotation of house ownership within the villages as these folks prosper and in many cases move to a town or city. Gentlemen, this will be one huge component of reviving capitalism and our free enterprise system which in turn will start the development of a new America. "

"Did I answer your question J.J.?" Robert said with a serious face. Everybody broke into a good laugh. "You sure did Robert; to say this is a breath-taking project would be to severely understate the facts!" "Robert," Pete Dawson said, "I think as far as I am concerned I don't need to ask any questions at this time, but I am going to suggest that those who get involved as developers should plan to have a conference call about once a month to share ideas and get questions we may have answered." Everybody else chimed in that they thought it was a good idea. Jed Davis said, "Besides that, I am so all fired up that I need to get out of here and get back to the ranch. It looks to me like we have a heap of work to do."

"The ladies also should probably be wrapping up their session soon," Ben said. "Before we adjourn, how about we set a date and a time for that first conference call one month from today at 10:00 AM Central Time?" That suggestion met with everybody's approval and Robert agreed to set it up.

CHAPTER TWENTY

During the time the men were engaged with their meeting, Sandy and Amber met with all the wives. After introductions were made and time was given for a chance to get somewhat acquainted, their meeting got underway. Amber passed around a schedule of items that she and Sandy thought they should discuss. "I hope you all are as excited as we are," Sandy said, as she opened the meeting. The response was very positive.

"As you may know, the mission of our Corporation is to assist in moving as large a percentage of shareholders out of poverty or near poverty and devastation as we possibly can. Ironically, they are finding themselves in this condition not through their negligence, attitude or ambition but rather by action of our leaders in Washington, D.C."

"Somehow, we have to give it all we are capable of to help these people reclaim their dignity and self-worth even if we have to spend the rest of lives doing just that." Sandy was given a nice round of applause for that statement and she couldn't help saying "It is so wonderful all of us are of such like minds when it comes to pursuing this amazing challenge!"

"Let's get right into some topics that we thought should be on our agenda for this meeting. A large number of the shareholders who will be joining us in our villages will have hit bottom and have been reduced to nothing in financial terms. We need to help them adjust to this current status and then move their lives forward to a new level."

"It will be important for all of us to keep remembering that we have a real understanding of life and what it is all about, having been raised and spent all or most of our lives in rural America. This knowledge will help us pass on a lot of wisdom to all of those coming to us. Most will be coming from the city and will have little knowledge of how to survive and move their lives forward under the circumstances they will find themselves living in.

Certainly they will be starting well ahead of our forefathers, who came west in covered wagons with nothing more than what they could carry. When they arrive at their new residence in a Village, they will find a good solid house to live in and the means to provide a basic living for themselves and their families. They also will be surrounded by like-minded people who will help to form a solid social bond among themselves."

"First, we will need to have to a lot of sessions or classes to discuss what will certainly be a culture shock for most of the new residents of the villages. The good thing is that we will be dealing with folks who for the most part are strong and have fantastic attitudes, given what they have been through. They will now be presented with the opportunity to eventually bring themselves out of from underneath all of those setbacks and misery, realizing they can build a new life."

"Next we need to set up classes on gardening, canning, and what I would call just plain old frugal living. In our case I have talked to our county home economics person and told her about our plans. She said she will be more than happy to assist us in these classes, so I think this can be a great resource for all of you also."

As we move forward into other areas of need, we will have to address items like the development of nurses' stations on site and having some kind of people mover or bus that can provide transportation to the nearest towns for the residents who either have jobs in town or have the occasional need for some supplies. Also we visualize that on Sundays, the Community Center will need to double as a church. Services would be held for the various Christian denominations as needed, and subject to having qualified pastors or lay people."

"Another area that has to be addressed is child care and home schooling. We will have a fair share of single mothers in our Village population plus married women who want to work outside the home."

"At this point Amber and I thought it might be best if we spent the rest of our time together opening our session up for general discussion. Does that sound okay to you ladies?" Everybody was in agreement with that direction and a real great discussion took place as a lot of ideas and subjects were aired by all. Both the men's and women's meetings concluded with a strong feeling of "Yes, we can do this and we will make it happen!"

When they had returned back to the ranch there was a short debriefing session and exchange of thoughts and ideas,

A Mark of the Divine

but the bottom line was everybody was on a high as a result of the meetings in Denver. Amber said she had taken notes throughout the women's meeting and would retype the information and send it out to all the women who were in attendance. This information could also be a part of the packet that goes out to the new ranchers who were joining the Developers' group. Ben said he would do the same thing for the men.

Prior to retiring for the evening, Ben stepped out on the porch and leaned on the railing, digesting the stillness of the night and the brightness of the stars. *How fast things change,* he thought. *It was just a little over two years ago it seemed like the Country might start getting back on track. The voters had finally sent a powerful message to the political candidates during the midterm elections, and it seemed like we might be have gotten through to those we were sending to Washington, D.C., to truly represent the wishes of the majority. But somehow the gains made to right the Country and get it going in a direction that would bring back a strong economy, high job growth and lower taxes all seemed to have been wiped out in one day when the results of the 2012 election were determined.*

He thought back on his days of playing football as a running back. When there seemed to be no opening to run through, many times spinning and changing directions achieved the desired results. Guess in one sense that is what we are about today as we forge out a new direction. Ben smiled to himself as he thought about his friend Bruce who referred to entrepreneurship and innovation out here on the Plains as 'Prairie Talent'. *Yep,* he thought, *that's a good handle for all of us involved in this giant movement.*

CHAPTER TWENTY-ONE

"As the plane banked left and continued its climb out from the airport, Ben said to Amber, "The more I think about the new priorities of our mission, I think we should quite doing membership recruitment meetings immediately and redirect our efforts to meetings with those who are already shareholders. It's important they have a good understanding of what is available to them. They need to know they can take their membership to the next level and consider moving into one of the Villages within the next few months as housing becomes available. What do you think Amber?"

"Funny you should say that Ben, I actually was just thinking along the same lines, since there is such incredible momentum now as far as new shareholder sign ups. At this moment, we don't know how large the movement to the Villages will be and that is something we definitely have to get a handle on real soon. I keep having the feeling that it is going to be overwhelming. By switching over to holding meetings with our shareholders, we will at least start to find out their thoughts and needs as far as it relates to the upcoming movement out to the Villages. In fact, when we have these share-

A Mark of the Divine

holder meetings, a signup sheet for those who would like to move this year should be available. This will help immensely as we and all the other developers put their operational plans into motion."

"That's a good idea Amber, as soon as we land I'll call Robert and Sandy and see if they agree, which I am quite sure they will. Then we can start calling shareholders together.

Robert is out on his last swing so it would be easy for him to switch over to also doing meetings with the shareholders. We can switch a lot of the others who are now engaged in recruitment meetings, to start holding shareholder meetings. We'll have to have at least one meeting with all of our presenters to go over what we want to talk about at these shareholder meetings."

Robert and Sandy were in total agreement with Ben and Amber about putting on meetings that were aimed at all the shareholders of the corporation, so their earlier plans were changed later that same day. This would really be the first beginnings of what would become known as The Mid American Beltway to start with and later just Mid America. Both Amber and Ben had separate shareholder recruitment meetings set up that night in Portland, Oregon, that they were committed to. These would be their last meetings with this kind of agenda. They agreed to meet for a late dinner and then they would put together their agenda for the meetings with the shareholders.

Amber said, "I talked to Sandy just before I met with you and she had just updated the totals figures for the number of shareholders. Can you believe the number of people buying shares in the corporation has now exceeded thirty million, and that number is increasing exponentially by the hour? Sandy said she has had to add three more people to the corporate office staff to help out on the administration side of things."

Amber and Ben had chosen a little restaurant off on a side street that Amber had run across the last time she was here. It was a cozy little place and provided them with plenty of conversation privacy. As she took a sip of her wine, over the top of her glass she fastened her eyes on Ben and thought *I don't know how or when, but somehow I am going to get this man to marry me, I really think he is the man I have been waiting for all these years.* Ben was absorbed with the menu and didn't notice the laser look he was getting from Amber.

"Amber," Ben said, "Now that we have finished with our membership drive would you be up to a little diversion this weekend?" I wonder what he is thinking. I sure hope he isn't a mind reader!

"Quite frankly, I think that a little diversion would be a good thing and help us get pumped up for our new meetings quest with the shareholders. That just might be what is needed," Amber said.

"What would you say if I said how about we fly down to a Puerto Vallarta, Mexico for a weekend of fun in the sun? We'll just hang out and relax, but don't worry, I'll get two rooms for us."

Amber was so completely taken aback that she just starred at Ben with her mouth hanging open. Finally she said the only thing that came to her mind. "But I don't have any clothes that I could take to a place like that." "That's okay, you won't need any," Ben said. Amber's mouth opened again but nothing came out. Ben started laughing and said, "That didn't come out quite the way I meant it. What I meant to say was that whatever you need, I'll get for you down there." Then Amber busted out laughing also. "Well that's a little bit more relaxation then what I was thinking of, but it sounds like a wonderful idea."

CHAPTER TWENTY-TWO

On beautiful white sand, they reclined on their beach chairs sipping sodas. Watching all the activity going on was almost overwhelming to Amber, as she had never experienced anything remotely close to this.

"Before you ask me to tell about me, if in fact you were going to do that," Ben said, "would you fill me in on who Amber is?" Amber smiled at the no-nonsense approach Ben used to inquire about her personal life. *Did he have some hidden agenda?* she wondered.

"Wait," Ben said as his gaze went to the ocean, where he spotted a whale breaching. Straight out from us are at least four whales romping together." "Wow," Amber said, "the only time I have seen a whale was in the movies or a magazine. They are awesome." She reminded Ben of a little girl in a candy store. Her enthusiastic and exciting demeanor was definitely contagious.

"Okay," Amber said with a little smile, "are you going to keep interrupting me after you ask a question?" "Sorry, but I just didn't want you to miss the whales!" "I was just teasing you. Now here is the life story of Amber Johnson. My folks were killed in a car accident when I was seven years old. I was in three different foster homes, and my experiences with those homes were not pleasant. I came to understand later that my foster parents were in it for the money and not much else. Love and comfort didn't seem to exist in their vocabulary or their actions."

"As soon as I graduated from high school, I left the last foster home I was in and struck out on my own. One of my high school counselors had highly encouraged me to go to college and to really consider majoring in business. He pointed to the work I did in the last two years of high school as a public relations apprentice for a utility company, saying that the accolades that I received indicated a real aptitude for working in the business world.

I had enough money saved up to get a small apartment and continue to work for the same company. I enrolled in a small local college and worked my way through four years to get my degree. Although I had several good job offers, I decided to take the risk of establishing my own public relations firm. Over the years, with a lot of hard work and a lot of luck I have been able to build a very successful business."

"I doubt if luck had much to do with your success Amber," Ben said. "By the way, did you know you are a very impressive and attractive young lady?" "That was a very nice thing for you to say Ben, particularly the young part." "Well, I consider myself still young at age forty, and I would suspect you are pretty close to my age?" "Absolutely not," Amber said with a very sober face, "I am only thirty-nine."

"Tragedy struck one more time in my young life, when my husband of two years was diagnosed with cancer. In three short months after that he had passed on." "I am so sorry to hear that Amber, it must have been extremely hard on you."

"It really was, in fact over the several years since then, I have just thrown myself into my work and really haven't had much of a social life."

Ben was shaken somewhat as he listened to Amber and realized how almost identical their lives had been. Besides the similarity in how they had lost their parents, the fact that they had both lost their spouses at an early age and had never remarried, seemed quite phenomenal.

CHAPTER TWENTY-THREE

"Amber, I know you are going to think that I have lost it, but I have to say something to you." Ben hesitated and seemed to be struggling to get the words to come out. "I just want to say that from the very first day that I saw you in that meeting I put on for the Rotary back in Denver, I felt and knew in my heart you and I had something very special.

Only once before had I experienced anything like what hit me that day." Amber's eyes had gone wide and her heart seemed to beating in triple overtime, but she held her tongue to hear Ben out.

"Amber do you think that if we gave our relationship a chance, we could discover that this is what we both have been waiting for all this time?" Amber started to speak, but Ben held up his hand. "Before you say anything, I have to tell you that I am in love with you."

Tears gathered at the corner of her eyes as she tried to get her voice activated but she was having a tough time of it. Ben left his chair, came over and sat down on the end of her recliner, reached into his beach bag and took out a small box. Amber watched him with curiosity. "Amber," Ben said as he opened the little box which held a beautiful diamond engagement ring. "Will you marry me?"

Amber was stunned and almost in shock. She couldn't get any words to come out. Finally she said the first thing that came to her mind, "Ben, you've never even kissed me!" Ben slid up a little further up the recliner, leaned down and kissed her with such passion that she thought she was going into an unconscious state of being. They looked at each other without words for several seconds and then a big grin spread across Amber's face. She reached up, put her arms around his neck and simply said, "Yes!"

They called Robert and Sandy when they got back up to the hotel and told them the news. Amber heard Sandy say to the kids, "Ben and Amber are going to get married." There were loud squeals and laughter as everybody was so excited they could hardly contain themselves. Robert said, "When are you planning to have the wedding?" Ben replied."If it is okay with you guys, we'd like to have the wedding right at the Ranch the day of February 10th." Sandy who was on an extension said, "That would be great. We'll start making some plans right away. Would you like me to call Father Tim to make sure he is available for that day?" "Thanks Sandy," Amber said, "that would be fabulous. We'll call you tomorrow night so we can finalize some of the plans."

CHAPTER TWENTY FOUR

After setting their schedules up for the next week, Amber and Ben combined their efforts in putting on the first meeting for the shareholders. The word had gotten out fast among the shareholders and when they walked into the huge ballroom in the hotel, they could hardly believe their eyes; the room was full.

Ben walked to the podium, introduced himself and Amber and then thanked everybody for attending. "Today marks the beginning of a new phase of our efforts as we are officially going to substantially reduce the recruiting of folks to become shareholders in A Mark of The Divine. I am pleased to tell you that we are now moving rapidly towards a shareholder base of thirty million which will continue to grow very rapidly." There was standing applause along with a lot cheering and back slapping as renewed energy was felt throughout the room.

"Today, I want to talk to you a little bit about what will be happening over the rest of the winter months and then the next step in this massive undertaking as we enter spring. We all know, the situation in the United States is continuing its downward spiral if you measure today's America compared to America as little as five years ago. Witness Federal take-over's of industries, continued constriction as it relates to freedom of speech and freedom of religion, extreme taxation, a declining health care program and the list goes on. It is a very frightening time for those of us who have embraced all that our country has stood for over its two plus centuries of life."

"By March, we hope to have at least 1000 ranchers and farmers throughout the Plains States and some of the bordering States who will become what we call Shareholder/Developers. They, like us at the O'Neil Ranch in western North Dakota, will be developing small Villages that will dot the Plains from the Canadian border to the Mexican border. Construction of these Villages will get underway as soon as weather permits, which will vary considerably from the far North Country to western Arizona. In fact, we expect that construction in the lower elevations of Nevada, Arizona, and New Mexico, plus the States of Louisiana and Texas, may actually be starting as we speak."

"Those who are shareholders in A Mark of the Divine and elect to start their lives over in one of these villages, are automatically invited and all you need to do is contact us to set that action in motion. Incidentally, we will have sign up sheets up here at the end of the meeting for anyone who wants to sign up now. Naturally, each Village will require enough space for the inflow of people so some patience will be needed on your part. As this migration begins, we need to match the availability of houses with the number of people planning to move into the Villages.

As the population steadily increases in the Villages, the rate of construction will also increase as we will have just that many more people building houses.

Within the next month, if you are one of the people who are requesting to move, you will be receiving a packet of information from us. This will detail what you can expect when you make this transition from where ever you live now to a new home in the new Mid American Beltway. Included in the information will be a listing of the developers and their locations and telephone numbers.

All the developers will be linked together. If your situation requires that you need to move right away and can't wait any longer, you will be directed to contact a developer that has immediate availability."

"Because this whole undertaking is so unprecedented, we have little on which to base our assumptions. However, it is our best guess at this time that two to three million people will be able to be accommodated and will move to the Mid American Beltway during the rest of 2014. In 2015, that number will easily triple. There was a gasp from the crowd as they tried to digest what Ben was telling them."

"Since we could spend hours talking about all the things that we are projecting, I think it would be better if we just open this session up to your questions. Don't forget, you will be getting detailed information in the mail."

"Ben, can you clarify the housing thing for us and how people moving into these Villages will be able to buy a house, get a job and live some kind of a decent life?" asked a shareholder. "If I answer your question in any kind of detail sir, none of you will get home for dinner tonight." That seemed to lighten up the crowd a bit and brought some good laughter.

"Much like the community you live in right now," Ben said, "each Village will have a broad mixture of people with many different skills, education, money, and so forth. Let me start with those who for whatever reason are for all practical purposes broke or close to it. Of course as you know this category has been expanding quite rapidly as small businesses have been shutting down right and left, and corporate capitalism is becoming a thing of the past."

"Unemployment, the real unemployment numbers which include those who are way Underemployed, those who have given up trying to find employment, and those who are working at a various part-time jobs just to try and keep food on the table and a roof over their heads, is now projected to be close to thirty percent. This obviously isn't the number that you hear coming from the cheerleaders in Washington, D.C., as they tout the tremendous number of jobs they have 'saved'. They give a number which is impossible to prove or dispute but most of us know what a crock that kind of rhetoric really is.

Be that as it may, reality is that in America today almost a third of our nation's working population is in trouble. So we have a large number of people who have now gone through any savings they had and are living on the brink of poverty." If these people who are shareholders and so desire, they will be processed into Villages as quickly as possible. The developers like ourselves will be financially assisted with funds from A Mark of the Devine."

"Those who join the Villages won't be digressing back quite as far as what our ancestors faced when they migrated west in covered wagons, but there will be a big cultural shock that most likely will take place as people learn to acclimate themselves and adapt from what was to what is. Most of these folks will have themselves as their only assets, but will be a real example of what I call true American grit. They will have a strong desire to succeed, but most likely will be putting a different definition on the word success."

Technology has been great asset to all of us, but unfortunately it also has led a particularly alarming percentage of our youth into a form of hibernation and a failure to acquire the social behavior learned by youth of previous decades. For them, the change will be probably be almost gut wrenching, as they adapt to working in gardens instead of playing electronic games, as just one example. Will that be a negative in the long run? We don't think so; in fact it will develop a much stronger younger generation with a great work ethic and moral foundation, something that is desperately needed in our America today.

"These families will learn to live comfortably on very little and hopefully be able to put new definitions on happiness. The houses that will be built for them will be quite simple and devoid of luxuries but nevertheless very efficient and comfortable. A family will have the opportunity to actually own their house through the accrual of credits for work they are doing without receiving direct payments. I should interject here so that you understand, in one sense you will be borrowing the money for the house you live in, but you will have no pressure for payments. Look at it as your house being like a savings account, the more you put in the more equity you will have in your house at some time in the future."

"That's one category of people and another category is those folks who have been able to keep some kind nest egg in terms of assets. They will have the opportunity to upgrade their housing to pretty much what they want since they would be paying for their houses up front. A lot of those in the first group I discussed will be able to earn money by working on construction and other projects, for these people."

"The financing gets a bit complicated, and I just don't have the time to expand upon it any further. We are hopeful that in the long run, the developers who will be putting in a lot of their own money up front, will have the opportunity to profit from their efforts, which may take several years. But you have to realize that these people are not anticipating a big bonanza. They are providing resources for development, because they have a deep-seated love for America and its people and are angrier than they have ever been at their Federal Government."

"Okay, one more question. Yes ma'am?" "Thanks for taking my question. My son and I live in an apartment and the violence we are seeing taking place in our area is definitely on the increase. Also the breakdown of authority in the school my son attends to seems to be increasing and it appears to be getting more dangerous all the time for the kids as there is a big increase in the number of gangs in the area. My question is two fold; will life in the Villages be safe and what about schooling?

Those are two excellent questions. First, let me talk about your safety. Our Ranch as well as all the other ranches and farms involved, will have a very sophisticated alert system all the way around their perimeters. This is to alert the Village of any impending intrusions that might be taking place. All the residents age sixteen and up will be furnished with rifles and be given shooting lessons on a regular basis. This may sound a little ominous to many of you, but preparation is very important.

It would be foolish and naïve for us to believe that over time the Villages will not come under some kind of attacks, and we want to be ready for that kind of an event. Our world, unfortunately has become a much more dangerous place and we have to have our thinking and preparation in sync with the way things are."

"The second part of your question is much easier to answer. Home schooling utilizing Internet resources and experts from around the world outside of education will be the standard by which the children in the Villages will be educated. There won't be any big surprises inside the textbooks the kids are studying like there is in so many parts of the U.S. today. Radical ideas have wormed their way into many textbooks throughout our school systems, starting at an early age and then on through college. It is downright criminal the way these radical and unfounded ideas are presented as fact. The education your child or children will receive will be far superior to the level of education that most of the kids are getting today. We will also be having on-going training for those who want to become home school teachers. So the bottom line to your questions is, the children in the Villages will be very well educated and you will be far safer in the Villages than just about any other place you could be."

"In closing let me just say this, in spite of the cultural shock that you may go through in moving to one of the villages, be assured the experience will be very positive and once you have made the adjustment, I think you will understand the true meaning of being a pioneer, because you will in fact be one in the truest sense. God Bless you and America.

CHAPTER TWENTY-FIVE

Western North Dakota was experiencing some especially balmy weather for winter time, although there still was a fair snow cover on the ground. After landing in Dickinson on a commercial flight, Amber and Ben hitched a ride over to the Private Pilots area, picked up one of the vehicles they had left at the airport and headed for the Ranch. It was a beautiful evening and they were enjoying the serenity as they drove. They were also utilizing the time to analyze the effectiveness of the shareholders' meetings they had held over this past week.

The sun was just setting and even though the temperature was falling rapidly, it was a wonderful January evening. They were chatting easily about their meeting successes over the last week when Amber shouted, "Stop the car Ben!" Ben instinctively pulled over, stopped and said "What is going on?" "I saw something off the side of the road, just a little ways back, and I swear it looked like a little girl". There were no other cars on the county road as Ben whipped the car around and slowly drove in the opposite direction.

"There!" Amber shouted pointing off to the side of the road. Ben stopped the car.

A Mark of the Divine

Sure enough, there was a little girl all hunched up and sitting off the road, half-way down in the ditch. They both jumped out of the car and ran down to the little girl. She had a thin jacket on but she was shivering uncontrollably and obviously scared out of her wits. Ben surveyed the area but couldn't see anyone else, as the thought had just occurred to him that this might have been a ruse to get them to stop and then get waylaid, mugged and left without a car. But that definitely didn't seem to be the case.

Amber sat down next to the little girl and put her arm around her. "Please don't be afraid. Where are you parents?" The girl just shrugged. It was obviously difficult for her to talk as she was shaking so badly. The tears were flowing freely.

Ben was mad as a hornet as he said to himself as much as to Amber, "How could anybody be so inhumane as to drop off a little kid out here in the middle of nowhere? If we hadn't come along it's likely there wouldn't have been another car come this way until tomorrow. The temperature will likely drop well below freezing tonight, so if the cold didn't kill her, quite possibly a coyote or two would have."

"Okay, "Ben said, "let's get her in the car, and we'll sort this out back at the ranch. Put her in between us and we'll crank up the heater and get this little one warmed up." As they proceeded towards the ranch, the little girl's tears ceased and she quit shaking as her little body's temperature got back to normal. "What is your name?" Amber said. "It's Zari Azar." "How old are you Zari?" "Thirteen." "Were you out there very long before we came by?" "It seemed like a long time, I was so scared and cold."

"Zari," Ben said, "I have to ask you this. Where are your parents and were they the ones who left you out there?" Ben had taken note of her darker complexion and was wondering about her nationality. Her name sounded Middle Eastern. She started to sob again and was unable to talk for awhile. Ben and Amber didn't say anything and finally she said, "My father dropped me off and told me that he would never see me again. He has always hated me. My mother had told me once he just wanted a son and had no time for a daughter. He told me that he and my mother were going far away." Then a new stream of tears rolled down her cheeks. Amber put her arm around the girl and hugged her tight.

Ben was positively steaming, he was so mad. "Zari," Ben said, "I don't want you to worry, Amber and I will take care of you. We'll see that no harm will ever come to you again." He glanced at Amber and noticed the agreement in her eyes.

After bringing Sandy, Robert and the kids up to speed on what had happened, they agreed that at least for right now, Zari should stay in the second bedroom at the cottage Amber was staying in. She seemed to be comfortable with Amber. Amber got her settled in and after Zari had taken a long hot bath to get the chill out of her bones they went back to the main cabin and ate. Sandy's children and Zari had quickly become friends. Zari seemed to be calming down and relaxing. The fact that the kids were hitting it off really helped the situation. Amber thought, how could any human being be so cruel as to leave their daughter the way they had?

After all the children had gone to bed the conversation between the adults centered on Zari and on how they would handle this unexpected turn of events. "I for one," Ben said, "feel we should do everything in our power to right all the wrongs that have been foisted on this little girl her whole life."

They all agreed and started putting together a plan for Zari, what she would need and how they would all handle everything. "What do you think about our adopting Zari?"

Amber asked of Ben. "Interesting you said that, because I was thinking the same thing, Amber," Ben commented.

"Oh, that is a great idea! It would be so wonderful of you to do that," Sandy replied. "I'll get things in motion tomorrow," Ben said. "I don't know how many obstacles we'll have to overcome to get this done, but hopefully it can happen and happen soon." "We'll have a discussion with Zari tomorrow morning and find out what she thinks about the idea," Amber said. "You know, one thing I have discovered about being around you O'Neil's? There definitely aren't any dull moments." That gave everybody a good chuckle. "Don't forget," Ben said, "you're going to be an O'Neil pretty soon yourself! "Believe me, Mr. Ben O'Neil, I could never forget that. You have no idea how excited I am.

CHAPTER TWENTY-SIX

As Zari approached the table Ben said, "Good morning sleepy head, how are you feeling this morning?" "That's the best sleep I have ever had," Zari said, "and I think it is because the angels brought me to you." "Come sit down and have some breakfast Zari," Amber said. "Ben and I have some things we want to talk to you about." Zari sat down at the table and before Ben or Amber could say anything she said, "Before I fell asleep last night I thought of two things that I wanted to ask you. When I was playing with Jimmy and Maggie yesterday we talked about being a Christian. I had friends that I use to play with who were Christians. Do you think I could become a Christian, Ben and Amber? Before you answer that I have one more question. Do you think I could change my name to Suzanne?

Ben and Amber were a bit flabbergasted at the content and directness of her questions. Nothing was said for a few moments and then Ben busted out laughing as did Amber. "I think perhaps you just answered the question we were going to ask you," Amber said. "What was that? Zari asked. "Well first," Ben said, "let me answer your questions." "The short answer to both your questions Suzanne," winking at her with a smile when he said Suzanne and that brought on the giggles, "is yes." Now before we talk more about your questions we have a question for you. "What do you think of the idea of Amber and I adopting you?" Suzanne's eyes went wide like saucers and she stared at them for a few seconds and then jumped up and went to Amber first and then Ben giving them each loving hugs, while the tears started to flow.

"Now I know for sure that the angels are looking after me Dad and Mom," she said as she smiled and cried all at the same time. "I have to go over and tell Jimmy and Maggie, is that okay?" "You go right ahead and we'll see you in a little while," Amber said. Zari, now to become Suzanne, gave each of them another hug and a kiss and ran out the door with her coat only half on, yelling as if someone other than Ben and Amber could hear her.

CHAPTER TWENTY-SEVEN

Pleasantly exhausted from all the activities of the previous couple of weeks, the four O'Neils knew they didn't have the luxury to bask in the glorious warmth of their successes. In fact, they all were quite humbled by what had been and was being accomplished as it was beyond their wildest expectations.

The work just kept piling up and on top of that, Ben and Amber's wedding day was only a little over a week away. So the next day they were back at it. "Let me lay this out for everybody for starters, then we can go over everything and fine-tune our approach," Robert said. "Over the next weeks, Sandy and Amber could you go through the shareholders lists that have been collected at the meetings?"

We need to develop a list of people who have indicated they would like to move to one of the Villages as soon as possible and also identify or highlight their skills. Next, please confirm with these folks that they are truly in a position to move and desire to do so. Then let's make up from this list, the names that fall into the following categories as of now: contractors, carpenters, plumbers, roofers, heavy equipment operators, heating, concrete specialists, electricians and clerical."

Sandy interjected, "I am sure glad that when we set up our computer program for shareholders we grouped everybody by their profession, skills or business, otherwise this would be an impossible task." "Can you guys do that for starters?" Ben asked. Both Amber and Sandy answered in the affirmative. Sandy said, "Let's add teachers to the list of skills. I think we will want to get our home schooling programs off and running at the earliest possible date."

"Ben, I think you and I should look at the shareholders that are listed under farmers and ranchers. We'll start sending out lists to the guys from the various States that were at the meeting in Denver, as they all said they would be glad to hold some meetings in their States with potential new shareholder/developers. This is a phase of our program that really needs to get into high gear.

Ben said, "We are so fortunate to have the kind of shareholders in this category that we have. I worked a lot with farmers and ranchers during my career and most fit the mold of having huge hearts, are as tough as steel rebar, very savvy, and very motivated. Being shareholders, they are also strong Christians or people of other faiths. So I think once we have a chance to lay out our plan as we see it at this time, these folks will be chomping at the bit to get involved and will be enthusiastically pushing forward."

Amber said, "Do you think that they will have a problem converting their farmland or grazing land into housing projects?" "I don't think so" Robert said, as most of the folks who will get involved have tremendous acreages and so the percentage of land they will be converting to this project will represent a pretty small part of their land. They will quite possibly even look at it as a good diversion of assets over the long haul."

"These people, like us, are usually ready, willing and able to lend a big hand to those who need help. I think most of them, because of these wonderful attributes, will open their arms to the challenge of developing these brand new communities. They will be motivated by the prospect of giving hope to those who are in desperate need of change. This need of change will not be just from financial needs. It will also be because of their need to escape from religious persecution and moral decay in their communities." "I'd like to suggest that we just relax and enjoy the rest of the day and then we'll start hitting it hard tomorrow morning," Ben said, "BUT we are working for a pretty tough task master and even though he rested on the seventh day, I don't think we have that luxury." Everybody got a good chuckle out of Ben's statement, and they all agreed, no rest was in order at this time.

CHAPTER TWENTY-EIGHT

The big day arrived for Ben and Amber, and as luck would have it, the weather, for a winter day in North Dakota, was perfect. They had planned to have the ceremony down by the creek if weather permitted. Robert had built an arch and painted it white. Sandy had strung some artificial flowers on it. There was a lot of hustle and bustle taking place, and the children were all taking part in all the activities.

A lot of neighbors had been invited and the day was turning out to be quite festive. When Father Tim arrived, everybody moved outside and went down to the area that was set up for the wedding ceremony. Amber looked absolutely gorgeous as Robert escorted her up the make-shift isle between the seats. He gave her a big brotherly hug as he gave her to Ben. Amber couldn't help the tears of joy that started to run down her cheek. *I am so danged emotional, I hope my tears won't freeze on my face,* she thought to herself.

With guidance from Father Tim, Ben and Amber said their wedding vows. Then they turned and kissed each other. After the kiss had ended, Father Tim said to the group, "I'd like to present Mr. and Mrs. Ben O'Neil!"

A Mark of the Divine

After all the congratulations and hugging and kissing, they all started back to the house. On the way, Father Tim made a quick snowball and let it fly right at Ben's back. "We don't have rice so snow will have to do," he hollered. A grand snowball fight immediately erupted and the laughing and screaming was contagious as everybody got into the act. Eventually they made their way back to the house where they enjoyed the goodies Sandy had made. "It just couldn't have been any more perfect," Amber said to everybody, "to have all of you here for our wedding was very special. At this moment, I am surely the happiest person in the whole world!"

All the guests had departed. As Ben and Amber made their way over to their house, Ben said, "We're really lucky. There is real gem of a blizzard moving our way, so I am sure glad we had the chance to have our wedding ceremony outside. It was a beautiful backdrop for a very special day. I love you Amber O'Neil." "That sounds so wonderful," *hmm Amber O'Neil, how great is that?*

CHAPTER TWENTY-NINE

The next evening, with the wind howling outside and the snow coming down pretty hard, Ben and Amber were relaxing on the couch in front of the fireplace. Amber said, "I know we have been over most aspects of this whole mission, but because it is so complex Ben, will you do me a favor?" Ben cocked an eyebrow as he looked at Amber and said, "Do I dare to ask what you have in mind?" "Please do an abbreviated run-through of some of the elements that are causing this whole mess we have in the United States and how A Mark of the Divine counterbalances all of that," Amber said.

"Did anybody ever tell you what a romantic you are?" Ben said as a smile played on his lips. Here we are all nice and cozy in our little cabin with a fire going while a blizzard rages outside and what do you want to talk about?, business!" Amber reached over and smacked him on the shoulder. "There will be plenty of time later for 'other' kinds of talking, I just need to get a couple things straight in my head, so indulge me." With a sigh of resignation, Ben met Amber's request with the kind of intensity born of conviction that truly defined who Ben was.

A Mark of the Divine

"What our plan will do, is to provide a new lifestyle to those who desire to make a change from where they are at now. The motivation for these people will come from their destitution, mostly caused by under employment or unemployment. It will also come from their inability to feel free to worship without danger. Another big motivator for a lot of people will be their seeking better educational opportunities for their children and the list goes on.

"There is another sector of people who have ridden a wave prosperity by being employed by either State or Federal Governments. The number of Federal civilian employees is rocketing towards twenty million, and that number is almost identical for all State Government employees. That is a staggering figure of close to forty million people that we, the taxpayers, need to support. A part of the fiscal problems for governments is this bloated number of employees who are receiving compensation that is almost double of what they would get in the private sector for similar jobs. Then add in the extremely generous benefits that are dished out by these governments, including the excessive retirement benefits and you have a recipe for fiscal disaster."

"I mention this group, because at some point both State and Federal Governments will come to realize this is unsustainable, and they will have to start laying a lot of people off.

Those who are laid off are going to have, for the most part, a real awakening and are going to need help transitioning to the private sector. This is going to compound an already bad situation. There will a lot of these people in trouble."

"At this time, unfortunately, approximately 55 to 60 percent of the population is dependent upon at least some government subsidies, which is exactly what our Federal

Administration set out to accomplish when they first came into office a few years ago. That is also unsustainable in the long run as the Country continues its transition toward Socialism."

"So you're saying that because of these things that are happening, the need for A Mark of the Divine is even going to become much greater as we move forward?" Amber said. Ben responded, "No Country can sustain a situation where more people are receiving benefits from the Government than are those who are paying in. Things will just continue to get worse.

We have examples of that happening in other Countries around the world. It's dependency in its worse form. People lose their dignity, they lose their will to succeed, and in essence, they simply exist. That's a long way from what we as Americans grew up to believe was our legacy and destiny."

"But how did this happen in the first place?" Amber asked. " The politicians went absolutely nuts by going on a spending spree that was unparalleled in the history of the United States. This put our Nation in so much debt, that the only way the politicians could work their way out of this mess was through taxation, at least that is what they wanted us to believe. It doesn't take a lot of education to understand that when you spend more than what you take in, there is a problem, and far be it for a politician to attack this problem by deeply cutting expenses."

"Underlying this whole politically led problem is the lack of term limits, huge governmental salaries and benefits in the form of retirement, health care and on and on. This encourages these people to become career politicians and that in turn leads to corruption and a less and less true representation of the people they are suppose to serve. It doesn't seem to make any difference as far as what political party a politician belongs to, they pretty much follow the same pattern to varying degrees."

"It appeared that perhaps the tide was going to be turned when 'we the people' finally had enough and really made our voices heard in the mid-term elections. This caused a big turnover in who was representing us. But the Administration remained the same and the Senate was still under the same leadership that had gotten us into all the trouble in the first place. So although there was a correction taking place it didn't have time to gain much traction before the Presidential election and we know what happened then."

"There was a movement that started out East a few years ago. They had a great slogan, 'Starve the Beast'. The idea was to legislate a big cut in sales taxes, income taxes and so forth, thus cutting off funds to the Governments and forcing them to start slicing away at all the fat." "Why didn't that really take off, it seems like a very practical solution?"

Amber asked. "In their super ability to spin the truth and in fact flat-out lie, the politicians were able to convince a big enough percentage of the voting population that this was really a bad idea, and they would be cutting off their nose to save their faces."

"So your saying that the tax burden on all working Americans is basically leading tens of millions of people toward the poor house," Amber said. "That's what I'm saying. Not only that, but it has taken the incentive out of the free enterprise system. Why work your butt off and take risks only to have a big chunk of what you earned, be siphoned off to the Government for redistribution to those who would rather not work and just collect a check? The answer is that many decided they wouldn't continue to do this. So the big thing that made this country what it became, that being Capitalism, was rapidly being replaced by a strong movement to Socialism. That is what has led us to the plan we have developed."

"There is one other major element that has slowly been changing during this time. That is our religious freedom. This pertains particularly to Christianity and Judaism, which have been taking a real beating. Now remember Amber, our plan in the final analysis is to merely stimulate and guide a movement that may well have happened eventually with or without us."

"I kind of remember this when I was in grade school and perhaps you do to, but there were a couple of doctor dudes from out East that developed a thesis called the Buffalo Commons, about 30 years ago."

"In essence, the Buffalo Commons was a proposal to create a vast nature preserve in the Great Plains. Needless to say, this really ticked off a lot people throughout that area. The researchers thought that returning about 140,000 square miles of the most arid areas back to native prairie and reintroducing the buffalo into these areas to roam wild would be a great thing."

"Ben, what the heck does that have to do with what we are talking about?" Amber said. Ben looked at her and busted out laughing. "Do you know that you always screw up your face when you get confused about something?" Amber couldn't hold back a laugh that bubbled up inside of her as they gave each other a big hug. "I do love you little Amber!" Ben said. "Love you more Ben."

A Mark of the Divine

Ben continued, "We believe, as do many of the governors in the Midwest, that there will be three huge areas of land that will be playing a major role, in terms of population in our future as a Country. It is thought that these three areas will split the United States of America into three America's: East America, Mid America and West America. The States identified in the Buffalo Commons thesis as compromising Mid America are: the same States that Mid America would consist of: The Dakotas, Minnesota, Montana, Wyoming, Colorado, Nebraska, Kansas, Oklahoma, New Mexico and Texas. Also included will be some adjoining States, such as Arizona in the southwest, and on the east most adjoining States plus most likely Alaska. A second area, referred to as West America, consists of: California, Oregon, Washington, Nevada, Idaho, Utah and Hawaii. The third geographical area will be the eastern seaboard and all adjoining States.

"This huge sprawling area which will be Mid America, will become known as the new frontier once again as it was in the early beginnings of America. It will also become known for its strong Conservative Christian and Jewish population bases. These are people who honor the wonderful and powerful phrase 'In God We Trust', which was very symbolic and meaningful with America up until just the past few years. 'In God We Trust' will once again be the guiding light for new, strongly revitalized America, known as Mid America.

Unique to this geographical split into three Americas is that both West and East America are characterized as more Liberal in their thoughts and actions. Mid America will be just the opposite and will follow along the lines of being much more Conservative in their thinking and actions."

"Just think about the vast differences that exist between geographical areas in terms of space and population. Here is but one example: in the more liberal-leaning States the population per square mile is over two hundred people. In the more conservative leaning States, the population per square mile is less than sixty people. There is a lot more that could be expounded upon, but let's just leave it at this for now."

"The word pioneer will have come full circle and will define the entrepreneurial spirit of these brave and adventurous people who will pull up stakes, pack their few possessions and move into the many different areas of Mid America to start a brand new life. These people will be the new symbol of hope, and their strivings will parallel our forefathers' adventures as they pushed west in covered wagons filled with dreams of new and wonderful beginnings. Mid America will demonstrate what a just and compassionate society firmly grounded in Christian and Jewish beliefs can accomplish. This is at the heart of the movement and what has necessitated a drastic change. We had traveled so far down the wrong roads with the way things were; that to fix what was ailing the Country was becoming impossible. "

"Ben darling, this has connected the dots for me and I thank you for helping me to develop a much clearer picture. However, I believe you could continue these explanations well into the wee hours of the morning, but how about we hit the sack and pick this up tomorrow when we get together with Robert and Sandy?"

Ben chuckled and agreed that enough was enough. Let's do it, we'll cuddle up under those big old quilts and listen to wind howling as Mother Nature flexes her muscle.

CHAPTER THIRTY

The next day although the blizzard was still in full force, Ben, Amber and Suzanne bundled up and managed to make it over to Robert and Sandy's place. Two days ago when they had heard the forecast for the possibilities of a very dangerous blizzard coming their way, Robert and Ben had strung a rope between the two houses, That proved to have been a good move as it would have been the only way they would have dared to cross the space between the two houses. The visibility was zero. Without the rope they could have missed Robert's and Sandy's house, and that could have spelled doom for them.

The children were off in another part of the house doing their own thing as the four adults, armed with hot coffee, descended on the great room where a wonderful fire blazed in the big fireplace. They had gotten into the habit of spending at least three hours in the morning going over intentions, debating various issues and continually revising some of their plans. Today would be no different.

"As you know, I hate politics with a passion," Robert said, "but I know we all have been getting questions about the Corporation's stance on endorsing political candidates

A Mark of the Divine

whether it be at the local level or Congress and the White House. Last night I put together a list of basic beliefs for political candidates. If A Mark of the Divine would agree to endorse them. This would be quite a significant move because the corporation, A Mark of the Divine obliviously now has considerable clout. This is what I put together, so let me run through it and then we can discuss it.

He began, "A Mark of The Divine, Inc. will take under serious consideration the endorsing of political candidates if the candidate signs an agreement to support the main issues we believe in.

1. That Christianity will be the Official Religion in the geographical area of interest for any given candidate. This does not mean that other religions aren't welcome in the involved area, for example, the Jewish people and their beliefs. Again, however, keep in mind that 'we can only serve one master'; this means there will be only one religion that will be officially recognized in the area served by the candidate and that religion will be Christianity.

   Any so-called religion that does not respect human dignity will not be tolerated in any way. All public places including schools, government buildings and grounds will honor Christianity as the Religion of the Land.

2. Marriage will **only** be defined as the holy union between one man and one women.

3. The English Language will be the only Official Language. The Federal Government should agree to set up and fund as many English language teaching stations throughout this new Country of Mid America as is necessary to see to it that all legal immigrants

have the opportunity to learn English. Again, this does not mean that other languages are not embraced and encouraged as a tradition and a part of cultures.

4. Candidates for a National office must agree to establish and support a direction and a means by which illegal aliens can achieve legal citizenship or be deported, no in-between. This pathway to citizenship would be for only those illegal's who have not been convicted of any felonious activity.

    As part of becoming a citizen they must acknowledge and accept the order of the land as spelled out in items one, two and three. Again this does not mean that they are not free to follow and practice their own beliefs as long as those beliefs don't interfere in any way with what Mid America stands for. If they cannot do this, they will not be accepted as a citizen and will be deported. Updated immigration laws will reflect these definitions, be acted upon and enforced.

5. That all elected officials from City Council members to the U.S. Congress and National Administration shall serve no more than one term, and that term shall not extend more than six years. The benefits of only serving one term are overwhelmingly positive and beneficial for everybody. This will be an immense help in putting down corruption within all publicly held positions. There is a tremendous wealth of very well qualified people to continually fill Government positions. By cleaning up the process and limiting everybody to one term, people will be much more willing to come forward and serve. The United States

Constitution foresaw government by the people, not government by professional politicians.

6. Taxation of the people must be closely monitored at all levels. No governmental agency should come close to imitating the abdominal sickness such as is present in the IRS. This kind of heavy-handed and intolerable type of organization in America goes against everything that America stands for. Rather the IRS will be replaced with a small tax revenue agency that administers and enforces a simple flat tax.

    Every governmental agency, State and Federal, will be reviewed by outside independent and accredited accounting and management firms. If it is determined that any agency is not serving an **essential function** or is not operating at peak efficiency, it's operations will be either corrected or the agency abolished.

7. There is to be total reform in terms of the current Congressional compensation, including only health care benefits that are available to the general public. Congressional retirement benefits are to be Social Security, Medicare and a reasonable retirement benefits package that is commensurate with having served one term in office.

    How it came about that the members of the current and previous Congresses elevated themselves to such a lofty compensation, health care and retirement package, one can only imagine and say shame on you!

8. National debt reduction must be a key component in the battle to achieve a balanced budget and become a fiscally responsible Nation.

9. Our National Energy Policy must be totally overhauled. We must tap into the vast and heretofore unused or scarcely used natural resources of our own nation including oil, gas and coal. We need a strong advancement in the use of nuclear energy while utilizing the best technology and the work of non-political untainted scientists available to totally minimize environmental damage. With continued research, the development of economically feasible alternative energy components will become a large part of our energy usage for future generations.
10. Principled and moral conduct by all National, Regional or State News Media is called for. Any reporter who deliberately or carelessly falsifies any verbal or written information to the public will face severe consequences.

    These are the main principles that will need to be agreed to before A Mark of The Divine, Inc. and its shareholders will endorse any candidate running for election in a Public office."

A lively debate ensued but in the end with just a few modifications they all agreed that this was great document and should be circulated to all shareholders as soon as possible.

CHAPTER THIRTY-ONE

As the adults were finishing up with the day's work, the kids burst into the room hollering for them to come into the family room right away. Startled by the ruckus the kids were making, they thought sure something bad had happened. They all jumped up and followed the kids. "Look" Jimmy said, as he pointed to the big bay window. Much to their astonishment, there was a huge bull buffalo right up against the house. "His head is so big, I think it would fill this whole room," Jimmy said. "He must have gotten separated from the herd during this blizzard and is seeking shelter from the wind by standing on that side of the house," Ben said. "By the time this storm blows through, we will probably have to get Joe to bring the front-end loader and we'll have to dig him out of the snow," Robert said.

"I think that it is time for a really exciting story," Ben said. "Seeing that big buffalo right by the house reminds me of a story that you kids should know about." "Is it a ghost story Uncle Ben?" Maggie asked. Ben smiled and said no, the ghost story is going to have to wait, but you will like this story even better."

A Mark of the Divine

The kids all sat down on the floor in front of Ben, eyes wide with anticipation. "Many years ago," Ben said as he started the story, "right where we live now there were thousands of buffalo roaming this land. The Indians who lived throughout this land and hunted buffalo and had many uses for them. Like we do with cattle today, they ate the buffalo meat. They used the buffalo skins to make blankets, moccasins and clothes. The horns they used to make medicine."

"As time went by, the white men started to move westward. They also hunted the buffalo, but in their case, too many of them hunted the buffalo just for the sport if it. Soon the number of buffalo became pretty sparse."

"It was at this time that Running Fast, a little Indian boy of about you guys' age, had gotten up real early one morning. Leaving his teepee, he walked up to the top of a nearby hill. He was sitting on that hill and thinking about what bad shape their tribe was in as they hadn't been able to find any buffalo and their food was getting really low. There was a heavy fog, so Running Fast couldn't see very far. All of a sudden, as he was looking into the fog, this huge bull buffalo came out of the fog and just stood there looking at Running Fast. He slowly got up and walked backward a little way down the hill until he couldn't see the buffalo. Then he turned around and ran like a rabbit down the hill to the camp, screaming at the top of his lungs as he neared the camp."

"It was still early and most everybody was still sleeping, but when the Indians heard Running Fast's screams they all came out of their teepees to find out what the commotion was all about. Pointing at the hill, Running Fast explained to everybody what he had seen. Suddenly the whole camp was in motion. Grabbing their bows and arrows and knives they all ran up the hill but stopped just before they got to the top and peeked over.

Sure enough, that big buffalo was still standing there. The Indians were pretty sure there would be a big herd of buffalo behind him that they couldn't see because of the fog."

"Slowly everybody spread out and crept through the fog until, all of a sudden they came upon a whole bunch of buffalo. They didn't kill the big bull buffalo, because he became a sacred omen to them, but they did kill enough other buffalo to provide the whole tribe with food and clothing for many months to come."

"The tribe had a big powwow that night and they honored Running Fast with a beautiful necklace that was carved from a buffalo horn. They claimed that he now had a special gift that would make him very wise as he grew older."

"Now here is the big deal, the Indians believe that when someone is the first to see a big bull buffalo, they too will be given that special gift and will become very wise. Since Jimmy, Maggie and Suzanne were the first to see the big buffalo, you guys are now like Running Fast and will be given a special gift of wisdom!" The kids were so totally engrossed in Ben's story that even after he was done they sat there looking at him without saying a word. Finally, they all got up and went over to the window and just stared at the buffalo in silence.

"I would give anything to get inside their little minds right now," Sandy said, "and find out what they were all thinking." "You did it again Uncle Ben," Sandy said, "good job."

CHAPTER THIRTY-TWO

The blizzard had moved on through, and everybody was busy shoveling snow. They managed to get the snow cleared away from the big buffalo that had become trapped between a huge snow bank and the house. He just shook himself and sauntered away. The next couple of days the sun was out and actually getting some warmth to it. Winter was flying by and some thawing was already starting to take place in the last part of March. Tirelessly, the four had poured over various plans of action, when Sandy's home schooling classes were not in session. She not only was schooling her own children, but she had Ben and Amber's adopted daughter Suzanne plus three other neighboring children. In addition, Sandy had started to hold classes in their home for several mothers who lived in the area, teaching them how to home school their own children and perhaps some additional children this summer when the new people started to arrive.

They had all agreed, in one of their planning sessions, that it was absolutely necessary to provide an outstanding educational service. They reasoned that the education of children is a critical element to the future of the Nation.

A Mark of the Divine

Education begins in infancy, which is the purest form of home schooling, and it is continued through vitally important lap time. The amount of lap time, when the parent holds the child on his or her lap and reads aloud, is the best predictor of later success in reading. So those who will come to the Villages, regardless of how busy they are, will be expected to dedicate an ample amount of lap time for each of their children. This sets the stage for the child when he or she enters a more formal or structured form of schooling. Those in charge of the formal part of schooling wanted to be sure the end result would be that they were providing a far superior service including the environment, when it was compared to the educational format and environment of schools the kids would be coming from.

In public schools the Christian kids were now often being singled out by other kids as being weird. They were subjected to a lot of ridicule and bullying. It was becoming almost intolerable for Christian children in most schools. Obviously, this was an element that those kids would not have to deal with in the Villages.

"Without a doubt," Robert said, "The biggest unknown is how much time we have to prepare and activate our plan and then the time we have to accomplish the plan." "You're right, Robert, but it would seem the only thing we can do is move forward and pray we have enough time to at least accomplish most of what we have to do" Ben said. "I guess we have to assume that regardless of what we accomplish, it may not be enough to fully handle the demand. So, we need to plan for the maximum we can accomplish."

"Sandy," Ben asked," what's the status with the membership and what is our balance on the books, as far as shareholder investment into A Mark of the Divine?" "We are right at a shareholder number of 50 million, which to me is totally amazing. Our current invested balance is now $2,535,000,000, which also is more than mind-boggling. We have had a number of people who have gone way beyond the minimum investment of $25.00, in fact it is amazing to me that we have had a number of people who have been so impressed with what we are doing that they have invested a million dollars each in shares of the Corporation. We have been fortunate to have realized some decent growth with this money, which has been invested quite conservatively."

"Well, based on the plans we have put together, it looks like that money is finally going to get a real workout," Amber said. "We are really on the threshold of an adventure, if you want to call it that, that will certainly change all of our lives," Sandy said, "and also the lives of millions. It just doesn't get any better than that does it?"

CHAPTER THIRTY-THREE

It was early afternoon the next day and the 'to do' list was completed for the day. The kids were all over at a neighbor's so Sandy, Robert, Amber and Ben went into one of their famous drills of sorting out ideas, bouncing ideas off each other and finalizing ideas.

The TV was on low and was barely audible in the background. They all stopped what they were doing when they heard the quite famous newscaster say "This is Eric Smith coming to you with an important update on what is happening in our USA today."

"Page 1. For the eighth straight Sunday, a bomb was detonated today in a Christian church in the Eastern United States. Just hours ago, a bomb was detonated in Atlanta, Georgia, where hundreds of people were worshipping at a Sunday service in a Lutheran Church. Seventeen people were killed, and it is estimated that another twenty-one are in serious condition. This brings the church bombing death toll to a total of two hundred and fifty-two."

"The violence against the Christians and all people of faith has accelerated to a frightening level ever since the Federal Government had stepped up their so called 'Clean Out' policy of totally eliminating any reference to God in all public places. Since this bill was passed into law, millions of your tax dollars have been spent on 'white washing' all Federal and State buildings, removing age-old symbols and references to God. It's hard for me to believe that our wonderful Country has sunk so low, and I am afraid this is just the 'tip of the iceberg'."

"Page 2. Capitalism seems to be in its last throes of life, as we just received word of another Government takeover. This one will be a shocker to many. All major broadcasting companies have been taken over by the Fed as of today. So I wanted to tell you that this will be the last time you will hear and see this broadcast, as you can rest assured that I will be immediately replaced."

"Page 3. Another tax hike has just passed both houses and is sitting on the President's desk. It is anticipated it will be signed into law before the day is out. Ladies and gentlemen, this means that for most working people, we will see our income tax soar to a minimum of seventy percent, and that is just the Federal income tax. It seems like they are trying to eliminate the workforce and put us all on welfare."

"Page 4. I want to take this opportunity to say thank you to all my loyal listeners who have tuned in over so many years. I firmly believe we will see our great Country 'rise out of the ashes' in another decade as we, the Christians and all American people of faith rebuild a ruined nation. In the meantime, be strong; do not waver in your faith and know in your hearts that you are on the right side. May God bless you and keep you safe. Here is a P.S. Ben and Robert I'll be in touch soon." Eric knew that last little bit would be appreciated by about seventy-five million people who would know exactly who he was referring to. The names Ben and Robert O'Neil were now recognized nationwide.

The screen went blank as did the sound. The silence was deafening. It was also completely silent in the house as they all sat and stared into space, contemplating in their own minds what all of this meant.

Finally Robert said, "It looks like the tempo of the music we have been dancing to just went from a waltz to a polka." "Thank goodness we are as far as long as we are," Sandy said. "Who would ever have thought just a few years ago that all this could happen"

Maggie, Jimmy and Suzanne had just come into the living room where the adults had been in deep discussion. "Maggie said, "Don't I remember someone saying, 'all work and no play makes for a dull day and a dull you'? "You are right Maggie, I think you have heard that little saying at times around this house," Sandy said, "just what did you have in mind?"

"Well, before the snow melts and it starts to get slushy out, Jimmy, Suzanne and I thought that a game of flag football would be fun. We already have the flags ready, and we have the teams picked out. Jimmy, Uncle Ben and Amber will be one team and Mom, Dad, Suzanne and I will be the other team. We'll play for thirty minutes and whichever team has the smallest score will have to do dishes for the rest of the week."

Ben jumped up and hugged Maggie and said, "That's a great idea, sure too bad you aren't on my team, because now you going to have to do dishes for many days!" An hour later, totally exhausted, especially the adults, they all filed into the kitchen for some hot chocolate. The laughter and giggling was definitely contagious. "What a great idea kids,"

Amber said, "and with the fact that it ended in a tie, there is no change on dish washing duty." "That is a real bummer," Jimmy said.

CHAPTER THIRTY-FOUR

Exceptionally warm temperatures were making for an early start to the spring season, and the snow was melting quite rapidly. The frost was now coming out of the ground which would allow an early start on construction. The grass was greening up and the cattle had been moved to their first summer pasture. It was like a beehive around the ranch as all the preparations were in high gear for what would probably prove to be one of the most hectic but amazing of all summers. But it would also probably go down in the history books as the early beginnings of Mid America.

The first other order of a business this morning was brought up by Sandy. "There will be an extremely large number of people settling here between July and freeze up, and these folks will not have had the time to plant and harvest the vegetables they will need for the winter. Because of this, I think it would be a good idea for us to plant a large field of vegetables this spring. Since we have the equipment for the planting of most varieties, we can accomplish this. By the time hoeing, thinning and then finally harvest arrives, all which require a lot of labor, we will have a resident population that will be able to nicely handle all of these activities." "Excellent point," Robert said, "I'll order the seed as soon as we figure out our needs. Big Joe can prepare the ground right away and get the irrigation set up.

Ben said, "Our first construction crews will be arriving tomorrow morning. As has previously been discussed and agreed upon, the houses in Phase One will be straight line structures, two or three or four bedrooms, with a bathroom for each bedroom. A large root cellar that will also double as a storm shelter will be dug under each house. There will be no need for air conditioning to be installed. Heat will be provided by wall space heaters that will run on propane. The refrigerator and stove/oven included with the houses will also run propane. No electricity will be provided, however all houses will be prewired for electricity as at sometime in the future electricity may be brought to the houses.. The artificial lighting will come from kerosene lanterns that will be provided. There will be small generators used for plugging in block heaters for the vehicles during the winter time as there would be no garages."

"The density of the housing would be primarily determined by water availability. Each house will have its own well for water and a septic tank for sewage, or will share a water well with one or more other houses. Each house will have a yard that will be large enough to support a large garden. Among the many other activities for residents, will be classes on gardening and canning of vegetables and the use of root cellars. The garden area will be tilled with big equipment so that it would be ready for planting by the residents."

"The whole project in Phase One will be geared for residents who come with little more than the clothes on their back. The houses contracted to them will be furnished, and work will be lined up for them as they are processed in. Prior to coming, each resident will be approved before hand and then given a pre-orientation so they have a reasonably good idea of what to expect."

"Amber and Sandy have worked out all the details on how these folks will be credited with work they perform, where they are not actually receiving real money. These credits will go against the charges they have for housing, and all other necessities they receive, but they won't be under any financial pressure, that is unless somebody is lazy and acting in an irresponsible manner. However, the likelihood of that happening is slim in my opinion, given the character and determination of all those who have been making application."

"We are hoping that eventually a lot of the people will own their own house, but in any event they will not have to worry about making payments. Should any folks choose to leave, then if they have a credit balance, they will be paid for their house and given any additional money due them. If they don't have a credit balance, then they do not have to worry about owing anything when they leave. Their house will be given up and somebody else will move in."

"All of this will undoubtedly need refinement as we proceed. We have also sent this information out to all the other developers so that they will be operating on a very similar plan."

"Its going to be a huge cultural change for most people. It will be almost like slipping back in time to the days when covered wagons made their way west as America was first explored by the white man," Sandy said. "It's very exciting for these people, as I expect many who will come, will have been reduced to living on the streets after loosing their jobs and everything else, "Amber said. "All those who will be invited will be shareholders of the Corporation," Robert chimed in, "so they will be in our database."

"It's so hard to believe that so many whom we talked to in meetings just a short year or two ago have been reduced to this situation. It will take some time for most to start adjusting to this whole new way of life, realizing that in the long run, their lives will be changed very positively and will look like nothing they could have ever imagined."

"Our preparation is done," Ben said, "and we are at the threshold of a great journey.

Let's take a minute to join hands and give thanks for the tremendous guidance I feel we have all received from God as we have hurtled through these many months of preparation."

EPISODE TWO
THE EXODUS

CHAPTER THIRTY-FIVE
Continuation of 2013

"Mom, Mom," Cindy said as she pulled on her mother's arm, "you're scaring me. We are the only ones left in the church." Jan gave a little jerk and looked around trying to orient herself. She couldn't believe that she and her daughter were sitting in the church all by themselves. Everybody else had left. "Are you okay mom?" Jan gave her a smile and said, "Yes baby I am okay."

Cindy, who had now reached the old age of 12, thought to herself *her mom would still be calling her 'baby' when she was a hundred years old*. "Why are we just sitting here?" "I guess I was having such an intense mental conversation with Jesus that I didn't realize what was happening around me." Since they were all alone, Jan thought this would be as good a place and time as any to have a serious conversation with her daughter, a conversation that she had been putting off in hopes something would change and somehow they would be rescued.

A Mark of the Divine

"Cindy you know mom hasn't been able to find work now for several months in spite of the fact that I have spent every day of trying to find a job. Yes, I could have gotten a minimum wage job, but the fact is that half of those wages would be taken from me for various taxes. Then, if I had paid for someone to look after you when you came home from school, I would have spent at least forty hours a week working and end up with not only no money ahead, but it would have actually cost me money." "Who makes those kinds of rules anyway?" Cindy said. *Leave it to Cindy to ask a straight away question that gets right to the heart of the matter.*

"There are some leaders of our Country who have caused a tremendous amount of problems and pain for a lot of people, because they believe that our Government should take care of all of us and that they, the Government, are far more capable of doing this than we are."

"But what I want to talk to you about is something that is very difficult for me and it is going to cause a lot of problems for us. I think that within this next week sometime, we are going to receive an eviction notice and are going to have to leave our apartment. I haven't been able to pay our rent now for a few weeks and so we are going to get kicked out. I have barely had enough money to put food on the table and now that is pretty much all gone."

"Where are we going to go Mommy?" Jan was prepared for that question but still dreaded it and dreaded what she was going to have to tell Cindy. How could this have happened? It was just five years ago when Jan had been literally beaten down and made to feel like an absolute nothing by her husband. She had somehow gathered enough courage one day to come to the conclusion she could no longer live like that. She had contacted a women's abuse shelter and made an appointment to go there with Cindy the next day. Jan had packed as much of their belongings as she could put into two suitcases, so when Cindy arrived home from school, they had walked out the door of their home and never looked back.

Through a quirk of fate, Jan had become acquainted and friendly with a lady whose name was Jenny Morris. Jenny did a lot of volunteer work at the abuse shelter and Jan and Jenny seemed to immediately hit it off with each other. Jenny's husband Jake, a roads contractor, was in a really tight employment situation. He needed qualified workers. After quizzing Jan, Jenny concluded that perhaps Jan just might be a candidate for a job with her husband, even though women were not normally seen as operators of heavy equipment. She talked to Jake about it, and he decided he would give Jan a chance.

Jan would have to go to a heavy equipment tech training school, but he would put her on the payroll during training. It turned out that Jan had a real knack for operating giant machines, those that looked like some prehistoric monsters working their way across the landscape. Jan was small in stature and when she was sitting atop one of the big machines it almost looked like no one was operating it. Thanks to hydraulics and power steering, muscle wasn't one of the criteria needed. Rather good common sense, a good touch and a good understanding of what was to be accomplished, were what was needed. Jan demonstrated unequivocally that she had those traits.

Jan had been putting away money, so that she and her daughter could eventually buy a house and regain her self-respect. Just as it began to look like her life was finally going in the right direction, bad things began to happen. The same year that she had escaped her abusive husband, both her mom and dad had died after prolonged illnesses. She had no siblings and no other relatives so it was just she and Cindy. Now she thought, look at what has happened. Jake had finally had to sell his equipment and go out of business.

The government had taken over some of Jake's huge competitors. It eventually became impossible for him to compete with the government. She knew that Jake and his wife Jenny didn't have a lot of money left, but had enough that they could make it through these dark times.

"Mom, you're looking off into space again and not saying anything," Cindy said. "Sorry baby, I guess I was in deep thought. Cindy, unless a miracle happens within the next few days, we are going to find ourselves out on the streets and will be homeless people. I know this will be one of the scariest times in our lives, but I promise that I will do everything humanly possible to get us going back in the right direction." They left the church both caught up in their own thoughts about what the future might hold for them.

CHAPTER THIRTY-SIX

Amber and Sandy were sifting through their shareholder lists making notes and making calls. Ben and Robert decided that on a priority basis, they needed to get a heavy equipment operator on the ranch. They needed to begin some major earth moving: grading roads and leveling sites, digging wells and septic tanks, digging root cellars and trenches for footings. They contacted shareholders who had indicated that they were heavy equipment operators, but all had declined at this point. Many did ask if they could be put on a waiting list of some kind. To the person they had said they were now employed by the government and although they were making pretty good money, the conditions seemed to be deteriorating by the day so they very well might be interested in discussing employment possibilities at a later date. Amber and Sandy stayed with their search by continuing to make calls.

"Good morning, my name is Amber O'Neill with A Mark of the Divine Corporation and I am calling for a Jan McPherson." "Hi, this is Jan." *Why did that corporate name sound so familiar and yet she couldn't place it. Was this another collection agency or perhaps it was a holding company for the apartment complex she was living in?* "Jan, you may not recognize our Corporate name, but you bought a share in the Corporation a couple of years ago. I think you had attended a meeting that we held in Pittsburg, Pennsylvania, as I see you are from south of there in Bethel Park." Now it all clicked into place for Jan. She remembered how enthralled she had been with their presentation. Rain had shut down their work and Jake had taken her to a Rotary meeting.

"Yes Amber, I do remember now. Sorry I was a little slow in recognizing the corporate name." Amber went through a brief description of what was now happening and explained specifically why she had called Jan.

"Jan, if this is something you'd be interested in, we can put you to work immediately."

There was a long silence on the other end of the phone, and Amber could hear her sobbing. "Jan, are you okay?" "I am sorry," Jan said and went on to give Amber a brief summary of their situation. "You are an angel sent from heaven," Jan said. "I take it you would be interested?" "My daughter and I could be on the road tomorrow." After a slight pause Jan said, "Amber this is kind of embarrassing, but I don't have enough money to make the trip out there." "Don't worry about that Jan, I will wire you a thousand dollars to cover your traveling expenses."

Amber heard a sharp intake of breath and then sobbing again. "Sorry, this is just so overwhelming that I am having a hard time assimilating all of what you have told me. You won't regret this Amber. I'll give you a one hundred percent effort."

When Cindy got home from school, she saw the car packed right to the top. She ran into the apartment and said, "Mom what is happening? I see our car is packed full." Jan sat her down and explained what was going on. It took Jan awhile to tell Cindy, because she was giggling and sobbing all at the same time while she gave Cindy the news. Cindy said, "Mom where is North Dakota?"

CHAPTER THIRTY-SEVEN

Early summer had arrived in all its glory on the Plains. The snow was all gone save for a few small drifts that were on the north side of a hill here and there. The grass had turned green from it's dormant winter brown color. The trees were starting to leaf out, and the creek was running at a full clip. Flocks of geese and ducks could be seen making their way north for the nesting season. When one stepped outside, it felt like you could fly right with them, the air was so fresh and crisp. Ben reflected on what was happening in their world, yet in spite of the turmoil and the continuing meltdown of their beloved America, he couldn't help but feel God's hand giving them all a comfort that a non-Christian sadly couldn't really understand.

"You ready Ben?" Robert yelled. "You bet. Let's get cracking." Armed with several rolls of prints which contained maps of the entire ranch, geological survey maps showing subterranean water locations and aerial photography, they headed out in their pickup with lots of stakes painted at the tops and a transit for surveying. "It's hard to believe the direction we are taking and what has been accomplished since we incorporated," Ben said to Robert as the pickup bounced down a trail towards the place where Phase One would begin. "It's pretty exciting, hey brother?" Robert said.

"Our first heavy equipment operator should be here in the next couple of days," Robert said. "I talked to an outfit in Dickenson yesterday, and they have a couple of tractors we can rent. One has a back hoe on it and the other has a front-end loader with a blade on the back. That should be adequate to get us started. They will get them out to us tomorrow."

As they continued the work they had to do Ben said, "Amber was telling me last night that they have heard from two medical doctors who basically had the same story. They were fed up with the whole mess. They are in very good financial shape at this point and although it is earlier than what they had planned, they are going to retire. They are looking for a place they can build a second home to have during the summer months, at least to start with and then perhaps reside there full time in a couple more years. I'll get back to them this afternoon and we'll get things underway for them.

"They also committed to do voluntary work at the Village. After Amber had explained what we are doing, they both became really excited. They immediately committed to buying a house and said again they would be glad to do some work for free for the citizens of our new Mid American Beltway Village. That's pretty exciting stuff!"

"That is fantastic Ben. I had been thinking about where we might develop a Phase Two which would be the area where we could build for those that are paying up front and want custom-built houses. I expect we will have a fair number of people in this category.

They will provide paying employment for a lot of people in the Village. You know we have a mile-long strip along the National Park border that could work out perfectly for this group of people. They could have west facing backyards that back up to the Bad Lands. These building sites would provide wonderful views and complete privacy."

"That's a great idea Robert. Amber said both doctors would be sending house plans to us in the next week. I think we should head up there after we stake out these first few houses in Phase One. We can start staking out that area and let's also take some pictures to send to them. I think they are going to be thrilled." "I agree and another real nice bonus with this is that it will provide some nice cash flow not only for us but for all of the residents in Phase One that work on building these homes." Ben said, "Let's make a note for the next developer's meeting that we talk about the need to try and maintain a decent ratio between those that don't have any money and those that are financially okay. Those people wanting to build in these new communities are an important element in the corporation maintaining good cash flow."

CHAPTER THIRTY-EIGHT

"Look baby, that sign says Welcome to North Dakota." Cindy rolled her eyes and said, "Mom, we really must have a serious conversation about your use of 'baby' when addressing me!" Jan broke up with laughter and almost had to pull the car off to the side of the road she was laughing so hard. "Alright, I promise that I will try real hard not to say that when anybody is around, okay?" "Well, I hope you are able to keep that promise because you really are driving me crazy," Cindy said with a grin on her face.

As they started across the bridge, a sign said Red River. "I was at the library right before we left," Jan said, 'so I could read up a little bit about where we were going, and it said the Red River of the North is one of the few rivers in the world that flows north. They have had some real bad flooding over the years, because since the river runs north the spring thaw often takes place at a faster pace on the south end of the river while it is still frozen Up North. This whole area, which is called the Red River Valley, has some of the richest soil in the world. But a huge area on either side of the river is flat as a table, so when the snow thaws, if it thaws too fast, all the

water runs into that little river and causes a lot of flooding."
"I guess, no matter where you go, people have problems," Cindy said. Jan thought, *sometimes she is twelve going on twenty.*

"We have a little over three hundred miles to go before we get to our new home. I think I might start crying again; I am so elated," Jan said. "Did you see what the sign said under where it said welcome to North Dakota?" Cindy asked. Then, instead of waiting for an answer, she said, "it read 'Discover the Spirit'. Do you think they are talking about the Holy Spirit?" Cindy inquired. "Well maybe, "Jan said, "but probably they are also talking about the spirit of the people in North Dakota and what nice people they are and how hard they work." Cindy didn't say anything, but Jan could tell she was deep in thought. "Since it is getting late in the afternoon, I think we have done enough driving for today. Let's stop in the next town and get us a room and something to eat. Then we'll get a fresh start tomorrow, and we can be at our destination by mid-afternoon."

"That sounds good to me, I am starving."

CHAPTER THRITY-NINE

"Good morning, you have reached A Mark of the Divine Corporation, this is Sandy. How may I help you? Hi, my name is Jeff Olson, and this may seem like a strange question, but I heard a rumor the other day that you are hiring people out in North Dakota, is there anything to that rumor?" "Are you by chance a shareholder Jeff?" "Yes I am." "Just a minute Jeff, let me see if I can bring your name up on the computer. Jeff Olson from Cleveland, Ohio, and you are a plumber, is this correct?" "Yes, that is me." "Good, can you me give a little background and tell me what your current situation is?"

"The job opportunities in our area are deteriorating quite rapidly. I have been an independent plumber with my own little business for several years and managed to provide for my wife and two sons quite adequately. However, in the last couple of years things have gone downhill big time. When I am able to get work, the taxes I am having to pay, make it hardly worthwhile to work. What little savings we had put away have almost completely vanished. The value of our house decreased to the point where we owe more on the mortgage than what the house is worth. We eventually had to walk away from it and rent an apartment. Now it looks like we won't be able to even hang on to our apartment. Are we desperate? Yes, I would say that would accurately describe our situation."

Sandy explained to Jeff what was happening and how everything worked. "Based on what I have told you, do you think you and your family would be interested in coming out here and literally starting over again?" "From my perspective, I would say absolutely yes, but I need to discuss this with my wife and boys. Would it be alright Sandy, if I called you back tomorrow morning after I have talked to the rest of the family?" "You sure can Jeff, and I appreciate the fact that you are discussing this with your wife. By the way how old are your boys?" "They are 10 and 13 years old." "Great, we have a ten-year old boy and if you decide to join us, I know he'll be excited to hear that there will be a couple more boys in his age group coming out."

The next morning Jeff called back telling Sandy the family was ready to tackle this new venture with everything they were capable of. Sandy gave them further instructions and she told Jeff that as soon as he arrived and got settled he'd be put to work.

CHAPTER FORTY

Robert, Sandy, Ben, Amber and all the kids were just finishing up breakfast and there was so much conversation going on and so much excitement in the air that it was almost electrifying. "Our first new resident should arrive this afternoon," Amber said, "along with her little girl. Suzanne and Maggie were talking about the new friend they would have when Cindy got there, and Jimmy was pretty quiet. *It sure would have been nice if the lady who was coming this afternoon would have a son instead of a daughter. How many more girls could he stand to have around here anyway,* he thought. But then his mom told him about the two boys that would be coming out soon, and he was all excited.

"Did you know in the last week, Amber and I have sent out close to one hundred packets to shareholder/developers that have requested information?. Also, the two girls we hired last week have been fielding calls from the developers almost non-stop. The shareholder farmer/ranchers who have now started on their developments are requesting shareholder names from our data bank, so I think it is safe to say the migration is well underway," Sandy said. "Pretty exciting stuff," Ben said, and pretty scary also, we are really plowing some new ground." "I wish we could figure out a way that would allow the developers to directly access our data bank, but the chances of someone hacking into our system and really messing it up are too great," Amber said.

"It will be nice when we get the first few houses up so we can start to get people going on this project," Robert said, but at least for starters we were able to pick up local help. I think Jan and Cindy's house should be ready in a couple of days. In the meantime they can stay in the bunkhouse that is available. Following the completion of the first house, we should be able to complete a house every four days, until we start getting bigger crews. Once we start adding people the number of houses we can construct in a week will just keep increasing. At the same time we will start laying the footings for the good doctors' houses toward the end of next week."

"Have you given more thought at this point about additional security?" Amber asked. "Robert and I have been talking about that. Not really having too much of an idea what kinds of threats and overt actions we might be faced with, we haven't formalized that part of the plan yet," Ben said. "However, one of the things we have talked about and are now ready to implement is the weekly gun safety lessons for all the residents sixteen and older. There will also be regular target practices. In addition, we'll expand our current security system to include the circumference of the entire property, especially after what happened to Amber.

We also have to talk to Sheriff Buck so he is aware of what we are doing, and we'll be developing some more strategies with him as time goes on and the population increases.

The good thing is, on an overall comparison, all the folks throughout all the new Villages springing up across the Plains, are going to be a lot safer in the Villages than any other place in America."

"Why do you think that we have gone for such along time without having any incidence of being attacked?" Amber asked. Robert said "Ben and I have also wondered about that. We have come to the conclusion that whoever was behind those early attacks on us, must have given up, at least temporarily. They probably thought when they couldn't snuff out a small flame, how were they going to extinguish the blaze of our movement now. We have grown so fast and become so large that they must feel, they have to take a different tack. Plus I think the ad Amber ran for us really put the frosting on the cake."

"But you don't think we are out of the woods now, with all the security measures you are implementing and adding more?" Amber said. "You can be sure, that the anti-Christian groups including our Federal Government will continue to be relentless in seeking ways to defeat this movement. The very fact that it has become so large will be a magnet in itself," Ben said. "Although I don't think we'll be under any potential physical harm from the Federal Government, they nevertheless could easily be the cause of others being a problem for us. Being on guard and constantly attuned to our surroundings are going to have to become a way of life and second nature for all of us."

CHAPTER FORTY-ONE

"You know what is going to really help people get into the right frame of mind as they transition from their previous life to life here on the Plains?" Ben asked. "That two-hour video Amber and Sandy put together. I just had a chance to view it last night, and it is terrific." "Thank you Ben," Amber and Sandy said, almost in unison. "I haven't had a chance to see it yet," Robert said, "can you give me a brief overview of the contents?" "Sure," Sandy said. "First, let me say that the thought of an introductory video occurred to Amber as we were talking about how so many people who were considering moving out here were going to be so ill-equipped as far as their knowledge and expectations. Most of the people we have talked to so far have little to no knowledge about the history of our pioneer era, unless they were fortunate enough to have grandparents who passed this information down to them. Most of them didn't learn much about this in school.

The reason we felt this was important, is although there isn't a direct parallel to then and now, there are enough similarities that we thought people would be able to feel a relation to what it was like back then. By understanding the spirit and drive of those pioneers, they might be able to process this whole new way of life they are entering. Also, it would be helpful if they understood the mind-set of those early settlers: their adventurous spirit and what motivated them to sacrifice so much to achieve their goals."

"So, we put together hundreds of old photos that are a big part of the video. One photo, for example, shows a woman pushing a wheelbarrow loaded with buffalo chips that would be used in a fireplace to provide heat in her hut. The video shows and tells about the pioneer home, which in many cases, were made of prairie sod. We show pictorially the hardships and the good times. We show how important relationships were; how much fun the simple things in life really were. It might be hard to visualize life without such things as radio's, televisions, computers, telephones, and Internet, which did not yet exist. What we want to accomplish is to make the transition into this new life easy for them to comprehend and then assimilate. The video is intended to help them realize that in many respects this is not a backward transition but rather a very positive step forward in their lives."

This realization will be really important for the younger ones as they transition from home computers, for example, to chalkboards: as they transition from video games to games like tag, hop-scotch, marbles, checkers, etc."

"The overall idea here is to get everybody to understand that as humans, we live in a world of comparisons. We want people to compare their new way of life with the lives of pioneering folks of the 1800's and early 1900's, rather than compare their lives in the Villages with what they have experienced before. Then they can realize this is a cakewalk. It is hope that the video and the comparisons it evokes will give them a very positive and enthusiastic outlook on life from today forward."

"What a splendid idea," Robert said. "That reminds me; very soon we will start on our first community building. It will be designed as a multi-functional building. One big part of it will be converted for church services of various denominations on Sundays. It will house a computer room where the young and old alike can avail themselves to the Internet. We will be encouraging people to sign up for various on-line learning classes. This building will also house a community library. It will be a place for everybody to gather in the winter time for various events such as dances and potluck dinners where everybody brings food to be enjoyed by all. We will also install a bank of phones for people to use. One corner of the building will house a combination pharmacy/first aid station. Hopefully, we will be able to hire a couple of nurses for this area."

"Have we had any priests or deacons or pastors indicate a desire to join us yet?" Ben asked. "As a matter of fact we have, and we expect that within the month we'll have our first church leader join us,"

Amber said. "One thing that is really interesting; more and more of the other developers are depending on us to provide them with information on shareholders; those we have talked to and know they are ready to move out to the Plains to one of the Villages. So we have started to become a kind of placement service for them and the other shareholders/developers. When a shareholder is ready to move, if we don't have the space or some developer is in need of folks with certain skills, we can direct them elsewhere."

A Mark of the Divine

"So far in the early going Amber and I are extremely pleased with the progress and how well everything is going at all levels. It seems like all the efforts we put into the preparation for this action are really paying off," Sandy said.

CHAPTER FORTY-TWO

Mark Anderson and his son Josh were walking along a path that led down to the bay, enjoying the quiet evening. Mark had asked Josh to join him for a walk after they had supper. It was time for a heart to heart.

"Son, I feel terrible about the situation I've gotten us into. I like millions of other fathers, stood by watching things slowly deteriorating. Morality, government leadership and excessive greed were rotting the core of our Country's so-called leaders. Unfortunately, when we finally realized enough was enough, it was too late. Our Country had been led down a path of ultimate destruction, as the national debt mounted to the point where it was breaking the Country."

Mark and his son Josh sat down on the banks of Manorhaven Bay, not too far from the apartment they lived in, in Manorhaven, New York. It was peaceful here; there was just a little ripple in the water. A pair of loons swam off to their right. Even the animals seemed to enjoy the solitude of the evening.

Mark had been putting off this conversation for a number of days, trying to figure how best to frame their situation and his suggested solution. Josh was thirteen, going on twenty, and Mark knew that he was very fortunate to have a son with such a level head.

He had a hard time trying to explain to Josh why his mother had filed for divorce and ran off with another guy. But that had been a couple of years ago, and since then he and Josh had developed a great relationship.

"Josh, I wanted you to come out here with me this evening so we could have a quite place to talk some things out." "Dad, we are in trouble aren't we?" Before Mark could answer, Josh continued," I have a lot of friends whose families are talking about the fact that they may actually have to live on the streets by this fall, if things don't straighten out." "Well, I guess that is jumping right to the heart of the matter," Mark said. *Was I that up to speed on what was going on around me when I was Josh's age?*.

"I had a long conversation with some people out in North Dakota today who are with a Corporation called A Mark of the Divine." Mark proceeded to tell Josh all about what they were doing and that they had offered to have Mark and Josh join them. "They said they really could use a person like me who was well founded in electrical engineering but with a broad base of work experiences." *North Dakota, I can't place where that it is,* Josh thought to himself.

"I told them that you and I would talk it over and I would give them a decision tomorrow. Josh, I know this will be tough to make a move like this, but our options are getting down to about nothing real fast." "Dad, if you think this is our best move, I say let's do it." It was all Mark could do to keep from getting tears in his eyes as he silently thanked God for being blessed with such a wonderful son.

CHAPTER FORTY-THREE

"Look Cindy," Jan said, "that big entrance with the sign says 'The O'Neil Ranch', we made it." They gave each other the 'high-five' sign as they drove up to the gate. The sign said to push the button to talk to the office. Jan pushed the button and a few seconds later, a voice came over the speaker. "Hi, my name is Sandy and if I had to guess I would say this must be Jan and Cindy that have just arrived." Jan had a big smile on her face as she said, "Hi Sandy, and yes, this is Jan and Cindy." The gate opened and Sandy said, "Just follow the road Jan, and it will take you right up to our house."

As Jan and Cindy emerged from the car, Sandy, Amber and kids came rushing out of the house. Introductions were made. Jan could hardly believe the warm welcome they received. It took about two minutes for the girls to disappear into the house, giggling and chattering like crazy. You would have thought they had been friends forever. Jan was having a hard time to keep from tearing up. *What the heck was the matter with me, I've b*ecome so emotional, I never used to be like this.

Sandy and Amber went through a little orientation meeting with Jan and told her that she and Cindy could stay in the guest cabin for a day or so until their new house was ready. Ben came in just as they were finishing up and so Ben had a chance to meet Jan. "We have a back hoe coming into the ranch this afternoon Jan, so if it works for you, let's plan on getting you into the work flow in a couple of days. Does that sound okay to you?"

"You have no idea how good that sounds, and I'll definitely be ready to give it all I've got." "We'll help you get settled into to your new 'castle' tomorrow. How does that sound?" Jan got up and gave Amber, Sandy and Ben a hug and said, "I don't know how I can ever repay you for this opportunity, but just know from the depth of my heart, I am eternally grateful."

Just then the children came bounding in, and Cindy was introduced to Ben. "This is my uncle," Jimmy said, "and he tells the best stories, Cindy." Ben laughed and said, "We'll probably have a storytelling session some night soon, but we have to be sure that the ghosts are around so I can tell the story right." That got the children giggling and they disappeared almost as quickly as they had appeared on the scene.

CHAPTER FORTY-FOUR

As they left the main highway and headed down the gravel road towards the ranch, Josh said, "look over there. What are those?" "Those," said Mark. "are antelope. Look over to the right. That antelope standing up on that knoll all by himself, is what is called the Sentinel. He is like a look-out for the rest of the herd. If he senses any trouble, he signals the heard and leads them away from it." "Wow, that's pretty neat," Josh said, "how did you know that?" *Feeling like he should brag a little instead of revealing that he had recently read about it on the Internet.* Mark said, "Well you know Josh, your old man is pretty smart." Josh didn't respond, and Mark could no longer hold the laugh that busted out, "I read about them on the Internet right before we left."

As they approached the gate, they could see the fence that surrounded the whole ranch. Sandy had told him to just punch the button on the intercom and someone would answer. Several signs were posted by the intercom and gate, telling anyone who approached that this was private property and giving them instructions to use the intercom. "I wonder why they have that fence and gate?" Josh asked. "From what

A Mark of the Divine

I was told, it is primarily just a security measure in the event some people would want to come in and make trouble," Mark said.

They had just completed the call to someone at the ranch, and the gate was starting to open when they spotted a tractor approaching, apparently grading the road. As it approached the gate, the blade came up and the tractor swung off to the side. Mark could hardly believe what he saw, as this petite little woman stopped the tractor, swung down and walked over to the car.

"I am guessing that you must be Mark and Josh, I am Jan." Jan was dressed in jeans and a sweatshirt, with her pony tail passing through the hole in her baseball cap. It took a moment for Mark's brain to start functioning properly. *Had he taken a wrong turn or something? How could he be out here in the middle of nowhere, have a very beautiful lady jump down from a tractor and call him by name?* "Hi, I am Josh." He reached across his dad and shook her hand. "Well, it's very nice to meet you Josh." Mark came out of his stunned silence and followed suit, "Sorry, for a moment I thought I was hallucinating, seeing an angle. It's very nice to meet you Jan," Mark said as he shook her hand. Jan busted out laughing at Mark's comment, and her infectious laugh brought a big grin from both Mark and Josh. "Come on, follow me and I'll take you up to the Ranch house."

As the three of them were walking up to the house after they had parked, Jan said, you're a pretty good looking young fellow Josh." "Yeah, my dad says I take after him." Jan looked at Mark and raised her eyebrows and said "Oh he does, does he?" That brought a laugh from Mark and then Jan and Josh also started to laugh. As they approached the house, Sandy opened the door and said, "Well, it looks like you three have gotten acquainted quickly." Jan introduced Sandy and said to Mark, "Go on in, I am going to put the tractor away for today." "Will you come back to the house when you get done Jan?" asked Sandy. "Amber had to go into town for some supplies so I am all alone. I'll give Mark and Josh a brief orientation and then if you wouldn't mind, you can show them to the open bunkhouse, where they can get settled in until there house is ready in a couple of days. Oh, by the way Josh, there is a bus taking all the kids into a little western town called Medora for ice cream and some other activities in just a couple of hours, would you like to join them?"

It was Josh's turn to become a little flabbergasted, but he quickly recovered and said "Sure, that would be fun." Sandy said, "The kids haven't had an outing for awhile and they have been working so hard between attending the vegetable gardens and school work, that my brother-in-law Ben, thought this little adventure was definitely in order."

"That okay with you Dad?" Josh asked. "Sure son, after that long ride out here it would be good for you and a great opportunity for you to meet some of the kids."

CHAPTER FORTY-FIVE

Amber and Sandy were enjoying the lull in the action, as they both stretched out on the porch with a glass of lemonade. People had been arriving in a steady stream for over a month now and the activity around the ranch was almost beyond comprehension. "I feel like I am in a daze most of the time," Sandy said, "the activity is almost overwhelming."

"I do to," Amber said, "but isn't it exciting? The people who have come to be a part of our village population are absolutely gems."

"I took a little tour early this morning," Sandy said, "and the changes in the landscape are unbelievable. The field of vegetables is looking great as are the individual gardens. The number of houses already built and occupied in Phase One is staggering. Also both doctors' houses on the perimeter are out of the ground. They are already being framed.

We had constantly talked about the huge transition that everybody moving here would have to make, but I overlooked the transition that we would be making from a peaceful and laid-back ranch setting to what is taking place now. I am definitely not complaining Amber, just trying to adjust."

CHAPTER FORTY-SIX

Mark and Josh had just gotten settled into the bunkhouse after their orientation meeting when Josh saw the bus pull up by the house.

"Dad, the bus is loading over by the ranch house," Josh said, "I better get going." "Okay son have a good time." "I will Dad." Josh was the last one to board, and he introduced himself to Ben as he boarded. "Well Josh it's nice to meet you and good you could join us. "Alright everybody quiet down for a second, I'd like you all to say a big hello to the newest member of our village, Josh Anderson." In one big "Hi Josh", all the kids greeted him.

As Josh made his way down the isle of the bus, he spotted one empty seat next to a pretty girl. *Well I suppose I'll get razed for this, but it looks like that is the only empty seat..* After Josh sat down he stuck out his hand and introduced himself again. *I've* never shaken hands with a guy before. Oh well, guess it won't hurt. "Hi Josh, my name is Cindy." "Is your mother's name Jan by chance?" Quite shocked Cindy said, "Yes it is, how could you possibly know that?" Josh explained how he and his dad had met her mother, and he remembered her talking a little bit about her daughter Cindy.

By the time the bus got back to the Ranch that evening, Cindy and Josh were best buddies. Departing from the bus, they spotted their parents sitting on the big porch that surrounded the Ranch house. "What are you guys doing sitting out here?" Josh asked. "It was such a beautiful evening, and so we both decided to sit outside and get to know one another," Jan said. "Oh," Cindy said and then quickly talked about their trip. "We had a really fun time in Medora, but I am totally worn out and am going to go to our house." "Hold on Cindy," Jan said, "Mark and I were about to call it night." "Yes, I agree, " said. Mark. "It's time to get some serious sack time. That long drive, the wonderful meal you fixed tonight, the great conversation and this wonderful fresh air is finally getting to me.

Before Jan and Cindy left, Mark said, "Jan, thanks for the wonderful evening. Somehow, I think we must have met in another life as it seems like I have known you for months, not just an afternoon and evening." "It's funny you said that, because that is exactly how I feel. I loved the time we spent sharing stories. I know more than a little about you, Mark." "Same goes for me Jan. We'll see you tomorrow. Good night now. There was a lot of 'girl talk' going on as Cindy and Jan made the way to their house.

CHAPTER FORTY-SEVEN

"Good morning you have reached A Mark of The Divine, Inc. This is Amber, how may I help you?" "Good morning, my name is Erika Solsburg, and I have a couple of questions about your organization. I am a registered nurse and live in Nashville, TN. I was talking to one of my friends, and she was telling me about attending a meeting you put on just a few weeks ago. She gave me your phone number. I am not a shareholder, but from what she told me, I would very much like to become a shareholder, and join your Village if that would be a possibility."

"Thanks Erika, for the information you just gave me. First of all we'd be glad to have you join our shareholder group. All you have to do is send us a check for $25.00 and we'll send you a stock certificate. But I am getting ahead of myself. However, before I do that, I need to ask you if you are a Christian or a person of faith? Since you didn't attend any of our meetings, you may have missed the fact that we are a Christian organization. But certainly welcome all God fearing people. I will gladly send you a packet that details our organization and what we are about."

A Mark of the Divine

"First of all let me say so that you know, yes I am a Christian. Part of my motivation for calling is that I am also wondering if it would be possible you might need a registered nurse in your village? If so, would you consider allowing me to come out to the ranch and further discuss the possibility of my filling that position? I have two children, one is a boy who is 10 and one is a girl age 12. Becoming a part of your village, would be a God-send to me and my family. We could be there right away.

Amber was a bit taken aback by this request, as they so needed a nurse to operate out of the Community Center, yet the Ranch was a long way from Nashville. It took her a few moments to react. "Erika, may I ask you a personal question?" "Yes, you certainly may Amber." "Is some kind of trouble causing you to feel the need to come all the way out here with your children immediately?" "Amber, I am in trouble but not with the law or anything like that.

My story is really complicated, and I don't feel comfortable talking about it on the phone. All I am asking is for the opportunity to sit down and tell you about it, before you make up your mind about allowing us to be a part of your group. If, after you hear my story, you feel that you would rather not have us as a part if your village, we'll graciously depart."

"Erika, please feel free to come out immediately if that is your desire, and we'll all sit down and talk this out." Amber could hear a small sob escape from Erika. "Thank you so much Amber, we will be out there in two days time." Amber gave her directions and they hung up. "What was that all about Amber?" Sandy asked. Amber relayed the conversation she just had with Erika. "Wow, that certainly should be an interesting session. We'll hold one of the bunkhouses open for her and the children.

CHAPTER FORTY-EIGHT

"Cindy!" Jan called out when she stepped into their house. Something smells absolutely fantastic. Cindy gave her mom a big smile and ran over and hugged her. "Sandy had a cooking class for us today during our home schooling. She showed us how to do a vegetable stir fry, I sure hope it is good." "Oh Cindy, that is so thoughtful of you. Before I came in the door, I wondered if I was going to have enough strength to make supper tonight."

From the day after she and Cindy had arrived, Jan had been going non-stop: grading roads, digging root cellars and trenches for footings for the new houses, and making trenches for plumbing to the septic tanks. But Jan had never been happier in her whole life. She still couldn't believe their good fortune.

"You're happy with our new home aren't you Cindy?" "Oh yes. Suzanne, Maggie and myself have really become good friends. I love having school in their house. Sandy is really a good teacher. I think I have already learned more in the short time we have been here than I did all last year in school." Jan smiled to herself; *my little girl is growing up, thank you Jesus for sending your angels to embrace us and help us.*

Just then there was a knock on their door. "Hi Jan," Robert said, "Sorry to bother you as I know you probably just got home from a very long day. I'll keep you for just a minute. I have just a quick question. You are about a week ahead of our building crews. We got an urgent call from another shareholder/developer about a hundred miles east of here wondering if there was any way he could borrow you for a few days. Apparently your reputation as a top-notch operator is starting to spread." Robert continued. "I talked to Sandy, and she said it is absolutely no problem for Cindy to stay with us while you are gone. Maggie and Suzanne, of course, voted immediately in favor of the idea."

Before Jan had a chance to say anything, Cindy jumped right in and said, "Mom, someday you'll be famous! This is the just the kind of start that you need to spread your fame and earn your fortune." Where does this little girl come up with all this? Jan laughed and said, "I'll be glad to help out." "Great," Robert said, "I'll get the flat bed loaded with the tractor tonight so you can take off at daybreak tomorrow. I'll leave the directions and everything else you will need on the seat of the truck."

CHAPTER FORTY-NINE

The buzzer on the panel above Amber and Sandy's desks signaled that somebody was calling on the intercom from the gate. "I am guessing that is Erika, as she was due in about now," Amber said. "Okay, I'll contact the guys on the two-way and have them come in so we can all hear what Erika has to say," Sandy said.

Erika and the O'Neill's were all seated comfortably in the big family room. Erika's children had bounded off with the other kids right after introductions had been made.

"First off," Erika said, "I want to profusely apologize for asking you all to meet with me, as I am sure you are tremendously busy." Ben jumped in at this point and said, "Erika, we don't know at this time what it is that you feel you have to tell us, but rest assured, we are not the kind of people to be judgmental and will hear you out with patience and empathy."

"Thank you all for this opportunity. When I have told you my story, if you feel we will not a fit here in your community, I will accept that and we will depart."

A Mark of the Divine

Everybody was at full attention when Erika started her story. "When I was ten years old and my sister was thirteen, we lived in an apartment just off of the Fort Leonard Wood Army Base in Missouri, where my dad was a drill sergeant."

"One day I was held over for some extra work in school and as a result I ended up walking home by myself. On my way home, a van pulled up along side of me, someone grabbed me and I was thrown into the van before I even knew what was happening." "Oh my God," Amber said and the others made similar remarks.

Erika continued, "To make a long story short, over a period of time, I was smuggled into Mexico and became a pawn of a big sex trade ring, which of course I didn't know at the time. By the time I was twelve I had experienced firsthand the underbelly of the Mexican drug cartel, and its sex division. I won't go into any details other than to say these Cartel men were the vilest, most horrific and dirtiest human beings on the face of the earth. I can't tell you how many times over the ten years that I was in my captivity that I wanted to kill myself.

When I was fifteen, I had a roommate that showed me how to siphon off and hide money without anyone knowing it. By the time I made good on my escape I had a substantial amount money stashed away. About two months before I finally made my escape, I had been sewing money inside the lining of my clothes. One night, there was some kind of disturbance in our building. I really don't know what was going on. There was so much shooting. I think it might have been some kind of gang war taking place. I had secretly been able to get some dye and I also had some heavy makeup hidden away when the disturbance broke out, I thought this was my chance to slip out unnoticed and escape. I put three layers of clothing on, which was all the clothing I owned. I dyed my blond hair black, and covered my face, neck and hands with the dark makeup so I could blend in with the rest of the population."

"I went out a back entrance during all the commotion and immediately disappeared into the crowd on the street. I had no plan other than to escape and try to make my way back to the United States. I knew that I was in Mexico, but I had no idea where in Mexico. I needed a plan for finding my way back to the States."

"Having been in Mexico for ten years, my Mexican Spanish was as good as the natives. I began carefully selecting people whom I thought I could trust to give me some information without informing somebody bad. Sleeping in rundown shacks, hitchhiking and doing a lot of walking, I made my way to the U.S. border in a little over a month. I made contact with a Coyote, one who takes people across the border for a fee. I was able to make the payment and joined a group going across. As we neared the river I slowly let myself move to the rear of the group and then slipped back further but not so far back that I couldn't see them up ahead of me. When I got to the river, I washed the makeup and dye out of my hair as best I could and then slipped across the border by myself."

"Using the same process that I had in getting to the border, I made my way to Tucson, Arizona. I was walking by a church. I believe there was some Divine intervention as something made me go into the church. I was exhausted, hungry and didn't know what I was going to do next. The church was empty. I walked up to the front row and sat down. I cried until I fell asleep. The next thing I remember was a kindly looking older man shaking me and asking if I was okay."

"It turned out that this man was the pastor of the church. I had a vague recollection of 'church' from before I was kidnapped and remembered going to church with my mom and dad. In retrospect, I know in the depths of my heart that God had my guardian angel accompanying me on that whole trip. After telling the pastor my story, he took me into his office and made a call. About fifteen minutes later a man showed up, and the pastor introduced us and told me this man and his wife would help me. The pastor repeated the story I had told him."

"As it turned out these people, Judd and Jenny Peterson, were angels themselves as they took me in and I worked as a maid for them. They helped me locate what was left of my family. We found my older sister in a hospital, dying of some kind of rare disease.

My father had been killed in the Iraq war about two years earlier, and my mother had passed away a year later with a broken heart. After working for the Petersons for a about a year and getting my head screwed on straight, I headed to Georgia where my sister was hospitalized. I am forever grateful to the Pastor and the Petersons who literally saved my life and still to this day I keep in touch with all of them."

"I should mention at this point that I will probably never shake off the need to keep looking over my shoulder, fearing that someone from the Cartel will discover my whereabouts and capture me again. It was always beaten into our heads that to escape would mean certain death and that no matter how far we tried to go to escape their clutches, it would be a useless endeavor as we would be found and dealt with. But more about that later."

"I found my sister Candice, and we had a very tearful reunion to say the least, both knowing she had very little time left to live. Candice's husband had also been killed in Iraq and she had been left with two small but wonderful children, a boy and a girl, Brekken and Andrea. I was Candice's only living relative. After a few talks, I said that I would adopt the children and treat them as my own."

"When my sister passed away, she willed her house to me and I proceeded to adopt the kids and get a job working as a receptionist/hostess at the local hospital. It was there that my interest in health care rose to the surface, and I started night school in nursing.

Because I was kidnapped when I was only ten, my formal education didn't amount to much. I took some correspondence courses and got my high school diploma. Then I went on to get my nursing degree and became a registered nurse. That pretty much summarizes things up to this time, with one exception. I think that I am being stalked. In the last couple of months I have become suspicious of being followed. I fear that the Cartel has finally been able to find me. I am scared to death that they might try to kidnap Andrea, who is the same age as I was when I was kidnapped. I did go to police about this but because I don't have anything really concrete they say there isn't anything they can do."

"The day that I called you I noticed a van that I had never seen before parked just down the street from our house, and it looked ominous. At the same time that I noticed the van, I saw the kids coming down the block from school. I was quickly out of the house, running to them. We walked back to the house with fear in our hearts. Maybe I am paranoid, but I truly believe that it's their intention to punish me for running away by kidnapping my daughter. When we left to come here we set up a plan so it wouldn't look like we were on the run. I spent most of the trip out here continually watching my rearview mirror and am not sure if we were followed or not."

"That is my story. I have to apologize that I may have brought danger to your doorstep. If you would like us to leave I will certainly understand. On the other hand, if you can see fit to let us become a part of your community, we will do everything in our power to fit in and contribute totally to the village."

Erika stopped talking and just folded her hands and looked at the floor, dreading what kind of response she might get from telling her life's story. Silence prevailed for about a minute. The grandfather clock ticking away at the other end of the room sounded like it was right next to her. As if by some kind of signal, Amber, Sandy, Ben and Robert all stood up at the same time and came over to Erika. They took her hands, pulled her up and each gave her an embrace that Erika would remember for the rest of her life. Nothing was said for the longest time as if all the emotions being discharged in the room wouldn't allow for any noise other than the few sobs and the grandfather clock ticking away.

Erika and her children moved into their new house within five days. Erika helped lay out a corner in the community building where a small pharmacy of sorts was setup and someone posted a little sign that said Nurse Erika's Medical Care Center.

CHAPTER FIFTY

Where had June and July disappeared to? Robert was just coming from the barn where he and their ranch foreman Big Joe had been discussing the need to move the cattle to a different pasture. "We are going to have a lot of help this year," Big Joe said.

"Maggie and Jimmy are becoming excellent riders and some of the other kids they have been teaching to ride are catching on really fast. We're going to have a whole wrangler team assembled for the cattle drive, and they are really excited." "That's great Joe. Thank you for taking the time to teach those little rascals how to become adept at riding, you are a real gem." "Not having had any kids of my own," Joe said "this has added a whole new dimension to my life, for which I will be eternally grateful. They are wonderful bunch of kids and very well-mannered."

"After those young wranglers got done with their ridding lessons today, I talked to them about the fact that we are planning on moving the cattle the day after tomorrow, starting at daybreak. They were fired up about helping move the cattle to a different pasture. I will be surprised if any of them will get much sleep the next couple of nights. By the way, I arranged for one of the construction workers to take a pickup and bring a grill along with a bunch of hot dogs and other good stuff out to the pasture where we will be taking the cattle. We are going to have us a wiener roast right out there along the creek after we get the cattle settled down. I thought the kids would really get a kick out of that." "With a big smile on his face, Robert said, "I expect Joe, you are one of the most important persons alive in those kids' eyes right now."

As Robert made his way to the house, he was in deep in thought. *Why not?* Joe's comment about the picnic put a bee in Robert's bonnet. It was hard not to be partial to some of the folks in the community, and there were a few that Robert felt really had earned a little bonus. He stepped up his pace on the way to the house. When he came in the door he found Ben had just arrived, and the girls were also there. "I've got an idea," Robert said, "and it's a good one." "Oh sure," Ben said, "it's strange that you didn't say it was brilliant." "Well, as a matter of fact, it really is quite brilliant now that I think about it."

When the chiding settled down, Robert said, "The day after tomorrow, Big Joe is taking Jimmy, Maggie, Suzanne, Cindy, Josh, Brekken, Andrea and Jeff's two sons, Mike and Don on the drive to move the cattle to the north pasture. The kids have been practicing and practicing and now think they are full-fledged cowboys and cowgirls. After they get the cattle settled down in the north pasture, Big Joe arranged to have a wiener roast up there. The kids are ecstatic."

"Sandy, Amber, do you have anybody scheduled to come in the day after tomorrow?"

Sandy and Amber checked, and both said, "No." "Then it's settled. Day after tomorrow We're taking the bus and all of us plus Jan, Erika, Jeff with his wife Betty, and Mark are heading into Medora for a fun-filled day." "That sounds absolutely wonderful," Sandy said, and there was immediate and mutual agreement from Ben and Amber.

CHAPTER FIFTY-ONE

Sandy had immediately called and reserved tickets to the Pitch Fork Fondue and the musical at the Burning Hills amphitheater. After Sandy secured the reservations, she sat at her desk for a moment thinking about what a treat this would be for everybody. *Coming from their backgrounds this probably wasn't going to be anything close to what they have ever experienced in their lifetime.*

It was a beautiful afternoon as they drove along the winding road, enjoying the scenery and just having a number of very relaxed conversations. After arriving in Medora, they strolled down the wooden sidewalks. Ben pointed out the various restorations that had been accomplished in this little old western town. He explained how the town developed and how it became the focal point for Teddy Roosevelt and his Roughriders.

"This is a little like stepping back in time," Amber said, "and it is really exciting to think that our forefathers were a part of this history." "Medora?", Jan said, "that sounds like a lady's name." "Well, as a matter of fact, that is absolutely correct. A 24-year old French nobleman, by the name of Marquis

A Mark of the Divine

De Mores, founded the town of Medora, in 1883. He named the town for his bride. Her name was Medora Von Hoffman, and she was the daughter of a very wealthy New York City banker. The Marquis had some pretty elaborate plans for this area. Unfortunately he went broke and he and Medora returned to France."

"It was in that same year that Teddy Roosevelt arrived on the scene in Medora," Sandy said. "Roosevelt fell in love with the area. He formed two big cattle ranches, one to the north of the Badlands and one to the south. It is said that he credited his becoming the youngest President of the United States, to his experience and love of the Badlands of North Dakota."

They enjoyed their stroll through the quaint little town. They indulged themselves with ice cream cones at one of the little shops. The sun was just setting. They were in the bus, following the road as it snaked back and forth, climbing towards the plateau atop the high butte. "People, what you are going to see and experience may not be the eighth or even the ninth or tenth wonder of the world but to those of us who feel an association with this area, rank it right up there with the Egyptian Pyramids."

Everybody's eyes were riveted to the scenery, yet they were surprised when they leveled out on top of the flat butte and pulled into the huge parking lot. They all looked at Ben with big question marks in their eyes. There didn't seem to be very much up here, save for the big restrooms and a kind of lean to where a large number of picnic tables were set around on the grass and a lot of people were lined up.

Ben busted out laughing at the look on their faces. "This is it," he teased. "Are you hungry?" Everybody said they were starving. "That's good, because you are going to have your belly's' expanded with one big North Dakota steak.

As they got to the front of the line, they could see a lot of big 30 gallon drums and several cowboys with pitch forks standing round them. "You are about to witness a North Dakota Tradition," Ben said, "this is called a North Dakota pitch fork fondue. T-bone steaks are put on the tines of the pitch forks, and then the pitch forks are immersed into the boiling cooking oil for about three to four minutes and bingo, you've got a fantastic steak."

Twenty minutes later, Ben and Robert looked around at the women's plates and said, "I can't believe it! I thought sure we'd get at least some of your steak. How is it possible for little birds of paradise like you gals eat so much food?!" Amber poked him in the ribs and said, "It's all in the wrist. That was fantastic; I'll never forget this experience." The others chimed in with their agreement. Erika said, "I sure hope those pitch forks were clean." That brought a big laugh from everyone.

As they walked out of the eating area Mark said, "Do we take the pickup to another area for the musical?" Robert said, "Do you see those people walking over at the edge of the butte and then they seem to disappear?" "Yes, I see them. What is happening?" "Come on. I'll show you." They all let out a little gasp as they neared the edge. Like some kind of magic, a huge Amphitheater appeared below them, carved out of the side of the butte. "This is totally amazing, they all said." Jeff said, "Look at that great big outdoor escalator for transporting people down into the Amphitheater, how are we going to get back up?" "When the show is over the escalator reverses and it transports everybody back to the top," Ben said.

As they were settling into their seats, Sandy pointed to a trail high above the stage with big spotlights illuminating a cowboy on horseback herding three huge bull elk up the trail. They all were thrilled by the live presentation taking place. As luck would have it, off to their left beyond the stage and high up on another butte, a huge yellow harvest moon had just climbed into sight. In front of the moon, outlined by it's light, a cowboy on horseback sat perched on a trail. It was like a painting. This would be something that they would never forget as long as they lived.

As they made their way back towards Medora and then on to the ranch, everybody was talking at once as the images of day and evening's activities were like a merry-go-round in their heads. One after another, they all expressed their thanks for such a spectacular outing. 'The musical was a fitting climax to an absolutely amazing day and evening," Jan said.

Robert was sitting next to Sandy and whispered to her, "I'll bet you five bucks that we have our first wedding at the village before the year is out." Sandy looked at Robert and then glanced up front a couple of rows to where Jan and Mark were sitting together. She smiled and said, "You may be right, no bet."

CHAPTER FIFTY-TWO

It had been a rarity when Ben and Amber, Robert and Sandy all had the opportunity to spend some quiet time together, but this evening was proving to be a wonderful exception. Spring and summer had been hectic. The crickets were in full song, the harvest moon was just rising, and it looked like something out of a fairy tale. The four of them were strolling along a small creek that ran through the ranch. "Don't you feel you could just reach up and embrace a whole bunch of those stars all at one time?" Amber asked. "Like tonight when they appear so close," Sandy said. "It looks like they are on strings, hanging down for us to gather."

"I hate to bring up business on a lovely night when I am with such beautiful people. Robert said, "But….." He was cut off by a loud groan from the other three. "Okay, I'll keep it short. As you know, we had hoped to complete a thousand homes this season, but it looks like we will fall a little short of that. Still, I am in awe of what has been accomplished. Do you realize the population of the O'Neil village is now approximately 2,950 wonderful souls? We have been so fortunate to truly have a great cross section of people and skills.

A Mark of the Divine

I am estimating that for the first year of A Mark of the Divine's operation approximately three million people will have made their way to one of the Villages. We all have learned a lot, and next year things will be smoother. They will have to be, because our goal will have to be ten times what we have accomplished this first year. If someone asked me what a good definition of America would be, I'd just say come to the O'Neil Village or anyone of a thousand other villages, and you will have your answer."

"But anyway, that isn't what I wanted to talk about. It's getting late in the fall, and we are going to have to shut down construction for the winter very soon. How many people do we have lined up to move into the Village before winter?" Robert asked Sandy. "As of right now, we have scheduled ten more families to arrive over the next five days." Ben said, "I think we are going to start pressing our luck if we schedule anymore folks in before freeze up. What do you think Robert?" "I agree, the fifteen day forecast predicts temperatures will start to dropping into the low twenties at night."

"Sandy, Amber," Robert said, "Who is the last family you have scheduled as of right now?" "A lady by the name Cassandra White, and her seventeen-year-old son Nick," Amber said. "Alright, if everybody is in agreement, we'll have her and her son be the last folks we will be able to accept until next spring," Robert said, "start checking with some of the other developers in the southern tier of States to see if we can refer some folks to them as they will be able to keep construction going for quite a bit longer and in some cases, they may be able to keep building all winter."

Also, let's have those same people who can keep their construction going start sending in requests for people they need to boost their labor force over the next six months. Some of the folks here may want to move to one of the other developments for the winter. This would be good for them, as they could keep busy and pick up some extra money. It would also make it possible for more people to join the exodus because of some of the developers being able to substantially increase the building of houses with the increase in labor." "We'll be on it first thing tomorrow morning Boss," Sandy said, and got a chuckle from the rest of them. "Now can we enjoy the rest of our walk?" "I solemnly promise to utter not a word that would have anything to do with business," Robert said.

The air was completely still. They could hear the howl of some coyotes that had to be at least two miles away. "It is nights like this, when Mother Nature is speaking to us, that we should count our blessings," Sandy said. They all agreed that Sandy's statement was right-on as they continued their stroll to the tunes of the night music of the crickets, frogs, coyotes and an owl that was making his presence known. "This is when you get a glimpse of the unfathomable power, glory and mystery of our universe," Sandy commented.

CHAPTER FIFTY-THREE

"Brrr," Jan said, "I am glad this is the last trench for footings and root cellars I will have to dig this year. I think the ground is going to be freezing up pretty soon." There was a big crew coming in right behind her, and the plan was to have this last house finished by the end of the week. She had just climbed down from the tractor and was observing her work when Mark came up behind her and gave her a big hug. "Can I warm you up?" She wiggled around to face him, gave him a big hug and kiss. "Jan, will you marry me?"

She was standing next to the ditch she had just dug and almost fell into it. "You picked a mighty strange place to ask me to marry you," she said. "But you know what, that is okay. I have been preparing my answer to your question, regardless of when or where it came. She stood on her tiptoes, gave him a great big kiss and with a smile that covered her face said, "Yes!" Then after a moment's thought she asked, "When?" "What would you think of a wedding right after Christmas?" "That sounds marvelous. I'll get Amber and Sandy to help me make it the best wedding ever," Jan said, "Shall we ask Ben and Amber if they will be our bridesmaid and groomsman?"

Before Mark could answer, she whirled around, leaving Mark standing there with his mouth open and ran like crazy across the field toward the ranch house. *Guess she is in a hurry to break the news,* Mark thought to himself as he stood there grinning from ear to ear.

CHAPTER FIFTY-FOUR

Introductions had been made between Cassandra, her daughter Stephanie, Sandy and Amber. "Please come in and sit down," Sandy said. After they were settled, Sandy said, "We'd like to give you a little orientation and introduction to our Village, but before we do that would you mind telling us a little more about yourselves?"

"I am, as I told you, an ordained minister of the Lutheran Church and was the pastor of our little church in Oregon. Two years ago, we had a lot of radical Muslims move into our area. It seemed like it only took a few months before they were attacking anything and anyone that stood for Christianity. They were able to do this without being apprehended for quite awhile as the authorities didn't seem able to positively place the blame on them for what was happening."

One night, I was over at the church getting some things ready for the next day and my husband had come with me to help out. We had just finished up what we wanted to get done and were ready to leave when four men dressed in robes and face scarves burst into the church. It appeared they were intent on destruction. My husband made the mistake of trying to stop them. In a destructive fury, they went crazy and killed him. Then they began beating me, knocking me to the floor. I was repeatedly raped and beaten. They left me lying there, and preceded to set fire to the church. A passerby saw the men run out of the church and saw the flames. He ran into the church, saw me on the floor and carried me out. Then he took me to the hospital which fortunately wasn't very far away. I eventually recovered physically, but I have to say that emotionally I am still struggling to come to grips with what happened that night."

"The violence against Christians is slowly escalating in that whole region, and I am so thankful I had the opportunity to be at a service club meeting when one of your people discussed A Mark of The Divine, Inc.. I bought a share in the corporation. I believe there must have been some Divine Providence involved in my action that day. I definitely think I must have been spiritually nudged to go to that meeting and hear what was said as it was the first service club meeting I had gone to since the terrible ordeal. Then after we talked on the phone, Sandy, I knew for sure that it definitely was Divine Providence that took me by the hand that day and led me to the meeting."

Sandy said, "Cassandra, I know you said you haven't been involved in your profession since that horrible time, but I hope you'll consider becoming one of our pastors at the Village. The people here need you and perhaps in some way you need them." "I think you're right Sandy. Yes, I have thought about that and will be glad to do whatever I can."

Amber said, "Stephanie, you've been awful quiet. I understand you are eighteen and have finished high school. Do you have any idea what you would like to get involved with in your future?" "Yes, I do, Amber. I really want to get into teaching after I get my degree, but I have to say that I am not impressed with our current systems for public education. I think that some new dimensions for education and some new models for schooling should be developed within our education systems."

"Wow," Sandy said, "You and I have some fun times ahead, I think you're going to be an integral part of the development of a new upper level educational system right here in the Village, while you pursue your degree." Stephanie was thrilled with what Sandy said.

They all stood and hugged. Cassandra thought, *it has been a long time since I have been this excited.* Cassandra and Stephanie were taken over to the bunkhouse where they would stay for a couple days until their house was ready.

When Amber and Sandy got back to the house, Sandy said, "What a couple of beautiful people and what a great way to bring our acceptance of 'immigrants' to the Village for this year to an end." "It's just hard to believe that we won't be taking in any more people until next spring," Amber said.

EPISODE THREE
MOLDING THE CLAY

CHAPTER FIFTY-FIVE
End of 2014

The first of November arrived with splendor on the Plains. The temperatures had soared to the middle seventies, which was highly unusual for this time of the year. After checking the weather report, Ben closed his computer and said, "You know Amber, I think we should have a harvest festival at the end of this week. The vegetables and all the other crops been harvested and canning is complete. The cattle that are going to market have already been culled out and moved to the loading area. The weather is going to be fantastic this week."
"That sounds wonderful Ben. Let's go over and talk to Sandy and Robert and get our plans made."

Excitement reigned high as the two families, including the kids, came up with idea after idea for the festival. In the end they agreed it should be at the end of the week, since the weather forecast was very positive for the entire week. A dance floor would be laid outside in the big area by the community center. There would a variety of bands. A long row of tables would be set up to accommodate food everybody would bring. The neighbors would be invited. There would be sack races, and all kinds of other fun contests with lots of prizes. The kids were so excited that they could hardly be contained.

Without question, word of this event would be spread throughout the community by afternoon. Ben, Robert and a number of the men had very successful hunting over the last couple weeks, bagging their limit of pheasants and deer. After getting a permit they had even shot a Buffalo. This was going to provide for a feast like none other.

The next evening, they were all sitting out on the porch discussing all the things that still had to be done. There wasn't a bit of breeze. "It is so quiet," Amber said smiling, "I heard a pine cone from a mile away crash to the ground." She had just said this, when they all became aware of a rumble in the distance, probably at least five miles away. They were all trying to put a name on the noise, when Ben jumped up and said, "That's a very large group of motorcycles." He pointed to a plume of dust rising into the sky. "I have a bad feeling about this," Robert said, "Sandy, run in and sound the alarm. Let's not take any chances."

In the lookout tower on top of the house Ben looked through the telescope. He said, "It looks to be what I would estimate to be about one hundred motorcycles." They came up to the gate. The buzzer for the intercom came on. Ben grabbed the microphone. "What can we do for you?" "We're not here to make trouble," came a raspy voice, "but we've been hired by some people to bring back a woman who lives in your village. Bring her out and we'll be on our way. Her name is Erika Solsburg. She's a valuable property for the people who want us to bring her back."

"Sounds like you're talking about a piece of machinery or something, not a person," Ben said. The rough voice blared again, "Look buster, we don't want to bring a lot of pain and suffering and maybe even death to you people. Just bring the bitch out and we'll be on our way with her."

"Well, I am afraid that you have come a long way for nothing, but at least it was a nice day for a ride." The leader didn't say anything more. Through the binoculars they watched the bikers take some planks that were laying near the road and build a ramp so they can ride their bikes over the top of the fence.

Robert was on the two-way radio talking to people from the Village, who were now hidden strung out along a ditch around the parameter. Many carried rifles, and some had shotguns. "It looks like they are going to try to breach our fence and will be coming in if they are successful." Robert said over the radio.

"These people will stop at nothing, so we shoot to kill. Ben and I will try to take them out as they come up the ramp and over the fence. If any get thru and keep coming, you people take them out. They won't be expecting this kind of resistance. I have notified the sheriff. He and his men plus any highway patrolmen in the area will be arriving to assist us."

Just after Robert said this Erika's voice came over the radio, "Robert, Ben: I can't be responsible for jeopardizing the lives of any of our people here. Tell them I am on my way out." Both Ben and Robert responded simultaneously

"No way Erika, you stay put. No more will be heard on that subject."

Ben said, "They're starting to line up in a single file with the idea of one bike after another coming over the fence." "Okay brother, looks like we are on deck. We'll alternate bikes as they come over. I'll take the first biker. You take the second and so on."

The first biker, presumably the leader, accelerated up the ramp and flew over the fence. As he sailed through the air, Robert nailed him. The second biker was up the ramp and flying over the fence when Ben shot him. Both lay in a tangled heap inside the fence. The third biker was just starting to go up the ramp when he realized the first two had either been killed or badly injured. He tried to veer off and stop but instead crashed into the fence.

There was a lot of commotion among the bikers as they seemed momentarily to be in a lot of disorder. After what appeared to be some heated discussion, they split into three groups. One group of about thirty stayed on their bikes at the gate. A second gang of the same size, started to work their way around the fence to the west. The third group of bikers worked their way around to the east.

When Ben and Robert had laid out the last of their security systems and their mode of defense, they had extended the ditch all the way around the property, about one hundred yards in from the fence. As a part of their emergency plan, people with guns were spread out in the ditch all the way around.

We'll have to try and determine where they plan to attack from and beef up our people in those areas," Ben said. "My guess is that they are planning an attack from three different directions at one time." Some of the folks had already started to move to both the east and west along the ditch when they saw what was happening.

As predicted, thirty minutes later the assault from three different directions began. As before, Ben and Robert took out the first five bikers that came over the fence by the gate. As the reports came in over the radio, they learned that the bikers who tried to breach the other areas had been disabled or terminated. Just as fast as it had started it ended. At the same time, five highway patrol cars came up the road behind the bikers that were left by the gate. The sheriff and his men were right behind them. Following them were ambulances, a fire truck and a unit of National Guardsmen.

All in all, sixty bikers had been killed. The thirty-eight who remained alive were badly wounded. They were handcuffed for their journey to the hospital at the State prison. "Robert told Sheriff Buck and the other law enforcement people who had gathered, "We have a pastor here at the village, so we'll dig a mass grave and hold a funeral service for the ones that were killed." "All right," the chief of the highway patrol said, "but before you do that, we'll go through and get any identification we can from the dead so we can notify any next of kin. We'll also get fingerprints so we can hopefully identify them sometime in the future."

"What do you want to do with all these wrecked bikes?" Ben asked. "I'd say they are the spoils of war. If you can use them, take 'em." "We've got some guys that can dismantle them and use a lot of the parts for something else," Ben said, "but perhaps you can send someone out to gather up the bikes that belong to the ones you have jailed or hospitalized. You can put them in some kind of holding area, and maybe have an auction later, I am sure you guys could use the extra money those bikes would bring for a variety things in your departments." "Thanks guys, Sheriff Buck said, we'll do just that. We all appreciate what you are doing out here and commend you for the heads-up security you have developed."

CHAPTER FIFTY-SIX

A few days later, the whole Village gathered at the new cemetery. Forty-two simple white crosses stretched across the back of the cemetery where the unclaimed bikers were buried. The podium and microphone had been placed in front of the crosses. Chairs had been setup in front of the podium and spread out over a large area.

Robert addressed the crowd first, "I know that the attempted invasion of our Village was a very traumatic and scary day for everyone and especially the children. I pray this type of incident will never visit our community again, but in reality our world has gone through some very dramatic changes, and they haven't been, for the most part, good changes. In all likelihood, other types of similar incidents may visit us in the future. I say this as a reminder so that we all will remain on constant alert. Yet we cannot allow the reason for our vigilance to taint our lives with fear. I want to thank you and congratulate you on your bravery and courage during the attack. Believe me when I tell you that if these people weren't lying in this mass grave, it would have been many of you. At this time I would like to call on Pastor Cassandra to perform a formal burial service for these folks."

"Thank you Robert. Before the formal burial service, I would like to say just a few words. I have experienced firsthand the treachery of the dark side of human behavior."

Cassandra then proceeded to reveal her story of the attack on herself and her husband. How they were attacked in their church one night; how he was murdered and she was raped and incurred a near-death beating. I feel good about the fact that my daughter and I are residents of this wonderful Village here on the O'Neil Ranch. In spite of the biker attack we both feel very safe and secure. We are surrounded by wonderful and beautiful people. We are so happy to be here."

There was a thunderous applause from the crowd. After everybody settled down again, Erika, who was sitting in the front row, raised her hand, asking if she could say a few words. Pastor Cassandra introduced Erika, then stepped away from the podium.

"I just wanted to say how terrible I feel that I am the one responsible for the assault on our community. I would like to tell why. The gang that attacked us had, I am sure, been hired by the Mexican drug cartel that kidnapped me when I was only ten years old. They smuggled me into Mexico and kept me as a sex slave for ten of the most horrible years anyone can ever imagine. Myself and the other girls that were in captivity were not treated as human beings by these evilest of evil people but rather as their property. Even though it has been over ten years since I escaped, they are still trying to get back what they believe is their property. So they hired those thugs that attacked us to bring me back."

"When I found out that I was the reason for that gang appearing at our doorstep, I told Robert and Ben that I would give myself up so that no one in the community would get hurt. Thankfully, they wouldn't listen to me at all." Erika broke down and cried.

After a short time Erika regained her composure and said, "Thanks to all of you for being so understanding. I have never felt so much love and caring in my entire life as I have here at the Village." As Erika left the podium, the response was both boisterous and tearful.

Pastor Cassandra then delivered the last rites and final blessings for those who had perished. At the end of the ceremony, she said to the crowd, "Please feel free to come and talk to me any time if you are having trouble dealing with what happened. In our Sunday school classes for the next few weeks I will be addressing violence and how we cope with it. As you know, this was quite traumatic for all the younger people. God Bless you all. Let's look forward with great anticipation to the Harvest Festival at the end of the week and not let this incident diminish our enthusiasm nor smother our fun."

CHAPTER FIFTY-SEVEN

As fall yielded to winter on the Great Plains of the north, you would have thought that it would have been quiet and serene in the Villages. But not so, activities abounded as skating rinks were built, there was snow sculpturing for prizes such as a jar of someone's special homemade jam and gatherings at the community center were happening every day.

Sandy and Amber and their team continued to be as busy as ever, fielding calls coming in from all over the United States from people looking to move out of the area they were in and join one of the Villages. Fortunately the weather in the southern sector of the Great Plains and some of the add-on States was staying quite nice and construction was still going full blast. Many of the Villagers at the O'Neil Ranch had temporarily moved to the south to help out with various construction activities.

"Didn't we just celebrate Christmas last month?" Robert said in jest. "Time has gone by so fast that it does almost seem like it was last month," Sandy said. Once again, Robert had found a huge Pine tree, cut it down and moved it to the community center. Once it was erected it stood almost 30 feet tall. Contests were developed that awarded prizes to the best handmade tree ornaments in several different categories and the decorating of the tree became quite a festival in itself.

Several of the fellows had built a Nativity scene, and it graced the foot of the tree. The entire Village gathered and surrounded the tree and the Nativity scene. For an hour they all joined in and sang Christmas songs, exchanged Christmas greetings with each other and mediated upon the meaning of Christmas.

A universal Christmas service was held after that. Then as dusk settled on the community, paper bags with sand in the bottom and a candle stuck in the sand, more commonly referred to as luminaries, were placed along the Village's main street at about 30 foot intervals, and then the candles were lit. "One of the meanings of this tradition on Christmas Eve or Christmas Day is the hope the light from the luminaries will guide the spirit of the Christ child to everyone's home," Amber said to kids as they were helping light the candles.

Just as people were thinking the Christmas Day celebration was coming to a close, the alarm sounded in all the houses, and the two-way radios came alive. "This is Robert; we have detected a breach in our security. A very strange-looking creature is just about ready to pull up in a huge sleigh by the community center. Everybody is requested to head over there right now but do not bring your guns!."

Ben had dressed up as Santa. Big Joe had hitched up four horses to the sleigh. They had loaded the sleigh with brightly wrapped packages that Sandy and Amber had been able to purchase and wrap without being detected. The children were ecstatic. Ben had a barrel of fun playing Santa, handing out gifts and teasing the children. It was a fitting climax to a wonderful Christmas weekend.

The next day, Jan and Mark were married in the community center and again the whole village was present. Ben and Amber had been delighted when Jan and Mark had asked if it they would be their bridesmaid and groomsman. They had also asked Robert and Sandy to stand up for them. So the founders of the O'Neil Village bore witness to the first marriage held there. Following the wedding, in typical Village fashion the music broke out, food appeared on long tables and the celebration of Jan and Mark's wedding was, as one of the kids put it, 'a dandy doodle dandy'!

"This is the best Christmas season ever," Suzanne said, "everybody is so happy and love just seeps through the crowd." "I know," said Cindy, "getting presents seems rather ridiculous now doesn't it?" Sandy said, "You have learned a valuable lesson in that 'things' aren't near as important as values and caring."

Robert was standing off to the side observing all the festivities, his mind in full gear as usual. He got a little choked up, recalling *where these people were when they came here and where they are today. It was a miracle in the making, and an extremely strong testimony to the tenacity and the determination of common, everyday Christian Americans. How fortunate we are to have been a small part of this huge movement.*

CHAPTER FIFTY-EIGHT

Sandy came into the kitchen where Ben and Robert were sitting, discussing the up-coming meeting with the developers, scheduled for next week in Wichita, Kansas. "Guess who I just got a call from?" Sandy said. Ben said, "Well, I was wondering when the Pope was going to call." Ben ducked the round house Sandy let go at him. "No, it was none other than the news commentator Eric Smith, wanting to know if we had a nice lot set aside for him. Also, could we build him a house next spring if he joined our Village, that is if we would accept him!"

"Robert said, "What did you tell him?" "I told him that the answer to the first part of his question was a definitely yes, but I wasn't sure if the Village would vote him in or not. We both got a good laugh about that. I said you'd give him a call back yet today, Robert."

"That is super news," Ben said. "We could also build him his own station for broadcasting right here at the Village. He could do his broadcasts with live feeds to every radio and TV station in Mid America." "You're right, this could be a really powerful tool for the movement as we move forward," Robert said. "He can become the official voice of A Mark of The Divine, Inc." "Aren't you taking a lot for granted?" Sandy queried. "No, and let me tell you why I am saying that. I had a long conversation with him on the telephone about a month ago, and I didn't say anything about it to anyone because he asked me not to. He wanted to be sure that this was the right move for him. I felt pretty confident he would join us, but I just had to wait. It was really hard, not telling you guys."

Just at that time, Amber came into the kitchen and said, "Oh good, you are all here. I have something I need to say. I was going through and summarizing the commitments that we already have for next year as far as new folks joining our Village. We are now right at five thousand folks committed to join us next year, and it is only December."

One after another they all chimed in with amazement and frankly, were quite stunned. Even Sandy hadn't realized that the figure had climbed into the stratosphere. "Alright," Ben said, "we have to do some planning and appraisals, to see how this might work. It will be an entirely different scenario this spring, compared to last year, as we have well over a thousand workers who will be in place when we start. I am glad we are having the developers' meeting real quick like. It will be interesting to see if the rest of them are getting this kind of early commitment.

CHAPTER FIFTY-NINE
JANUARY – 2015

The convention for the shareholder/developers in Kansas City had been rescheduled to the second week in January. Because the numbers had grown so large, it was agreed by the developers that each state would elect twenty representatives. These representatives and their spouses would attend the convention. Their reservations alone exceeded six hundred, and the excitement was felt all the way back to the O'Neil ranch.

Ben and Robert had decided they really should expand the conference to two days. They thought that having a two-day conference would serve everybody better and allow for a much more complete program. They invited the governor of each state to participate in the conference and also the mayors of all the cities and the towns within the convention area. It now appeared that fifteen governors and over three hundred mayors would be participating. So it looked like reservations might exceed the one thousand mark on the second day of the conference.

A Mark of the Divine

While Ben, Amber, Robert and Sandy were finalizing and fine tuning their outlines and material that would be used at the Kansas City meeting, the children were involved in similar activities. After Cindy had come up with the idea that perhaps they should also have a program for the children from other villages, that concept was accepted and formalized. Two children representatives from each village would attend the convention; they would have their own program.

The idea was received by the other villages with accolades and enthusiasm. This moved the attendance figure up considerably, but thank goodness they had secured a site which could handle this many participants.

Conceivably, this conference could turn out to be one of the most important get-togethers in decades. It could be a giant first step in grabbing a chunk of the United States by the boot straps and heading it down a road toward rebuilding the great American dream.

Of course, they all knew they were still in the very early stages of that dream, as millions were still in desperate straits. It was calculated there would still be many millions who would migrate to the Mid America States before the political carnage had run it's course. There was a chance to see real progress in the rebuild of the United States, but there was a tremendous amount of skepticism because too many fundamentals remained the same and the hole that had been dug was far too deep. The alternative, which was being discussed very heavily between all the governors of the attending states, was that as a block, they would file for secession and form a new Country called Mid America. The way things were progressing with A Mark of the Divine, Inc., witnessing the unbelievable response of people desiring to move into the Villages, the governors were very close to polling their constituents to get a sense of how the general public would feel about secession and the formation of a new America. That poll was scheduled to happen in about two week's time. They knew that Eric Smith had conducted a similar poll, but now they were considering conducting a vote that would involve their entire voting population, rather than a poll. One difficult hurdle to overcome in all of this was that the population in these states was literally increasing by thousands on a weekly basis.

CHAPTER SIXTY

Robert brought the meeting to order and addressed the group. "Ladies and gentlemen, welcome to the Mark of The Divine, Inc., Shareholder/Developer conference. This is what we hope will be the first of many such conferences. I doubt any of us could have ever imagined this setting even two years ago. What we have all been through during this period defies all logic as we mounted a movement that is phenomenal to say the least.

You could say that over last two years, we have set about to reclaim our identity. We talk about the phrase 'identity theft'; well folks, as a run up before the establishment of A Mark of the Divine, we witnessed the biggest identity theft in the history or our Country. Not just the stealing of our identities, but the identities of our children and potentially those of their children. What has been accomplished to regain our identities up to now is nothing short of amazing. The resilience of those who believe in what America has truly represented for over two hundred years plus has been the backbone of our success as we shifted from talk to action."

A Mark of the Divine

"We all are very aware that our nation became great because it was founded in the belief that there is but one Higher Power. Our Federal and State Governments were formed only for the purpose of serving the people. Governments should engage in only those things, such as military defense, that did not lend themselves well to private enterprise."

"We also knew that freedom was the precious gem that anchored our determination to maintain a democracy which valued life and the pursuit of each individual's goals. With the Ten Commandments, the Constitution and the Bill of Rights as our guides, our ambitions and our entrepreneurial spirits led to rapid growth of our great Country. These documents also provided the parameters for those who came to America.

"We place no value on skin color or any other physical attributes. Rather we believe in the Golden Rule '**Do unto others as you would have them do unto you**,' and that all mankind was created equal under God. We value hard work and detest laziness. Our word is our bond and to be careless with that responsibility at the expense of someone else is not tolerated."

"Over the years, so many of these values and beliefs began to erode within the general population and within the leadership of our Country. As the 'decay' continued to ripen and the steady drift away from the multitude of attributes that had made our Country great became more and more prevalent, the dire consequences of these actions and of failures to take actions also became apparent."

"All of this plus a lot more have been the catalysts which has propelled ten's of millions of people to the brink of financial ruin and devastation. Through your brave leadership and selfless action we are gathered here today. Our overall goal is to continue to launch the rebuilding of the American dream. Now, I would like to introduce my brother Ben, so that we can get to the meat of our program as we have much work to do. Don't forget tomorrow will bring a very different and exciting program as we join hands with our neighbors, our state' governors and city and town Mayors."

Ben took to the podium, thanked Robert and addressed the attendees. "I truly believe we are at the threshold of something that will continue to be extraordinary in scope and positive results. As many of you may know, by this spring we are estimating we will have approximately eight thousand developers spread across fifteen states from Canada to Mexico and from Wisconsin to Arizona. The average size of all our villages ranges from one hundred for those who just recently got started to almost ten thousand in a Village in southwestern Arizona. The total population of all villages we are estimating will be thirty-three million folks by the end of this year." This brought a standing ovation from all the attendees.

Now in just a few minutes we are going to break up into the pre-assigned work groups based on the information you received earlier in the mail. This is going to be the 'sleeves rolled up' work that we all are going to have to attack for the rest of the day. As you also know, there are three separate work sessions that will be going on simultaneously. The men in one group, the women in another and the young folks in yet another group. Every person has his or her work group assignments, and we ask you to turn in your summaries at the end of the day. These will be further summarized and mailed out to you and all other villagers not in attendance, so that

A Mark of the Divine

you can all share in the wisdom garnered in these sessions. On everybody's folder you have a room and table number that has been assigned to you and your group. Good luck, God bless and we'll see you all at the combined session tomorrow."

CHAPTER SIXTY-ONE

Excitement prevailed. The enthusiasm of the crowd was electric and definitely contagious as the second day of the conference was about to get underway. After everyone in the auditorium was seated, the invocation had been given, and the welcoming address by Robert had been taken care of, Ben stepped to the podium.

"In this second day of our conference, we are going to be addressing some issues that for many may seem pretty far out or at least a little over the top. However, these extraordinary times call for actions that keep step with or outpace the actions of those who seemed bent on destroying the America we know and love."

"Our first guest speaker today is someone whom most of you have seen on National TV before the Federal Government added the National Broadcasting industry to its collection. After getting the boot, most likely because of his conservative views, Eric joined our Village up in North Dakota. Although he won't be moving in with us until spring, he has been a very busy individual, preparing for this move. Please welcome Eric Smith."

A Mark of the Divine

"Thank you Ben and it is a real pleasure to address this group of pioneers extraordinaire.

Ben has instructed all of us who will be addressing you today to keep it short and to the point, so that is exactly what I am going to do. Over the last couple of months I have been conducting a number of polls within the Great Plains' and bordering states. I think you are going to be interested in hearing those results.

In a poll concluded just two weeks ago, we asked the following questions of one hundred thousand people who lived in towns and cities within this area. Question One: Do you feel the huge migration of people to the Villages that are developing in your area and becoming your new neighbors is positive or negative? Ninety-one percent said it was a positive. Question Two: Do you think your state should consider seceding from the Union and join with other states in forming a new Country? Much to our surprise, an overwhelming majority, eighty-eight percent, said yes. This was no small sampling folks; this was a sampling of over one hundred thousand people who all live in the Plains States. Does this tell you that a majority of people have had it with our Federal Government? All members of the audience were on their feet applauding.

"I think there is one other very important item that should be considered in the many debates that will begin to take place over the next few months. That is the persecution of Christians and Jews taking place at an ever increasing rate. I know you may think that word 'persecution' may be a bit too strong, but believe me we are under attack, and it is becoming less and less subtle all the time."

"I am reminded of the appalling times back in the 70's when a Nazi organization within the United States was flaunting the German Swastika and parading in Jewish communities, raising the ire and fear of those who were either directly involved in theHolocaust or were but one generation removed. It was a devastating time for those Jewish communities, and they rallied around the chant 'Never Again'!"

"Many of you were motivated to move to these new Villages because of the deterioration of America's values in so many places. The removal of religious symbols and lack of respect for Christianity were probably at the head of your list. No longer do we seem to be 'One Nation Under God'. Churches have been burned. The striking of any reference to God in schools, government buildings and grounds and all public places are but a few reminders that our Christian God is under siege. I believe very strongly, as do the O'Neil's, that the trench which appeared in the Amargosa Desert a few years ago and still to this day has the exact same measurements as when it was first discovered, is definitely a message from God. Many of us might easily interpret this as God saying 'people you need to shape up or suffer the dire consequences of your inappropriate actions'. Thank you; keep your courage and fortitude in high gear. I look forward to visiting with you in the future."

"Our second guest is a long time friend who is well-acquainted with all the other state governors who have honored us with their presence today. I'd like to introduce to you Governor Jon Helmquist, of Kansas."

"Thank you Ben. This is a pretty monumental gathering, and I appreciate being able to be a part of what should prove to be a very memorable day for all of us. It may well be the

A Mark of the Divine

beginning of a new America! This brought a standing ovation. I also want to thank you for holding your convention in our State. We are honored by your presence."

"We all recognize the disastrous situation we have endured and continue to have in Washington, D.C. That situation is the root cause for the magnificent direction the folks with A Mark of The Divine, Inc., have so bravely embarked upon. I have come to the conclusion that the differences between Liberalism and Conservatism have become so great that leaders on both sides can no longer effectively function on the same playing field. In addition, I think all of this has moved to a plateau that renders it impossible to rectify.

It is for this reason that I am appointing a small team I hope will work with many other state teams who also feel the proper path for us to take is to join together in an effort to form a new Country. To put it in terms of a popular TV show, we need an 'Extreme Makeover'." The whole auditorium was on its feet, applauding and chanting 'Never Again, Never Again'!" This is what they were waiting for and desperately wanted to hear, it was like the start of a once-in-a-lifetime race."

"You'll be pleased to know that through the efforts of the O'Neil's, the governors of the Great Plains States along with several bordering state's governors have already formed a task force to start this ball rolling. It's going to take some time to put all this together. We will be reporting our progress through Eric Smith, as he has now been syndicated in over five hundred radio and TV stations throughout the Midwest."

"Your comments and thoughts are extremely important and we urge your communications to be constantly flowing to us on a constant basis throughout this whole process. Now

I would like to call on Governor Jan Schroeder of Arizona." There was another big applause as the gavel was handed over to Governor Jan.

"Thank you very much. What a pleasure it is for me to be standing here today. As you know, over the last few years our state has been fighting a tremendous battle with our Federal Government over immigration. In the midst of this battle I have come to realize just how totally incompetent the White House and Congress really are. For the most part, these people are so under qualified for the work of the positions they are holding that it has become an embarrassment for many of us who have such pride in our America."

"Because of this, we started the ball rolling last year to secede from the Union. This was a tremendous undertaking just to get to the point where we (finally) said, we have no other alternative. I have met with members of the task force that Governor Jon mentioned and have offered the support of the State of Arizona and will share what we learned about the process of secession."

"To have fifteen to nineteen States, go together and secede from the Union and form a new Country is probably the most exciting and challenging event that has happened since the birth of America over two hundred years ago. After these last few years, to be able to accomplish this will be like finally being able to take a shower after being denied cleansing over a very long period of time. I look forward to working with you, God Bless you and God Bless our efforts to form what undoubtedly could become the newest and greatest Country on earth." Instantaneously the whole auditorium erupted. The morning had put a huge electrical charge into the audience and everybody was anxious to divide into their assigned groups and get to the real meat of this conference.

As the afternoon wore on, there was an increase in the sound level of the hundreds of goup discussions throughout the huge auditorium. The molding of desired actions was now entering the final phases of these discussions. By the end of the day a preliminary agreement of discovery was reached and signed by the Governors of sixteen states: North Dakota, South Dakota, Minnesota, Wisconsin, Nebraska, Montana, Wyoming, Colorado, Kansas, Iowa, Missouri, Oklahoma, Arkansas, New Mexico, Texas and Arizona. A representative from Alaska was present. She felt quite certain Alaska would join the group and would confirm this within the week. Both Utah and Idaho had representatives at the conference. They felt their states would join with the Western states but again would confirm this within the week.

The agreement to pursue discovery was centered on these sixteen states seceding from the United States and forming their own Country to be called Mid America. A highly talented and respected team was tagged for this Herculean job. The Governors would serve as a part of this team but the heavy lifting would be done by the core members of the team. They were given a maximum of one year to develop and formalize this document for presentation. It was also agreed that a preliminary report would be processed at quarterly intervals, seeking comments. The core members of the team agreed to take a leave of absence from their regular careers to work on this project and it was agreed that an appropriate salary and reimbursement for incurred expenses would be granted to these individuals.

During this highly charged conference, Ben and Robert slipped out separately and joined up with General Elizabeth at a place they had agreed upon. In her usual 'get to the heart of the matter' demeanor, General Elizabeth conveyed several messages from their task force regarding the actions that were taking place. After a lot of discussion on issues related to the conference and where everything should move toward following the conference. Ben then asked, "Elizabeth, will you consider representing Mid America on what will have to be a newly formed Joint Chief of Staffs with representatives from all three countries, if this all comes together as we hope that it will?"

A slight smile appeared on her face, something that wasn't usually present, and said, "I have been actually anticipating you would be asking me that question and have given it a lot of thought. Yes, as a matter of fact I am already planning to move into the Midwest within the next few months, so I will look forward to discussing this further when the time is right."

EPISODE FOUR
CONCEPTION AND GESTATION

CHAPTER SIXTY-TWO
Conception and Gestation Of
MID AMERICA

In the few months since the big conference, corporate headquarters at the O'Neil Ranch had been hectic. Hundreds of reports were summarized, collated, packaged and mailed out to the members involved in the conference. These would assist the various committees. They would also be valuable to the transition team charged with developing the discovery presentation which would undoubtedly include detailed steps necessary for secession from the Union by the current seventeen states that would form a new Country called Mid America. Everybody was extremely pleased that Alaska had opted to join the group but a little disappointed that Utah and Idaho had opted to remain with the West Coast states.

Sandy and Amber were just taking a break when Erika came bursting through the door. "What a morning," she said, all out of breath. "What has happened?" Sandy said. "Two really wonderful events," replied Erika, "Jan McPherson

Anderson just gave birth to a beautiful baby boy, and both are doing great. Mark is strutting around like a peacock with a smile on his face that is from ear to ear." "That is wonderful. I'll bet Cindy and Josh are pretty excited also, now that they have a little brother," Amber said. "We'll have to have a celebration real soon, probably at the same time that he is baptized." "Great idea," Sandy said, "now didn't you say there were two big events that happened this morning?

Another big smile appeared on Erika's face. "Guess what?" she said as she produced a check from her pocket and handed it to Amber and Sandy. They looked at the check which was for ten thousand dollars from Draper Publishing House. They both shouted at the same time, "The manuscript for you book has been accepted!" Tears were running down their cheeks as Erika embraced each of them. "If it hadn't been for your encouragement, this would never have happened," Erika said.

"I had a long talk with the publisher this morning. They are setting up the release date and planning a big promotional push. It's a little scary and although laying my life out for everybody to see is a bit uncomfortable, I realize that there could be some real positive things come from this. If it strikes a little fear into the teenage and pre-teenage girls, I guess that is a good thing." "We are so proud of you Erika," Sandy exclaimed. "Look how many positive things have happened since you joined us."

"I know, I owe my life to you guys. When I first came here and asked for a meeting, all four of you were there for me. You have no idea how hard it was to tell you about being kidnapped at age ten and what my life had been like after that. What you have done for me is beyond belief and for the umpteenth time, THANK YOU!"

"Erika, always know in your heart that you are family to us. We are with you all the time, if not physically then in spirit. After the publication of your book, you will do fantastic things. The only bad thing is you will be on the road a lot once you start the promotions for your book. We're going to miss seeing your smiling face around here," Sandy said.

CHAPTER SIXTY-THREE

Ben was on his way up to the house. When he heard the alarm go off, he grabbed the radio off on his belt and turned it on all-call mode. "We have an emergency situation over at the Jewish Village. Most of you know where it is, about fifteen miles from us. They issued a call for support as they are under siege by a band of terrorists. All those who can possibly make it, please meet at the gate in fifteen minutes. We'll head right over to their Village," Robert said. "Bring your weapons."

As they approached the Village, gunfire could be heard. They stopped about a half mile short of the Village on a hill where they could observe the situation and then determine how to proceed. According to the last communications from the Village, the terrorists hadn't been able to breach the Village security buffers, but it did look like the terrorists were about ready to mount a charge. Under directions from Robert, approximately five hundred armed men and women spread out and advanced on the terrorists from their rear. The battle lasted for only a few minutes once they were close enough to start firing on the terrorists. Many of the terrorists were killed or injured as they tried to fend off the assault from the rear. They soon realized that it was matter of dying or surrendering. Shortly afterward the sheriff and his deputies along with a team of highway patrol people arrived and took over. Almost one hundred were arrested. Fortunately none of the Villagers suffered fatal wounds. It was later learned that the terrorist attackers were a large contingency of a group whose hate for the Jewish folks was running rampant in other parts of the U.S.

As Robert and Ben made their way back to the Ranch Ben said," Well, hopefully that group has learned their lesson. Terrorists will come to realize that any type of attack on either the Jewish or the Christian people in any of the villages will be met with vigorous and deadly defense." "Amen brother," Robert said. "The message must be spreading since it seems from all the reports and our own experience that the attacks are becoming less and less frequent. The other thing that factors into this is the populations in the Villages have grown immensely, which in itself will discourage this type of invasion." "It certainly would seem you are right Robert, but on the other hand we must continually encourage all villages not to let down their guard in any manner."

Ben continued, "Speaking of populations: this year's new people will start arriving next week and according to Sandy and Amber, it appears we will grow by another five to six thousand people, the number being dependent on our ability to construct housing before next fall's freeze up."

"The construction of houses is now under full swing. Considering the size of the work force we should have no problem keeping up," Robert said. "I think we also should start construction on another community center and park area. The other one is going to be overwhelmed in no time flat." "That is an excellent thought. I'll get that started immediately," Ben said. "It was a good thing that Jan started her heavy equipment company last year. She has trained and developed a real good team. She understandably wants to take some time off after just giving birth to their new baby, and she can do it now and not feel pressured," Ben said. "I know we all keep saying this over and over, but when I think of all that has happened in just the last two years, it's hard to get your head around it," Robert said. "We really have been blessed."

"I am thinking of one more thing. How about we have a big Fourth of July celebration at our ranch and inviting Saul Loestein and his village to join us? I am also thinking of asking Joe Miller, head of the Hutterite Colony, and all his people." "That would be quite a gathering wouldn't it?" Ben said. "Also," Robert continued, "if we want a big neighborhood celebration, why not invite folks from the surrounding small towns? After all, they are our neighbors, and we do interact with them frequently. A number of the villagers work in these small towns." "You know that is a great idea Robert, and Sandy could get cultural teaching materials out to all the home school teachers. This could become a part of their classes. The children would learn much about the Jewish and the Hutterite religions, and also about their customs and traditions." The home school teachers could encourage their charges to talk about these cultures when they are having their family meals together, and then the adults would also get educated on this subject." "It sounds like a plan," Ben responded.

"I was just thinking about when we met Joe a number of years ago. His pickup had slipped off the road just as we had come from the Ranch, and we were able to pull him back onto the road. He absolutely insisted that we join him and his people for lunch at the Hutterite Colony. I still remember being a little caught off guard when we went into the dinning area. The room was filled with long picnic tables, and all the men sat down to eat first and were served by the women. Then when the men were done eating, the women got to eat." "I remember that to," Robert said. "I also remember how delicious the food was and how hospitable everyone was. It was a very nice experience." "They have been good friends and neighbors," Ben said.

CHAPTER SIXTY-FOUR

Two weeks after Ben and Robert got the consent of Amber and Sandy regarding the grand plan to have a big whoopee-do over the Fourth of July, activities were ready underway to support this huge undertaking. Amber and Sandy, who now had twenty ladies working in the corporate office, welcoming and going through orientation with all the folks arriving on a daily basis, had time to work on other things. The building crews were doing a magnificent job of staying ahead of the new residents coming in at average of forty families a day.

"Thank you all for coming over here to the community center on such short notice," Sandy said. There were about a hundred ladies, all of whom had gone through Sandy's home schooling teaching classes. Sandy explained to the group about the upcoming Fourth of July shindig. "Over the next month or so, I'd like to suggest that you incorporate into your lessons for the children an overview of the Jewish traditions and beliefs as well as the same for the Hutterites. This is going to be an excellent opportunity for the children to develop an understanding of these cultures. They in turn, should be encouraged to talk about what they learn with their parent or parents at the evening meal. I will be sending you periodicals and study guides that you can use in your teachings."

"Yes Mary?" Sandy said. "Can you give us a real brief explanation of differences culture and beliefs now Sandy?" "Sure, I can do that. All that I tell you today and much more will be in your teaching packets you will receive within the next couple of days. "The Hutterites originated in Austria in the 16th century. Under the leadership of Jakob Hutter, they formed a communal type of living which was based on the New Testament books of the Acts of the Apostles and Corinthians. This distinguishes them from other groups like the Amish and Mennonites." "So they are a form of Christianity?" Jessica asked. "Yes, a basic trait or practice of the Hutterites is what is called absolute pacifism. They are forbidden from serving in the armed forces, the wearing of formal uniforms , like police or military, and they cannot contribute or pay taxes that are targeted as war taxes. Persecution led them to migrate to various countries over a period of time, and a small splinter group even converted to Catholicism.

In late eighteen hundreds three different groups migrated to North America and initially settled in what was then called Dakota Territory. This area encompassed what was to eventually become the States of North Dakota and South Dakota. Then later someHutterites migrated to Montana and the prairie provinces of Canada, Saskatchewan, Manitoba and Alberta.

Today, approximately seventy percent of the estimated population of fifty thousand live in Canada. The larger part, the other thirty percent, live in the Dakota's and Montana. These colonies, like our neighbors, are rural as they depend mostly on farming and ranching. They are literally self-sufficient. They are what they call male-managed, while the women are engaged in cooking, medical decisions, and the purchase of fabrics for the making of clothes. This will give you at least a basic idea about the beliefs and customs of our Hutterite neighbors."

"As for our Jewish Village neighbors, I'll just give you a quick overview of Judaism. Judaism is their religion and it dominates their way of life and their philosophy of life. There are three large Jewish religious movements, distinguished by their approaches to the practice of Jewish law. These are Orthodox, Reform and Conservative Judaism. Our neighbors are mostly followers of Reform Judaism which is more liberal in its beliefs than the others. Reform Jews view the Jewish Law as a general guideline rather than a list of restrictions to follow.

The worlds Jewish population is estimated to be somewhere around thirteen to fourteen million. The Jewish religion is more than three thousand years old. It is the oldest religion to survive into the present. Approximately six million Jews live in the United States.

Today, Judaism lacks a central authority. As a result there are many branches within the basic beliefs of Judaism, but in general all of Judaism is centered around the Hebrew Bible. The Biblical covenants between God and Abraham and God and Moses are at the core of Judaism. We also know that Judaism rejects the belief in Jesus Christ. They believe there is only one God, no Trinity. This is a quick summary of the history and beliefs of our Jewish neighbors and I hope it has been helpful."

"Although there are a lot of big differences in cultures and religious beliefs between our invited guests, this get-together can be a tremendous learning experience. Hopefully, all the children and adults can mingle and enjoy a day of fun together. We are going to have a lot of talent contests along with exhibitions and dance presentations. Also there will a lot of booths where arts and crafts and a lot of other homemade items will be available. There will be judging and awards for best pies, jams and on and on. We are also sharing information with our Jewish and Hutterite neighboring Villages, along with a number of small towns in the area. This will help everybody enter into the spirit of the day."

The plans for this one-day event and all that it would entail put a buzz through the Village that was electrifying and exciting. It quickly became the main topic of conversation at any little gathering and all the new people coming in were also immediately absorbed in the activities.

Even Big Joe got caught up in all the commotion and decided that some of his riding students from the Village would put on a show that day about horseback riding, and about horses themselves. His current crop of students picked up on the idea right away and started to develop all sorts of ideas as to how they should proceed and what their show would like when they were ready to present it on the Fourth of July.

CHAPTER SIXTY-FIVE

The first draft of the first quarterly report had just arrived from the task force commissioned to write a discovery report for what was now seventeen states who plan to secede as a block of states from the Union and form a new Country. Sandy made three copies so that she and Robert along with Ben and Amber could each have copy.

"It's a good thing this is just the summary, as I imagine this part of the entire document would probably be 1000 pages long," Sandy said. "By the way," Robert said, "there is a web site address at the bottom of the first page where we can go to view the document in it's entirety should we have a need to look up further details of any part of this summary."

That evening they started through the two hundred page report. Discussing and throwing out related ideas to enhance or change, as they took it section by section. This first document dealt entirely with the justice system that was being proposed for Mid America.

The opening remarks for this section said in part, *"The justice system that we have had in the United States is recognized as one of the most unique of all justice systems in the world. But being unique is not in itself a commendation for it's operative qualities.*

Admittedly, although it may be far better than most systems, there is a lot of room for improvement and now the opportunity is present to make the justices system in Mid America the best in the world. With this in mind, we have formed our proposal around the current system while making minor adjustments and in some cases complete changes to it, so as to craft a twenty-first century Justice System that corrects the failures of the current system."

"You know," Ben said, "I keep forgetting what a unique opportunity we have in that we are starting a brand new Country with the benefit of what one could almost call twenty- twenty hindsight. "

Robert, having been an Appellate Judge, was able to quickly pick up on the changes as they moved through the document. "I like these changes," Robert said,. "Whether a trial is being held in civil court or criminal court, at the lowest court or all the way to the Supreme Court, the format will be identical. Other than the Supreme Court, there will always be three judges hearing the case. In the case of the Supreme Court, State or Federal, there will be nine judges. This will certainly cut down or practically eliminate the appeals process which is so costly and time consuming. I also like the idea that all judges must be elected, none will be appointed, and again this goes all the way to the Supreme Court. I also like the idea that no judge shall serve in his or her elected capacity for more than six years, including the Supreme Courts in the states or the Federal Supreme Court. In my opinion no man or women is so all-knowing that he or she should be appointed to a lifetime position within the court system or any other system for that matter. These are all positions of honor and power. To serve our Country in any of those positions is an achievement that should positively mark the individual for life as a human being who has served his or her Country to the maximum. Individuals have paid a horrible price in some cases because of the inconceivable lack of professionalism and judgment on the part of some judges who can only be labeled as corrupt."

Ben said, "I agree and I also like the changes being put forth in jury selection and jury duty. Developing a professional reasonably paid jury pool in all areas will eliminate most of the jury selection process. Screening, qualifying and hiring into these pools will be done by a panel of three judges. This should eliminate such fiascos as was demonstrated years ago in a murder trial out in Los Angeles where race became the dominate factor in finding a guilty person innocent, not the weeks and weeks of testimony and presentation of facts, but flat out, it came down racial decisions. Speaking of which, there is zero room, and there should be zero tolerance for anybody who tolerates or promotes racism in any area of our lives."

"I am in awe of what is taking place and the fact that we are participants in such a tremendous undertaking," Amber said. "Tell me honestly Ben and Robert, did you foresee all of this taking place when you first started A Mark of The Divine?" "I'd like to say that I was that brilliant," Ben said. "But no, we seem to be directed by the Divine, and I agree it is hard to get your arms around such awesome events taking place."

"It sure would be fun to skip ahead and peek at what the conference or perhaps the confrontation will look like when the team goes to Washington and hand delivers our contract of secession," Sandy said. "That will be the final chapter in the document that we have in our hands and yes, it should be a show," Robert said.

"What happens if the White House and Congress reject our secession?" Amber said. "When it comes right down to it, they have no choice," Robert said. "Over the years, through Constitutional amendments, more and more power has gradually been shifted to the Federal Government. Doesn't that sound familiar? It is that slow and gradual movement that allows for the conditioning of the American people to the will and ways of the Federal Government. But in spite of that, the Constitution is quite mute on secession. The only document that might be used to try and block our secession is an old ruling back after the Civil War when the Supreme Court ruled that secession was unconstitutional."

'Two things that make this rather benign are that one, since the Constitution is quite silent on this, it seems ironic that the Court was able to site the Constitution. Second, if we secede, we become a sovereign nation and the current Supreme Court has no jurisdiction over us. So who cares what they rule? It would be meaningless to our new Nation. Oh yes, they'll puff out their chests and rattle the cage, but in the end, it will be just the same old thing, rhetoric!" "I do love how you boil things down Robert, and make the opposition look like they are dancing on a string," Sandy said.

Discussions had been on-going for several hours on the first part of the document they had, and it was quite unanimous when Sandy said that she had come to the end of her day. They agreed to pick up where they left off, tomorrow night.

CHAPTER SIXTY-SIX

"Pete, will you be our lookout?" Maggie asked. "We don't want anyone seeing us practice for the big show we all are going to be putting on for the Fourth of July celebration." "Okay," little Pete said, "but I sure wish I could ride with you guys." "In a couple more years Pete, then you'll be old enough, and you will be a fantastic rider." Little Pete grinned from ear to ear and said, "Do you really think so Maggie?" "I sure do." "Okay then, I'll be your lookout and yell if I see anyone coming this way."

The five ponies that Big Joe had the kids riding for their final act were perfectly matched and their temperament matched the task that they were expected to do. Maggie, Jimmy, Cindy, Josh and Suzanne were practicing standing barefoot while riding on the back of a horse. They were now practicing on a fake horse that Big Joe had rigged up. It gave them about the same motion as they could expect when they were actually on the backs of the horses.

"How much longer Big Joe, before we can start practicing on the horses?" Josh asked. "You all are catching on pretty fast, so it won't be too much longer, but then there will still be a lot of work to do. Don't forget, when you fall off a real horse that's going to be a lot different than if you fall off this practice horse. It's a lot further to the ground."

Ben and Robert decided that as a part of the recreation area they would dig a huge ditch like amphitheater and tier the sides. The design was such that it would have enough space for about two thousand people on each side and the flat bottom would be where any type of performance could take place. This project got underway immediately. They expected to have it dug, tiered and the grass planted by tomorrow. So they figured by the time the Fourth rolled around it would be in great shape. In the evenings small gatherings throughout the Village could be seen practicing dance routines. There were music rehearsals, both instrumental and singing groups. A lot of spectators were just enjoying the frenzied activity.

Word was coming from the Jewish Village, Hutterite Colony and a number of small towns in the surrounding area, that they also were in high gear developing dances and music that reflected their respectful traditions. While having fun was the prime motivator, there was no question that the upcoming competition was also spurring the momentum.

Recipes were all of a sudden not so generously shared as much thought and creativity was being given to what and how would make the best entry in the various baking contests, BBQ sauce contest and many others. There was even a contest to determine the best 'traditional' meal.

Prize ribbons for each event were being designed and sewn by several of the older children. All the grounds, yards, and homes were being groomed for showcasing their Village to the other two Villages and those coming from the surrounding towns.

Most of this activity was taking place in the evenings after their regular work was completed for the day. The energy level was amazing. It wasn't uncommon for people to put in a ten hour workday. During the summer months the sky would still have some brightness at ten o'clock at night, so work on other projects and activities in preparation for the upcoming event of the year, could take place in the evening.

It was all Sandy and Amber could do to keep up with supervising the day-to-day activities. This included providing orientation to a steady arrival of new residents, then seeing to it that they were being properly taken care of and introduced into the community. Ben and Robert were also inundated with overseeing the unbelievable progress of the housing construction. It was hard to find the time and energy in the evenings to finish off their report back to the transition team working on Mid America. Several truckloads of building materials moved into the Village daily. Managing inventory was, in itself, a tremendous challenge.

However, for all the stress and strain of their new lives, the O'Neils were constantly pumped up. They served as outstanding examples of the real meaning of motivation and living your life to the fullest.

CHAPTER SIXTY-SEVEN

"You know Ben," Robert said as they labored over all the document information that the transition team had sent them, "when I take time to reflect on all of this, I really have a lot of mixed emotions. On one hand, I feel a certain betrayal to what we have always known as the United States, but on the other hand I realize like so many things, there comes a time when circumstances dictate that you have to abandon the old and move forward and develop the new."

I have the same feelings from time to time," Ben said. "But what we are doing in this whole process of forming a new country and a new beginning feels so right. It's so-over-the-top that I swear my adrenalin is constantly registering near maximum. You would have to say, brother, that this movement and all that it entails is definitely working. "

The discussion shifted to a section outlining education goals in Mid America. Robert said, "I love the ideas that the team has put forth. They have boldly stepped forth with very innovative ideas which I feel should be implemented. The titles for the key items are descriptive. The Continued Pursuit in Home Schooling, Public High Schools Now to Be Just

A Mark of the Divine

Two Years, then they go to Two Years of Prep School Before Formal Higher Education. The latter is like having a middle school in between high school and college or tech school. What a great idea."

Ben Said, "In keeping with a preceding document where labor unions will be discontinued and no longer will be a part of the scene in Mid America, the teachers unions will be dismantled. The transition team is advocating a huge increase in technical schools. They have also very positively revamped the financing of education both from a government and individual standpoint."

"These changes will be critical for Mid America over the next decades. Energy is going to be the next big industry and will be like nothing we have seen in the past. Mid America will emerge as the leading energy producing Country in the world in my humble opinion." "No question Ben," Robert said. "We will establish our own environmental agency. That agency will have very little resemblance to the politically motivated and managed monster we have been saddled with for several decades. If there was a way to weigh the good accomplished by EPA against the negative aspects of this agency, I have a hunch that the scales would tip drastically to the side of negative."

"As technology pushes forward, just think of what we have in the form of recoverable and undeveloped oil resources now and in the future: ANWR (Arctic National Wildlife Reserve) in Alaska; readily accessible, and with extraction causing very minimal environmental impact. Then there is the Bakken Formation, which is right in our backyard with 3 to 4 Billion barrels of oil, this is in eastern Montana, western ND and southern Saskatchewan. In addition to that, it is estimated that there is enough oil under Colorado to last us for two hundred years.

With all of these vast resources lying undeveloped plus so many other areas in Louisiana and Texas and several other States, we will establish ourselves as the leading oil producer in the world. Another huge energy resource is natural gas. Investments in production of natural gas have not increased to any degree for over a half century. This has to match our investments in oil production. Then we will kiss good-by to our dependence on other countries when it comes to energy."

"Addressing all of this now and working feverishly for an immediate turnaround of our energy dependence is a must," Ben said. "I don't think that there is any question at all," Robert said, "that our Mid America will be a huge part in the Americas gaining back our own dominance and then have the ability to greatly assist many other nations, all of which we have lost over the last decade. We will emerge once again as the leader: an example of what a great Nation should look like."

"There is one more very important factor that will be critical to this particular subject of oil production. Although we don't know what the dollar figure will be yet, our share of the current national debt, which as we know has been blown totally out of proportion, is going to start Mid America with a pretty big deficit. We need to pay that off as quickly as is possible," Robert said. "Very good point," Ben said, "but with the right operative mode in place for the Nation, we'll definitely succeed.

"Let's look at one more section and then we better see how everything is going with the last-minute preparations for the big fourth of July celebration tomorrow," Ben said. "Agreed," said Robert.

They picked up the packet titled Moral Contemplation and Discussion. "I briefly glanced through this yesterday," Robert said, "and I think the idea is brilliant. Basically what they are saying is that there must be recognition of the inherent responsibilities we all have when putting forth any kind of document, statements of importance, and guidelines of all sorts in just about any category you can imagine. This ranges, for example, from curriculum and presentation in our schools to corporate actions and all actions by public servants from the Federal level all the way down to the city councils." "This certainly underscores those four powerful words which will be an underlying theme in governance, management, teaching and so forth, in Mid America, that being of course 'In God We Trust'," Ben said.

"It is hard to imagine the fantastic impact this would have on all of society if this is taken to heart and actually adhered to," Robert said. "We need to put that into the report we send back," Ben said. "The transition team has done a magnificent job in what they have developed to date."

CHAPTER SIXTY-EIGHT

After weeks of preparation, the day of the big event, July 4th, had finally arrived. It was only six in the morning, but already activity was at a fever pitch. Hundreds of booths lining the street and recreation areas were being stocked with all kinds of goods, most of which were hand-made or homegrown. Members of the guest Villages and surrounding towns were also starting to drift in and were setting up their booths, displaying an outstanding array of goods.

"Its ironic and sad," Sandy said, "here we are celebrating America's Independence Day, a day set aside to remember the signing of the Declaration of Independence on July 4th, 1776. It has taken us just a little over two hundred years to severely shake the very foundation that this celebration is based on. I have a hard time controlling myself when I start thinking too much about how a few people in our Nation's Capitol have practically destroyed nearly everything that America has stood for."

"I remember teaching this to children and talking to them about how important real freedom is. The Declaration of Independence was scheduled to become official, by actions of the

Second Continental Congress, on the 2nd day of July in 1776. But it was delayed by two days and approved on July 4th.

On July 1st, 1776, John Adams wrote a letter to his wife saying, 'The second day of July, 1776, will be the most memorable epoch in the history of America. I am apt to believe that it will be celebrated by succeeding generations as the great anniversary festival. It ought to be commemorated as the day of deliverance, by solemn acts of devotion to God Almighty. It ought to be solemnized: with pomp and parade, with shows, games, sports, guns, bells, bonfires, and illuminations, from one end of this continent to the other, from this time forward, forevermore.'"

Sandy continued, "What would John Adams and the rest of that gang think, if they knew what a pickle we let ourselves get into. In spite of the fact that so much has been taken from us by our own government, we must never lose hope or give up. We simply cannot let the lives of so many thousands of young men and women who have fought and died for our freedom go unchallenged and ultimately have been for nothing."

"So it is fitting that wonderful celebration is bringing thousands of people together here in the Plains. It is a celebration of the fierce determination of many brave people who have stood tall in the face of adversity and fought for freedom and independence," Sandy said. "Wow, Sandy," Robert said. "That was a dissertation that should be repeated this afternoon from a platform in front of all the people gathered here." Sandy smiled and said, "I guess I did get a little carried away didn't I?" "You were right on the mark," Amber said "and you know, this is going to be a fantastic day and the best 4th July celebration ever."

CHAPTER SIXTY-NINE

"Come on Amber," Sandy said, "the guys are busy doing a bunch of stuff and children are who knows where, let's you and I take a stroll down through the area and sample some of those fantastic foods from the booths."

"I am just flabbergasted," Sandy said. "Look at what these people have done with so little to work with. It's amazing!" It was like attending a state fair. There were hundred's of little booths set up with everything: wild game barbeque, jams and jellies, breads of all sorts, homemade candy and what seemed like a million different kinds of cakes, pies, cupcakes, doughnuts, and the list went on endlessly. "I think there will be a few tummy aches by nightfall," Amber said. Sandy laughed and said, "I think you are absolutely right."

As they made their way through the crowds, constantly being greeted, they stopped to listen to a small band that was playing everything from bluegrass to folk songs to polka's. They had just swung into a toe-tapping polka when Ben and Robert showed up, grabbed them and swung them out onto the grass area that was serving as a dance floor.

Laughing and hooting like little kids they got right into the swing of things. The rest of the dancers cleared the space and formed a ring around the four. Ben and Amber and Robert and Sandy put on quite a show and what with all the clapping and hollering by everybody you'd have thought this was the main event for the day.

"Come on," Ben said, let's work our way over to the amphitheater and see what is happening over there." "Great," Sandy said, "it won't be that much longer before our kids will be making their grand entry." "Oh look," Amber said. "There are Jan and Mark. I am sure they will want to join us as Josh is also going to be riding in the final event." As the six of them continued to make their way towards the amphitheater they kept running into friends. Erika came up and grabbed Amber and gave her a big hug. "It's so good to see you guys," she said. "Come on and join us," Sandy said. "Okay, but first I want to introduce you to someone who recently moved here that you may have not had a chance to meet. Luc McCannon and his daughter Beth, I'd like you to meet the O'Neil's."

After all the greetings took place Robert said, "Luc, why does your name seem so familiar?" Luc chuckled and said, "You probably remember seeing my name associated with The Line in the Sand, or as you have dubbed it, A Mark of The Devine. I was the pilot that discovered the trench." "Of course," Ben said. "Now it fits into place."

Luc went on to explain that after his wife had died from lung cancer, he had taken early retirement from the Air Force so that he could properly take care of his little girl. "I had been at a meeting that you held in Las Vegas and was really impressed with what you guys were doing. I had bought a few shares in the Corporation.

Little did I know at the time how profound an action I had taken. After my wife had passed on, Beth and I struggled trying to find the right kind of environment for her to grow up in."

Erika said, "I was at a book signing and the very last person to get a book signed by me was this really good looking guy." Ericka gave Luc a poke in the ribs and said "I guess you could say there was instant chemistry." "We went out and had coffee after Erika was done and got all her things put together. I guess we must have talked for three hours straight," Luc said. "Erika told me all about her life and about what she calls the 'miracle on the O'Neil Ranch'. The next day Beth and I made the decision that if we could get into the O'Neil Ranch, that's where we were going. We have been here for about two months now and we want to thank you for what you have done for so many and especially for what you have done for us and for Erika and her daughter."

"Ben, Amber, Robert and Sandy," Erika said, "We want you to be the first to know, Luc and I are going to get married!" There was so much hugging, dancing and shouting going on that they started to draw attention from a bunch of other people in the vicinity."

Why don't you guys all come with us? We're heading over to the amphitheater to watch the goings-on over there," Robert said. "We'd love to," Ericka said. "Wouldn't we Luc?" As Ericka said that her eyes twinkled with love.

CHAPTER SEVENTY

Several thousand people were gathered on the tiered slopes of the amphitheater: picnicking, laughing, chatting and watching all the activities taking place below them on the floor of the arena. Right at the time that the O'Neils and their group found a spot and started to watch, there were several dance troupes taking turns performing special and traditional dances. The crowd loved the performances. Sandy glanced at her watch and said, "Can you believe that the day is already starting to come to an end? It won't be long before the finale starts. There is to be a parade, probably like none that has ever been seen before." They all laughed and continued to enjoy the dancing that was taking place.

The sun was just setting when there appeared to be something close to chaos at the one end of the arena. Big Joe was in charge of the parade and was desperately trying to get everybody into some kind of marching order. All those in the parade would enter from the one end, march or ride all the way around the edge and back to where they started. Finally with a loud crash of cymbals, the first band entered the arena. In spite or their ragtag appearance and a little clowning to go with it, they actually made some pretty good music and every once in awhile, they would all be in step.

They were followed by an assortment of riders on horseback, bicycles, tricycles, and a couple of old cars all decorated with ribbons, banners, streamers and balloons. The Hutterits had a little band that stepped out smartly as did the Jewish contingent. As the first band exited back out where they had entered, new entries to the parade were stillmaking their appearance. The clapping and yelling that continued for all the entries was absolutely wonderful, and it highly encouraged those in the parade. After almost two hours the last unit of the parade exited the arena. It suddenly became very quiet and people wondered if that was the end of the event. The sun had set, but the sky was still fairly bright. It was an absolutely beautiful evening.

Suddenly from the far end of the arena, a drum roll was heard. Then an unisonous 'ah' was heard from the entire crowd as five young riders burst into the arena. They were riding at full gallop, standing barefoot on the backs of five perfectly matched horses. It was a sight to behold and the crowd showed their appreciation with enthusiastic applause and cheering.

Amber grabbed Sandy's hand in a nervous gesture and fought back tears as her emotions were overwhelming her. "That's our kids!" Amber said. Now the O'Neil's knew why they had been barred from rehearsals for over that last two months. Jan and Mark were sitting right next to them and were hardly able to catch their breath. They watched in awe as Jimmy, Maggie, Suzanne, Josh and Cindy flew around the arena.

The kids had their arms straight out and locked with each other as they circled the arena to a loud applause and lots of yelling and screaming from the crowd. They galloped all the way around, then came to the center of the arena and stopped, facing one side of the audience. After the horses had stopped, a small command, almost like a loud whisper, could be heard and all five horses went down on one knee, as if they were genuflecting. The crowd went nuts, and the smiles on the faces of the riders were from ear to ear. They then pulled the horses to a complete stand again and whirled them around one hundred eighty degrees to face the audience on the other side of the arena. They repeated the same prayer-like performance.

Needless to say, this was a fitting climax for a most unforgettable day. Everybody was sure to remember those kneeling horses for years to come. Big Joe could be seen beaming as the kids wheeled the horses around and made their exit to the wonderful applause and cheering of several thousand people gathered on the plains of North Dakota. The day was a fantastic tribute to the ingenuity and the spirit of everybody there, plus demonstrating the obvious love for their fellow human beings. It was a real celebration of life in America.

Within two hours most of the people had disbursed, the booths were dismantled, the grounds cleaned up and the visitors had all gone home. "Could this day have gone any better than it did?" Sandy asked, as they all sat around trying to relax from a wonderful but stressful day. "All the people I talked to, from many of our Village residents to our guests, they were all thrilled with what took place today," Amber said. That seemed to be consensus from everybody else. "I think you were right Amber," Ben said, "this was the best 4th of July ever."

EPISODE FIVE

CHAPTER SEVENTY-ONE
THE BIRTH OF MID AMERICA

Latter Part of 2015

The air in the Oval Office of the White House could only be described as electric, filled with tension. It was day three of discussions, negotiations, and threats. Voices were often a couple of octaves higher than they should have been. The development and transition teams of the soon-to- be official Mid America, and the President of the United States of America and his teams were getting close to wrapping up all the details.

The Mid America teams knew that when they left, the current Administration would prefer not to be cordial to the new 'upstart' Country. Yet the U.S. Administration had little choice but to be amiable, realizing the necessity to work together. The official date for the birth of Mid America was set for November 26th, Thanksgiving Day.

This would add a whole new dimension to the United States' observance of Thanksgiving. The fourth Thursday of November would be celebrated as both Thanksgiving and

A Mark of the Divine

Independence Day for Mid America. Because of the tremendous significance of this anniversary, it would be designated as a four-day weekend holiday.

It was interesting to note that a part of Mid America's Constitution declared Sunday as a day of rest and stated that no activities related to commerce would take place on Sundays. Emergency personnel would be required to be on duty, but they would need to alternate that duty on an every-other-Sunday basis. Family activities were strongly encouraged.

The Western Seaboard and most of the adjoining States had also followed Mid America's lead and would now become West America, so the United States of America was now going to become three separate Countries. Yet the three remained joined by common interests such as a multinational military that would defend them. Also it was agreed that the three Countries would allow free trade between them. It was determined and agreed upon that Mid America's Capitol would be established northwest of Kansas City, Kansas.

Ben felt that it would have been nice and convenient if they could have a common currency between the three America's. However, that wasn't going to work. The citizens of Mid America had to tackle this issue real soon and develop their Country's own currency.

The new Nation's Capitol would be very adequate but quite austere in comparison to Washington, D.C. This diminutive stature was intentional. It was symbolic and a constant reminder that the Federal Government of Mid America would remain small, and that the real power of this new Country would be vested in its people. Its architecture would nicely portray the commitment to a balanced budget and the maintaining of low taxes on the people of this new

Nation. Government was to be seen as the servant of the people, not the other way around.

As the three Nations continued to hammer out details, agreements and border issues, several concepts were developed and eventually agreed upon. Citizenship issues were debated and decided. Mid America, although not officially a independent Country for two more weeks, immediately started to organize their own National Guard. It was planned that the Guard would seal off the border between the United States and Mexico in the Border States that made up Mid America.

This would be the start of a legitimate pathway for any foreign person who wanted to be become a citizen of Mid America. This pathway to citizenship was immediately laid out and published. Regardless of nationality, the rules to becoming a citizen in Mid America would be followed and strictly enforced. However, East America, as many were calling the remaining states that represented the old United States, had some real issues to overcome. However, the current Administration refused to change the name and said they would remain the United States of America.

West America had determined that their Country's Capitol would be located in Redding, California. This allowed for separation from the State Capitol in Sacramento, yet be geographically centered.

The process continued night and day for the birthing of these new Nations. There were definitely some real 'labor pains'. As the magic date rapidly approached, for the transition teams, sleep became a luxury for the transition teams.

On November 26th, dawn broke over the Country that for over two hundred years was the United States of America, recently consisting of fifty states. Now this massive land mass was going to be divided into three separate and distinct Nations. After much agony, negotiations, polling, and certainly prayer and also lots of indecision, two more states joined the Mid America conglomerate. So the fifty States were divided into the three Countries: The United States of America (East America), consisted of twenty-four states: Maine, New Hampshire, Vermont, Massachusetts, New York, Connecticut, Rhode Island, Pennsylvania, New Jersey, Delaware, Maryland, Virginia, West Virginia, North Carolina, South Carolina, Georgia, Florida, Michigan, Ohio, Indiana, Kentucky, Tennessee, Mississippi, and Alabama.

Mid America consisted of nineteen States: Wisconsin, Minnesota, Illinois, Iowa, Missouri, Arkansas, Louisiana, North Dakota, South Dakota, Nebraska, Kansas, Oklahoma, Texas, Montana, Wyoming, Colorado, New Mexico, Arizona and Alaska.

West America consisted of seven States: California, Oregon, Washington, Idaho, Utah, Nevada, and Hawaii.

What was happening was almost impossible for most people to completely comprehend. However, people did realize why this was happening. There were several causes. As politics had replaced common sense, Christianity was being forced into the background. The state of joblessness and poverty continued to rise. There seemed to be no end to the reckless and ceaseless spending on the part of the Federal Government and also some of the State Governments. All of this added up to the extreme weakening of a once powerful and great Nation.

So it was that Independence Day for Mid America finally arrived on November 26th, 2015. It was certainly one of the most momentous days in the annals of history. On this day the sun seemed brighter and the sky much clearer than normal for a big percentage of the people of Mid America: in every household there was so much excitement that a new energy seemed to radiate from all across Mid America. West America had followed suit and was also declaring independence as a separate nation on this very memorable day in history.

West America and Mid America had agreed to hold their Countries' first elections on January 31, 2016. This didn't give a whole lot of time for candidates and the people to get acquainted with each other, but transition teams could not be expected to run the Countries for more than a couple of months. It was also agreed that the three Presidents would hold a summit conference on February 28th, after they had been sworn in. The primary goal of this conference was to give notice that the three American Nations were as strong or stronger from a military standpoint as they had been when united. But obviously there were certainly a myriad of other details to work out by the three Presidents.

CHAPTER SEVENTY-TWO

"Robert, I got call from Richard on the transition team, they want us to throw our hats into the ring for President and VP," Ben said. "No way Ben, you know how I hate politics." "There is something I have been thinking about for some time, which I'd like to bounce off you. I need your honest take on the idea," Ben said. "Alright brother, but if you think you're going to talk me into this by coming in through some kind of back door, forget it." "I understand Robert, but that doesn't mean you couldn't be my right-hand man!"

"The Democratic and Republican Parties were founded in the 1800's and I frankly think they have outlived their usefulness. In fact, I fear that there are so many who vote for one Party or another, not because they really believe in that Party or the individuals or even know much about what they are voting for. Rather they are casting their vote because a parent, a relative, or a friend said this is the way I voted. Do you think these people can really define either Party?

Also I think many people are really fed up and tired of the rhetoric the politicians spew in both Parties, and especially the 'professional' politicians. Most people have come to realize that far too many politicians have as their main concern not the people they represent, but what they can say that will help them in getting the votes to be re-elected.

We have the opportunity to make the needed changes right now as we form a new Country. What a shame it would be if we messed up this fresh start."

"What I am thinking is that anybody who is running for public office needs to stand on his or her own two feet. He or she shouldn't need to be defined by a Party Affiliation. The voter's decision should be about the individual: who she or he is as a person and the actions that have defined him or her. We know that old saying, 'talk is cheap'. We have had plenty of that from the politicians in both Parties as they have demonstrated time and time again the extent of their real commitment to their words. Everybody needs to pay less attention to what is being said, and to be more aware of the actions taken."

"Alright Ben," Robert said, I am following you on all that, but are you saying we would not have any political Parties anymore? No Democratic Party or Republican Party?" "Robert, can you honestly say that having these two Parties is a good thing for America today?" Robert thought about that before answering. "To be honest I have never given anything like this any thought, but now that I do think about it, you are right, they both became crippled some time ago in terms of 'looking out for the American people'."

"What I am proposing is that there be no more political parties, no more big union money or corporate money being invested in political parties per se. Anyone who serves in a public office must be judged, again not by what he or she says, but by what actions have been taken. We have to educate the populace on the meaning of Liberal and Conservative. A rating system becomes a part of all communications when it comes to defining where any particular person is with his or her thinking and direction. Let me give you an example of how this might work. We would develop and agree upon a definition of a 'Conservative'. The core principles would consist of: limited government, the realization that 'we the people' must take personal responsibility for our destination, and as George Washington said in his Farewell Address that.... '**Religion and morality are indispensable supports**'." We would incorporate what former President Ronald Reagan said which was: "**The basis of conservatism is a desire for less government interference, a desire for less centralized authority and more individual freedom, the kind of freedom that is necessary for people to pursue their own goals and the empowerment to solve their problems.**"

"Liberals would be defined as: those with the core belief that governmental action is needed to achieve equal opportunity and equality for all, and that it is incumbent upon government to alleviate social ills and to protect civil liberties and individual and human rights. They believe the role of the government should be to guarantee no one is in need, regardless of their behavior and willingness to accept personal responsibility for themselves. They also believe government is far more capable of solving everybody's problems, than are the individuals themselves."

"With both of these definitions we would put forth comparisons for people to gauge where a particular individual falls in his or her particular beliefs on different issues, such as abortion, marriage, public display of God and prayer, education and the list goes on and on."

"We could have a grading scale of zero to ten. Zero being an ultra-Liberal, ten being an ultra-Conservative and five being a moderate. Depending on the issue, a person might be a seven on one issue and four on another. In this case the person might be judged to be a moderate on average. No parties to hide behind, just each individual's actions standing on their own."

"Robert, this is a pretty skimpy outline of what I am thinking but at least you get the idea." "I am really impressed with your thought process brother; it's bold and very innovative"

Robert said, "So now going back to what we were talking about, if you want to throw your hat in the ring, I am all for it. I'll help in any way that I can, but I am not going to run for Vice President or any other office." "Okay, I hear you and understand. I have talked it over with Amber, and she is okay with my making this move. So I'll let the team know tomorrow that I am in." "This is going to be one heck of a ride brother!" Robert said.

CHAPTER SEVENTY-THREE

The decision was made and the plan of action immediately developed and implemented. The Eric Smith Radio and TV Talk Show was now carried on over five hundred radio stations and the National Cable Network with powerful, state-of- the-art broadcast facilities located right at the Ranch. His show would become an integral part of communications with Mid Americans.

Amber had been hesitant about Ben running for the Presidency but was finally persuaded and came to realize Ben would be the logical choice for our new Country's first President. She had real mixed emotions as she knew that on one hand he would make a fabulous first President for the new Country. But she also knew that he would be exposed to more danger and that bothered her. *I guess I just have to suck it up and pray that nothing bad happens to him. I think he has had some Divine guidance and protection so far in this amazing project, so there certainly is no reason to believe that won't continue.*

"Sandy," Ben said through the phone line, "did Robert leave the ranch on time this morning?" Her heart jumped into her throat as she said, "Yes he did Ben. He left early this morning for Dickinson, where he was going to pick up the plane and fly into Kansas City to meet with you as you both had planned." They were in the final planning stages of their campaign and if Ben won, they would have the early plan of attack from which Ben would launch his presidency. *Robert should have been there hours ago* Ben thought to himself. "Okay, stay calm Sandy, I am going to do some calling, and I'll be back to you in just a few minutes."

Ben immediately called Flight Service in Dickinson. "Hi Jerry, this is Ben O'Neil. Can you look up when my brother left Dickinson this morning? He would have filed a flight plan for Kansas City." "Ben, I have been on duty since six this morning. Robert has not checked in. Let me call over to the hanger just to be sure your plane is still there. Hang on." Jerry was back on line with Ben within a matter of minutes and told Ben that the plane was in the hanger.

Ben called back to the Ranch and talked to Luc, who had become the Village's Security Officer. "Luc, I have a real bad feeling that something has happened to Robert." Ben relayed the information that Robert was supposed to have met him in Kansas City, late this afternoon and never showed up, in fact never showed up at the airport in Dickinson. "I need you to round up Big Joe, Mark and a couple of other guys and start a search of the immediate area. He was driving the navy blue Ford F150 and I am going to call sheriff Buck and bring him into the picture. Give me a report about every hour as to what is happening."

Ben called Sandy back and relayed the information he had. "I have a bad feeling about this Sandy, but there also might be some kind of logical explanation." "Thanks for trying to make me feel good Ben, but you know as well as I do that Robert would have called if he had vehicle problems or whatever." It hadn't taken long for word to spread across the Village that Robert was missing and something had a foul smell to it.

CHAPTER SEVENTY-FOUR

No clues had been turned up by the Sheriff's Department; Luc and his security crew had come up empty-handed so far. Robert's truck had been found five miles from the ranch, but there wasn't anything that indicated foul play or evidence of any kind, in or around the truck. It had been three days since Robert went missing, and everybody was sitting on pins and needles.

On the fourth day, a typewritten letter arrived. It was postmarked from Denver, Colorado, and addressed to Ben. "We have Robert O'Neil in our capture. Our message and demands are simple. You have five days to withdraw your bid for the Presidency of Mid America. If we do not hear on the news that you have withdrawn from the race by this deadline, you will start to receive your brother's body parts on a daily basis. When he is finally dead, we will send the remains. If, on the other hand, we read that you have withdrawn from the race and publicly stated that you will not run again, your brother will be released and returned to his family."

Soldiers of Allah

A Mark of the Divine

Ben sat dazed with his emotions running the gamut from terror to rage. Within just a couple of hours, every law enforcement agency and anti-terrorist agency throughout several states, were made aware of the lettert Ben had received. "Ben," Director Miller said, "we firmly believe that your brother has been captured by a Muslim Terrorists' Nest located somewhere in Mid America. We believe their motivation is to try and level the playing field in Mid America, since the big percentage of the population is made up of Conservative Christians. We do not believe this is idle talk on their part, and we are quite sure they will carry out their threat.

Every available law enforcement person in Mid America has been assigned to this case, and we will do everything in our power to find your brother." "I have one question," Ben said, "based on your expertise and knowledge of these cowards, how likely is it that if I don't withdraw from the Presidential race and they kill my brother, that they will continue to try and bring me down by trying to take other family members?" "I think that you can expect this to be on-going, as they are committed to carry out their missions with little regard for human life."

CHAPTER SEVENTY-FIVE

That evening, Ben called two meetings at the ranch. The first was with the family. He really didn't want to involve the children, but he felt there was no alternative. After Ben explained to Sandy, Amber and the children everything that had happened up to that time, the discussion ranged from panic to rage. Finally Ben said, "As soon as we are done with our discussion, I am having a meeting with several of the men Luc has gathered. They are waiting for me at the Community Center. The meeting will have two main thrusts. One will be a massive hunt for Robert. We will cover several square miles in this area. The other issue we will discuss is security here at the Village. We will review the security measures in place and ensure they are sufficient, so that you and all the others do not have to worry."

Sandy said, "Let's all join hands and say a special prayer together for Robert. We pray he will be alright and that all of us will be kept from harm." With heads bowed, the O'Neil family threw their entire concentration into prayer.

Ben hustled over to the Community Center. Waiting there were one hundred twenty men and women that Luc had recruited. "Thank you for such a great response to an urgent call," Ben said. Ben went on to explain the situation so that they all had as much information as he did.

"Here is the plan," Ben said, "I may be going out on a limb a bit with this, but if my thinking proves to be wrong, well at least we'll know that we have done our best. Our time won't be wasted. There is a large number of personnel sweeping through many other areas. Most everybody involved agrees that the odds are likely this act of terrorism is coming from a radical Islamic nest somewhere in Mid America. Even though the note I received was postmarked Denver, Colorado, I have a gut feeling that was a ruse. I think the nest is somewhere in western North Dakota, northwestern South Dakota or western Montana."

"Based on that assumption, I have laid out the following: Eric, you and your one hundred captains that are present, will each be assigned a sector of this vast area. Each captain will recruit fifty men and women who will be assigned a sector within that captains' assigned area."

"Now this is very important, people. This is a search mission but not a rescue mission at this point. When I get done here, Luc is going to take you through a quick course in reconnaissance and then you captains need to do the same with your fifty persons. You will not be conspicuous as you move about the countryside since each of you will be alone and covering a fair amount of geography. The cover which you will use will be that you are calling on farm owners throughout the area representing a buyer who is interested in purchasing several farms in their area. You may explain that you are just in the initial stage of discovery so you won't have to get into a lot of detail. Be extremely observant because the folks on any particular farm you visit might even be held hostage and the terrorists could be listening to what you are saying. If you have any suspicions at all, after you leave, immediately call into our control center and talk to me or Luc."

"We are also soliciting help from someone most of you know, and that is Eric Smith.

He is going to be continually broadcasting the story of Robert's kidnapping over radio and TV. He will also be asking rural people throughout Mid America to call in with any suspicious activity they have noticed, including rural neighbors who seem to have disappeared or have been absent from their farmstead for a period of time.

Anything received that comes from this area will be immediately forwarded to a command center right here in the Community Center. This is where many of you ladies will come in. We are going to need you to handle the phone banks we are setting up. You will be recording incoming information and immediately transferring that information to the appropriate sector captain."

"There are just a couple more final comments. One, these people who have captured Robert are extremely dangerous and ruthless. You are not to engage them in any way. We just need to determine if there is reasonable justification to send in a trained squad. So it's observe and report, okay?" There was a strong response from all the men, "OKAY!" The second thing I know probably doesn't need to be said because you all are aware of the message we received, but I just need to reiterate, that we all have to function like a very well-oiled machine, because time is not on our side. Thanks to all of you and Godspeed, now let's go find Robert."

A Mark of the Divine

By the next day as the broadcasts about the horrendous act committed against the O'Neill family spread throughout the Nation, outrage was being voiced from the Canadian border to the Mexican border. Never had there been such a massive search conducted by all law enforcement agencies. Within the first 24 hours, ten Islamic training nests had been discovered and dismantled with over two hundred people arrested and on their way to prison. But unfortunately, there was no sign of Robert. Those who had been captured either had no information or weren't about to give any up.

Meanwhile, the phone calls coming into the command center at the Village were steadily being relayed to the teams out in the area. Ben and Luc had set up cots in the Community Center so that they could grab a few minutes of sleep from time to time. "I hope we're not on a wild goose chase," Ben said to Luc. "From everything I have heard and know about you Ben, your gut instincts and intuitions have always served you very well."

CHAPTER SEVENTY-SIX

Robert couldn't believe his luck. His captors had thrown him into an old box stall within what appeared to be a real old barn. They had chained the door shut, so there appeared to be no way out. But he was totally surprised that they hadn't frisked him. His retractable hunting knife that slid into a pocket behind his belt had not been found. Now as he surveyed the situation he thought *my best bet at a chance to escape will be to work on the wood that surrounds the rebar which is a part of the door. It had originally provided a window for both the owner and the horses: the owner could look in and check the horses and the horses looked out from the stalls; they (the horses) liked to check out what was going on also. The wood appears to have begun to rot, so hopefully the rebar isn't buried too deep into the wood. If it isn't, I might be able to chip a couple of those rebar out.* That *would give me enough space to squeeze myself through the opening and out of the box stall.*

Since his capture two days ago, he had seen no one. No one bothered to come and check on him nor did anyone bring him any water or food. Through a small window high on the wall, Robert could tell it was starting to get dark outside. He had managed to extract one of the rods from the door and thought *it shouldn't take much more chipping and the second rod should come free.* He was drenched in sweat and totally dehydrated as he labored to extract that second rod. Finally it came free. Listening to see if he could detect any sound, then getting a firm grip on the two outside bars, he carefully pulled himself up to the opening, worked himself through, and dropped to the floor outside the stall. He stood motionless for several seconds, trying to determine if anybody was on guard in the building. But the only thing he could hear was his own heart beating at a pretty rapid pace. Silently he made his way to a rear walk-in door, eased it open and stepped outside. Slowly he made his way to the corner of the barn and tried to get a feel for his surroundings. He had been blindfolded right after they had kidnapped him. But he estimated they hadn't traveled more than perhaps sixty miles. He guessed that it had only taken them about an hour to reach what appeared to be an old and abandoned farmstead. There was just enough moonlight making its way through a thin layer of clouds so Robert could make out the various old buildings, including an old house where lights were coming through the windows.

Robert knew that he couldn't dillydally. Someone could come out to go check on him at any time. He spotted a water pump about twenty feet away and wondered if his luck was still holding, and he could get some water out of it. He knew when he pumped the handle it would be noisy, but fortunately there was a wind blowing away from the house toward him, so that would help cover some of the noise. He spotted and old tin cup hanging by the pump, so he ran in a crouch to the pump and started to work the handle. Luck was still with him as after about four strokes he felt the pump prime itself and then yield some water. Apparently his captors were also using this pump.

After hydrating himself, Robert decided he had to put as much distance between himself and this farmstead as he possibly could before light, even if he was heading in the wrong direction. He moved out and got to the gravel road and decided that as long as he didn't see any lights from any direction he'd stay on the road so he could make better time. *thank the good Lord, that I have been running every day and keeping myself in reasonably good shape,* Robert thought to himself as he started a steady jog down the road. There was just enough light so that he could see any holes or obstacles that might appear on the road.

As dawn started to break, Robert felt that he must have covered somewhere around twenty-five miles. He found a spot where the trees were growing real close to the road and decided he needed to rest and try and figure out what to do now that it was getting light out. He hoped that his captors still hadn't bothered to check up on him.

He was just dozing off when he heard a vehicle approaching in the distance. It was coming from the opposite direction from the old farm where he had been held captive, so at least that was a plus. He had to formulate a plan. Did *he dare expose himself to the driver of that vehicle? What if the vehicle operator was a part of the group that had kidnapped him?* The vehicle was drawing closer. *I have to decide and do it real fast.* He immediately formulated a plan. *I'll stay hidden from the driver's sight. I am at a vantage point where I can hopefully determine what the driver looks like and if he or she looks okay, still have time to jump out from the trees to get attention.*

A Mark of the Divine

His heart was doing double time as the vehicle closed the gap. Robert could see it was a white half-ton truck and thankfully the driver wasn't going at an excessive speed so that he had more time to look and then decide. As the truck approached, Robert could make out that the driver had a baseball cap on and then seconds later he determined the driver was white. On instinct, he jumped from his hiding place and waved the truck down. As the truck skidded to a stop, the driver immediately opened the door and jumped out and yelling "Robert!" The driver was one of Luc's team captains. After they gave each other a big hug, they jumped into the truck, made a U-turn and headed back the other direction.

CHAPTER SEVENTY-SEVEN

A shout went up from one of the girls answering the phones. "We have Robert, and he is safe!" she yelled. Ben and Luc were catching some shut-eye but heard the announcement and bounded off the cots as the whole place went wild. There was dancing, and shouting and crying and hugging as the word quickly spread throughout the Village. Ben was immediately on the phone with Robert. After determining for himself that Robert was okay, he talked to his rescuer, got his location and the estimated location of the nest.

Within one hour, three helicopters with cargos of Special Forces troops converged on the abandoned farm house. The Special Forces immediately sealed off the entire area. The fight was soon over. Seven Muslims were arrested and cuffed. They wouldn't be seeing daylight for a long, long time.

About the same time as this was taking place, Robert got to the Ranch. What a reunion there was as family and Villagers surrounded Robert and even though it was only late morning, the Village band had assembled, and a celebration erupted, welcoming him home. When things finally calmed down a bit both Ben and Robert addressed the group, praising and thanking them for their excellent work.

Eric was already broadcasting the good news. As the Country learned of the rescue more celebrations erupted across Mid America. When the dust had finally settled, the Country learned that over twenty-five radical Muslim nest's had been identified and crushed in that huge sweep that took place across the land. It also was a lesson learned for this upstart Country.

One can never take freedom for granted. Somebody will be standing in line to deprive you of that freedom. Because of this incidence, very positive changes took place within all law enforcement branches and departments. Also, a new and heightened realization was developing. An awareness of what was happening around them was starting to become second nature for most citizens of Mid America. This was an absolute must as all people needed to be a part of the effort that would keep their Country safe.

CHAPTER SEVENTY-EIGHT
CHRISTMAS – 2015

The timing could have hardly been better. It was Christmas Eve, and the first snowfall was underway. No one could remember when the first snowfall had come this late. It had been a blessing for Robert, allowing him to escape without being hampered by heavy snow underfoot. It also allowed the Villages in the North Country an extended time for construction.

The birth of their new Country had happened, and Ben had officially kicked off his bid to become the first President of Mid America. Robert was managing Ben and Erika's campaign. Yes, Erika had been persuaded to join Ben as his running mate. Erika's speaking skills had become very polished as she moved across the country talking about her book. She also had become very savvy about the intentions of the Constitution and Bill of Rights. She coupled that knowledge with a deep-seated understanding and passion for championing right from wrong, and good versus evil.

A Mark of the Divine

The Village at the O'Neil ranch continued to be extremely busy as were all the villages scattered throughout the Plains and adjoining areas. Things were changing and evolving as so many people who had been destitute when they first moved in were now self-sufficient. Many were moving into nearby towns so they didn't have to commute to work. This was also bringing about a big change in rural Mid America, as literally thousands of small rural towns that were rapidly moving toward extinction were now seeing a reversal. They were starting to grow again. All this was a positive sign that the economy of this new Country was heading for some very robust times.

The 'five horseman' as Maggie, Jimmy, Cindy, Suzanne and Josh were called every since their big riding show the last fourth of July, were (with the exception of Jimmy) now in their final year of high school. Like hundreds of other kids in the Village, they would be heading for college, a tech school or pursuing their degrees on the Internet next year.

Many of the residents had now installed electricity in their homes and were upgrading from where they started when they first arrived at the Village. The number of new people continuing to move into all the Villages was still very substantial, but some of the building pressure had been reduced because houses were now being sold as people moved out and new folks moved in.

Things had also progressed to the point where the developers/farmers/ranchers of A Mark of The Divine were now starting to see some return on their tremendous investment in people and the future of Mid America. A few of the developers were truly shining examples and role models for the citizens of Mid America. They agreed to serve in the early development of Mid America, take a four-year break from their operations to serve in the new legislature if Ben was elected. The governmental leadership roles would be a completely 'new look'. Leaders would model efficiency and morality. They would be responsive to the will of the people.

Sandy and Amber's roles were starting to change, as well. And if the upcoming election favored Ben and Erika, then there would be really big changes in the two O'Neil families. Amber would become the First Lady. Robert and Sandy would become an integral part of the new Government over the next four years as Robert would become the Administration's Chief Legal Counsel. Luc's life was also destined to come under some big changes. If Erika became the Country's Vice President, he and Erika would have to balance home life with a whole new life wrapped in politics. It was planned that Luc would be appointed the Nation's first Security Chief.

Mark and Jan now owned one of the largest big equipment operations in Mid America. Jan was no longer operating equipment as she had for so many years. Now she was engaged in the running of the company. They were one of many families who continued to stay in the Village, because it had so much meaning to both of them. They figured the Village at the O'Neil Ranch would be called home for the rest of their lives. They were now looking at building a house out along the border of the Bad Lands.

Big Joe continued to direct the operations of the Ranch: he over saw all the crop plantings, irrigation, harvest and cattle management, and continued to teach hundreds of young people the skills of horseback riding.

Now as approximately a hundred close friends gathered in the yards of the O'Neil's homes. Darkness was just settling in, and a light snow was falling. Robert threw a switch, lighting up a huge Spruce tree with hundreds of colorful lights. There was also a beautiful Manger and the Nativity scene. Everybody applauded enthusiastically. Then most Reverend Cassandra White, who had an angelic singing voice, led the group in one Christmas song after another. The moon appeared, putting 'the frosting on the cake' for this beautiful and wonderful Christmas Eve celebration. Then everybody moved into Robert and Sandy's ranch house where hot chocolate and lots of goodies were laid out for everybody to enjoy. They continued to engage in light conversations.

Robert had suggested to Ben that Cassandra should be appointed as the official Pastor of all the Capitol's religious functions if he should become President. Ben had readily accepted the idea. He conferred with Cassandra, and she humbly agreed to accept the appointment.

Naturally, it didn't take long before the Village knew about this possibility, so as everybody stood around that evening there were a lot of congratulations being given to Cassandra. The comments were so overwhelming to her that she needed some time to settle down. She excused herself and went out on the deck to have a little time by herself. *You operate in strange ways dear Lord,* Cassandra prayed. *Who would have thought, after I was raped and beaten by the terrorists who murdered my husband, that I would survived and be here today. It was only by your grace that it is so. I have felt my hand in your hand as you have led me and my daughter to this point in our lives. Humbly, I say thank you dear Jesus.* Cassandra remained on the deck for a few more minutes then wiped away her tears, straightened her shoulders and went back in to join the festivities.

Fortunately, the next day's weather wasn't typical for North Dakota. The wind wasn't blowing as nearly the whole Village turned out for the Christmas service that was held in the outdoor arena. People were bundled up in heavy coats, scarves and mittens, but their enthusiasm wasn't diminished a bit, nor were they anything but enthusiastic and cheerful. as they took part in this beautiful Christmas day service. A small platform had been built on the floor of the arena to serve as an alter. After the service, everybody returned to their homes for a bountiful meal and an enjoyable but relaxing day with family and friends.

CHAPTER SEVENTY-NINE
The Year of 2016

January 31st had been established as the date for the Country's first national election, with the new administration and delegates officially taking over on March 1st. This was an incredible short timetable, but it was necessary under the circumstances, according to the transition team. It was also determined that the newly elected should begin working at their new job within a week of the election. In other words, when the public hired you for a job, you need to get on it immediately.

Ben and Erika were firing on all eight cylinders as they moved their campaign into high gear. Their message was simple and straightforward. There would be as little government as was absolutely necessary. Taxes would be held as low as possible. There would be a stringent and balanced budget. Every expenditure would be examined to be sure it was necessary and within the budget. If something was possible to efficiently accomplish through the private sector, the Government would leave it alone. The burden of performance would be on private enterprise. Competition and the consumers would provide the oversight needed to hold all companies accountable, spurring entrepreneurial activity the likes of which had been absent for a long time.

This upstart Country would be a shinning example to the world. The whole population would know how to spell 'entrepreneur' and understand it's powerful meaning.

Aid to those in need would be available, but it would be a far cry from what was called welfare in the programs of the old Government. Anybody receiving aid who was of reasonably sound mind and body would be required to participate in programs designed to bring them out of the need of having to accept charity. The programs would be designed to lead people out of a welfare state, encourage them to achieve self-sufficiency and restore their dignity and self-worth. It would be an exciting and humane segment of government that would be closely monitored to avoid abuse.

Those who were professional 'takers' of government handouts were in for a big jolt and would be subjected to a whole new modus operandi. To act as a leech was certainly not in the best interest of the taxpayers nor the Country. Leeches would be treated accordingly.

Those people who were poor and in desperate need of medical attention would be provided for. These folks would be given first priority when Federal funds were distributed to those in need. We will take care of our own first, before billions of dollars would be funneled outside the Country to other people in need.

A very large percentage of people had been forced to learn some hard lessons in the difference between 'need' and 'greed'. That lesson had been learned by literally millions when they were forced out of their jobs and their homes. Now was the time, as things started to turn around, to remember those hard times and those hard-learned lessons. Repeating the mistakes that had been made in the past was not an option. We as a Country or as a people cannot let ourselves slip back into a groove that once again, in the long run, could prove disastrous. We all must learn from our mistakes.

Ben was at a meeting when the question was raised about how our new Country would handle incarceration, the death penalty, prisoner rehabilitation and release. "That is a great question, and I appreciate the way you framed it. I feel it is time to move into the Twenty-first Century with this issue. I'll give you a brief overview of my thoughts and convictions."

"First, I think that we should build a National Prison that would replace all other prisons. This mammoth prison would be located in central Wyoming and cover approximately four hundred square miles. The prison itself would be state-of-the-art and would include the best technologies available to assure orderly conduct within the prison and throughout the entire property, assuring that escape was impossible.

Prisoners would be assigned to work projects. They would be expected to work a minimum of forty-five hours per week either within the compound or on closely guarded work sites outside the compound. Any prisoner balking at working would be incarcerated in the isolation section of the prison and would stay there until his or her attitude changed."

"No prisoner would be released without approval of a psychiatric board that would be housed in a medical facility on site. Likewise there would be a psychiatric aspect to the sentencing of all prisoners. No prisoner would be released because of the fact that there wasn't enough room to house all the prisoners: that horrific act would be a thing of the past. No prisoner would be released without developing at least one saleable skill that could serve him or her well upon release. A fundamental goal of all prison programs would be a zero return of inmates."

"In addition to the work programs, all inmates would be required to engage in a specified minimum number of hours attending various classes. The classes chosen would support the development of prisoners' marketable skills. The relationship of the classes to the skill must be obvious or clearly demonstrated. There would be little free time, and there sure would be no 'work out' areas within the prison. Physical workouts would come from working, not lifting weights! This would be a prison not a social hall. In addition it would be set up so that there would be no outside contact of any kind without close supervision."

"Robots would be used in place of guards in as many environments as possible, and again the best of what technology has to offer would be used within the system. You'll be reading and hearing a lot more on this subject in the weeks to come."

"As for the death penalty, I favor it's abolishment. I feel death is a far to easy a way out for an individual who has committed the kind of horrific crime that results in the death penalty for him or her under the current system. The type of incarceration he or she would receive would fit the crime and would result in a lifetime of work with no compensation and no retirement, no social life whatsoever. "

"From a cost standpoint, the states would fund the big portion of this operation on a cost- per-prisoner basis. However, because of the tremendous number of hours of productive work that would be achieved by the inmates, there would be a huge credit against the operating costs of the Prison and Rehabilitation Center which would reflect positively in the cost to the states. These credits would reflect positively as far as the taxpayers were concerned. The net result is that the sale of products produced by the prisoners' work and the essential services provided by the prisoners would go towards the cost of operating and maintaining the prison."

"Thank you for your attendance today. We look forward to serving you in Mid America's first Federal Government. Have a wonderful rest of the day and God Bless each and every one of you."

CHAPTER EIGHTY

Several thousands of people had gathered in the stadium. When Erika was introduced and took the microphone, it took several minutes for things to calm down enough for her to speak. Erika had huge name recognition as a result of her book which continued to remain in the number one spot on the nonfiction best sellers' list. She was a tremendous inspiration to so many people.

"Today, as Ben and I wrap up our campaign, we wanted to leave you with one more tidbit to think about before you all hit the voting booths tomorrow. Ben has secured an agreement from Adam Marlinski to administer our Nation's energy policies. He is broadly recognized as the leading authority on utilization of fossil fuels. As most of you know, eighty-five percent of our current energy use comes from fossil fuels which are oil, gas and coal."

"The wonderful thing about our position as a Nation is that we are rich in fossil fuels, from Alaska to Texas and Louisiana. We will become one the world's leading producers and exporters of fossil fuel within just a matter of a few years. So much of our resources have been underutilized because of the greed and corruption of politicians, often operating under the guise of environmental preservation and correctness. That will no longer be the case, as one of the huge benefits which will accrue to us as a new Nation will be the ability to shape our own environmental needs and stewardship: not on politics, not on votes, not on rants and raves of radical minorities but on a sound scientific and moral basis. None of us can even begin to realize what a straightforward approach to preserving the environment will do for our Nation and other Nations around the world. It will be like throwing off a heavy winter coat during the mid-summer heat of Arizona. It will be like unshackling a race horse like Secretariat."

"Over the next several years, safely and in concert with nature, we will tap into those vast, unused resources. At the same time there will be the building of modern refineries and all the rest of the infrastructure needed to fulfill the energy needs of this Nation. As quickly as we can, we will bring our Nation to a status of total independence when it comes to foreign energy needs. We will no longer have to rely on people who for all practical purposes are much closer to being our enemies than our friends."

"During this same period, on another playing field, we will call on the brilliant minds of many scientists and engineers to form a new task force. This task force will lead us away from our current heavy dependence on fossil fuel energy. Their involvement in research and development of alternative forms of energy will probably never result in the total replacement of fossil fuel, but it will lead us away from the heavy dependence we have on these resources at the present time."

"You are a part of one of the most dynamic movements that any nation in history has ever made. We have all been through a lot in the past few years. We have been through things that we thought would never be possible in the former United States of America.

But we have become like stretched steel. We have become much stronger. Let the slogan of 'In God We Trust', ring constantly in your ears and may God Bless you all."

"Well," Eric Smith said as he started his wrap-up of Erika's speech. "I think we have just been given much more than a tidbit of what we might expect in the next four years if Ben and Erika are elected into office. "Truly," Eric said, "I have to say the excitement of being a part of the launch of this new Nation, actually gives me goose pimples. It is so exciting, so refreshing and so dynamic that I have a hard time trying to comprehend the possibilities of our future. Tomorrow, under the new flag of Mid America, it's citizens will go to the polls for the first time. We'll be broadcasting all the returns as they come in starting right after the first polls close. Until then, as Erika said, may God Bless you and may He also Bless our new Country."

CHAPTER EIGHTY-ONE

It was 7:00 P.M. and the polls had just closed. All the O'Neil's, Erika and Luc and several other friends were gathered in the large family room at the Ranch, glued to the TV screen. The Community Centers were also jam-packed. There were several big TV screens in both Centers, held large audiences hostage. They were breathless as they awaited the election's outcome.

Just two hours after the polls closed, Ben received a call from his opponent, conceding the election. The opponent wished Ben the very best and said that if there was anything he could do to help make Mid America a better Country, to please call on him. The shouts of joy, the hugging and crying went on for quite a spell in the O'Neil house and as the information was announced on TV, the roar that came from the Community Centers which were over a mile away could be heard from inside the O'Neil's ranch house. Ben was now the Country's first President and Erika was the Country's first Vice President. Amber was numb as it hit her that she was now the Country's First Lady.

They all made their way over to the Community Centers. When they walked in, the crowds went ballistic. After things finally settled, Ben and Erika mounted the stages and thanked the audiences for their tremendous support. Ben concluded, "Of course as you all realize, our work has just begun, so we urge you to stay tuned to what is happening and please communicate with us. We need and respect your inputs. Now, what say we do a little celebrating?!"

CHAPTER EIGHTY-TWO
THE BALANCE OF 2016

Hernandez was anxiously pacing back and forth in his spacious study, stopping every once in awhile to stare out the window at the huge pool area where scantily clad young women and girls were entertaining older and old men. Trays of drinks flowed around the patio of the pool area, and drugs followed the stream. The entertaining antics of the girls were well matched to the consumption of alcohol and drug induced highs of the men. The weather in Mexico City was hot and humid.. Hernandez appeared to be a man who led a life of ease, possessing everything that he wanted. However, no one was more ruthless and unforgiving than this king of the drug and sex trades.

Even after all this time, Hernandez was still haunted by the memory of Erika slipping away from his organization, escaping from deep in Mexico to make it to America. This still gnawed at him. It was not so much that he needed her, but that she had outwitted him and all his people. The one attempt he had made to get her back by hiring a group of

A Mark of the Divine

hoodlums to ride into the place where she was residing and bring her back, had been a miserable failure.

Now she had become the Vice President in an upstart Country that had split away from the United States. It was time to cure this sore that continued to fester inside of him. He was a man who knew few failures. "Juan," Hernandez shouted at his right-hand man who was in the next room. "You called boss?" "I have an assignment for you and I don't want it screwed up. We have the opportunity to make a huge amount money. I want the new Vice President of Mid America, kidnapped and brought here. I don't know how you are going to do it, and I don't care what it costs to get the job done, but I will not tolerate failure. Do you understand me?" "Boss, what you are asking for is practically an impossibility. She will be guarded like royalty." "Quit whining. I want results not excuses. Just get the job done! We will demand a ransom of one billion dollars for her return, and her government will pay it."

Juan packed a few necessary items and left the Hernandez Palace, as it was so often referred to outside of earshot of Hernandez. The Palace sat on a high hill overlooking Mexico City which quite often disappeared from view because of smog. It was early morning when Juan departed. He had spent most of the night stewing about what and how he should do what his boss wanted. He knew that his mission was virtually impossible and on top of that, he was really not motivated, despite the implied threat of his boss, to even try and accomplish this assignment.

That night he rolled out a blanket and slept under the stars. He had finally been able to formulate a plan and was feeling the most positive he had felt in years, at least as far as his conscience was concerned. He knew that in many respects, he was no better than Hernandez, but he was planning a change. Without a major change in his situation, he knew he was a dead man: no matter what he tried to do, the end result would be the same.

Moving under the light of the stars, Juan blended in with a one hundred of his fellow men, headed for the Arizona border. As they approached the fence, Juan slowly slipped to the end of the line and then disappeared into a place where he was alone. A ruckus broke out in the area where all the rest of the people had headed. They most likely had been spotted by a Border Patrol unit. One of his possessions was a thirty foot rope with a double hook on one end. He threw the rope up and over the fence and pulled. The hook held. Being a powerful man, he had no trouble pulling himself up and over the fence, landing on his feet in Arizona.

Over the next four nights, Juan moved only in darkness, making his way north and avoiding all people. On the fourth night, Juan connected with a contact who lived in Mesa, Arizona, a city that was a part of the Greater Phoenix Metropolitan area. He spent the next three days researching information on the Internet and finalizing his plan.

Juan took a deep breath and dialed Luc McCannon's office at Mid America's administrative and operations center outside Kansas City. It took some tough talk before he was finally put through to Luc. "Mr. McCannon, first let me tell you that it will do you no good to try and trace this call. When we have come to an agreement, I will show myself." As head of security, Luc got a lot of nutcase calls so he was naturally cool and not totally in tune with the caller. Juan said, "What I want to talk to you about has to do with your wife, Erika." That got Luc's total attention immediately. He almost crushed the handle of the phone.

"I want to set up a meeting with you," Juan said, "but it has to be just the two of us. I don't know if that is possible given all your technology of long distance listening and location devices, but at some point we are going to have to trust each other." Luc interjected, "You're going to have to give me a real good reason why I should meet with you or believe what you have to say."

Negotiations continued for thirty minutes. In the end, Luc decided to chance the meeting. They were to meet in a junk yard. The exact location had been laid out by Juan. The meeting took place at 6:00 A.M. the next morning. Ben had insisted that a couple of sharpshooters be placed so that they wouldn't be seen but could still take out Juan if things went south.

Juan told Luc the assignment he had been given from Hernandez and Hernandez's motivation behind the intended kidnapping. Juan then informed Luc in no uncertain terms that although he was obviously not going to carry out the order, Hernandez would not give up. He told Luc the only way to put this to rest would be to see to it that Hernandez was eliminated. Juan asked for Mid America citizenship and to be put under protective custody including plastic surgery.

Later that morning, Ben, Robert and Luc held a strategic discussion about Luc's experience with Juan. "I set up another meeting with Juan at the same time tomorrow to finalize some kind of agreement and direction," Luc said. "Alright," Ben said, "I have an idea floating around in my head but I need a little time to formulate it into a plan. Let's all get back together in an hour. Is that okay with you guys?" It was affirmative.

At six a.m. the next morning, Luc and Juan again met at the junk yard. "I need to ask you a few questions, Juan," Luc said. "How many young women and girls are usually at Hernandez's house?" "Why are you asking that?" Juan inquired. "You'll know soon enough. Just give me a straight answer." "There are about twenty females that are there on a daily basis, serving customers with more than just drink." "How many other servants and guards are there on a regular basis?" Luc asked. "Hernandez has two bodyguards and then there are five servants" "Could they all be bought off?" Juan hesitated before answering, and then said, "All the people that serve Hernandez are poor and if they were convinced there would no repercussions, like getting tortured and killed, they could be bought. What are you getting at, senor?"

All right Juan, here is our proposal. "You will go back to Hernandez, tell him you have contracted with a very reliable and powerful gang. They guarantee they will have Erika within three weeks. You tell him that they are so sure of themselves that they will not expect any payment until she is delivered."

"He will be ecstatic when he hears that, " Juan said, "but how can I possibly say that when I know it is not true so therefore it will not happen and in three weeks I will be a dead man?"

Luke explained, "Here is what we want you to do during that time period. One by one you will get to each Hernandez employee, the two body guards and the five servants. Tell each of them they will be paid one hundred thousand dollars each, in American currency if they will turn on Hernandez and take him out.

You will lay out the plan, and you will all act in concert with the others to end this evil man's life. You will send me the name of each servant and bodyguard, and when the deed is done, a bank account will be set up for each of them with the one hundred thousand dollars in each of their accounts. Comprendo?" "Yes but...." Luke held up his hand, "Hang on. I am only part way through this plan. You will also offer each of the young women and girls free transportation back to their homeland. Tell them that they will get enough money to help them start a new life and that they will no longer live in danger. They are to assist in your plan in the take down of Hernandez."

Luke went on to outline how Juan should go about the execution of the plan. When you have achieved this mission you will have immediate access to transportation that will return you to Mid America. You will be given a million dollars, as well as protective custody the plastic surgery you requested. You have to agree to never engage in any criminal activity. Should you be convicted of any criminal activity, we will know and you will be immediately sent to the slammer for the rest of your life."

Two weeks later, the news was dominated by details about an accident that had claimed the life of a notorious criminal in Mexico. The crime leader's staff had disappeared. It was well-known that this head of a huge sex and drug ring had a lot of young women and girls in his employ. All had been kidnapped and forced into sex slavery. They also had disappeared. There was a warrant out for the arrest of Hernandez's second in command, Juan Golez, but he also had completely disappeared.

Prior to this, Luc had refrained from bringing Erika into the conversation as he didn't want to worry her. Now that chapter in her life was closed for good. Luc sat down with Erika to tell her all about what had happened. She had continually harbored a frightening image of being recaptured. It had been a shadow, hanging over her since she had escaped from them.

After Luc had finished with this riveting story, Erika sat in her chair stunned by what Luc had told her. Then when the real impact of what he had said dawned on her, she jumped up and ran into his arms sobbing with relief and joy. Now she was free from this evil veil that had covered her for most of her life. A huge weight had been removed from her thinking. "There really are no words that can describe how I feel right now Luc, other than to say this is like bringing closure to something that has been lurking in the shadows of my mind for so long it almost felt permanent. I love you from the bottom of my heart, Luc."

CHAPTER EIGHTY-THREE

A new holiday was fast approaching. Formerly called Labor Day, it was now designated in Mid America as Freedom Day. It was defined as a day to celebrate: freedom to work, freedom to worship, freedom to pursue goals and freedom from government leaders with a 'control freak' attitude.

Ben and Erika were constantly on the move throughout the country: talking to folks, getting their ideas and comments and having some very frank discussions. Ben was at one such get-together in a smaller town in Illinois. "Mr. President," the gentleman in the front row said. Ben held up his hand, "Excuse me sir for interrupting, but would you mind addressing me as President Ben? That's a little less formal and still maintains the dignity of the office of President." That drew a nice applause from the gathering.

"Now as you were about to ask before you were so rudely interrupted......" "Thank you President Ben, the man said with a bit of a smile, I was wondering, since you obviously believe in and vigorously promote our free enterprise system, if you could expound upon that for us? It seems like there are so many definitions?"

A Mark of the Divine

"That is a wonderful question. You know that you hit my hot button with that request," Ben said with a smile. "In very simple terms, there are two basic elements of free enterprise. One consists of a Government just like the one that we campaigned for and are operating in the way we said we would—which is keeping it's hands out of your pockets as much as possible. In other words, the people should not rely on their Government for anything more than is absolutely necessary. Three words that really sum this up are 'very limited government.'

So if we have limited government, this brings us to the second element. We must rely on entrepreneurship and the rewards that accrue from it, as well as free market forces. It has been well-documented over much of the entire history of America up until a decade or so ago, that the free enterprise system identified us as a Country and set us apart from all other nations. It was the driving force behind our success."

"Our forefather's demonstrated willingness and a desire to move beyond the status quo, a willingness and driving desire to see innovation as the springboard for achievement. This was a lesson that has been passed on for two centuries. It's called entrepreneurship, and although usually associated with starting or further developing a business, it can also relate to almost any type of job or activity, because it means innovation. Innovation is what moves us past the status quo." Ben addressed the individual who had asked the question, "Sir, would you mind telling me what kind of work you do?"
"I am a high school math teacher."

"My sister-in-law is a teacher, and she is one of the most innovative persons I know. She says the only reason for her to be in front of pupils is to pass her knowledge of how things work on any given subject to her students. She is constantly experimenting and innovating with ways that help her in this quest. Utilizing a pedagogy which addresses the needs of her students makes her an entrepreneur. Compare that to the teacher who is just putting in time, doesn't have the needs of his or her students at heart. Huge difference isn't there?

What has made America successful, and what will make Mid America exceptional? Not Big Brother, but you and every person in this room and in this Country putting your best efforts forth, day in and day out, willing to continually innovate, willing to take a leadership role, and willing to take some risk. Even if that leadership role goes no further than the classroom or the factory floor, when you act in this mode you are an entrepreneur. We are a people who enjoy rewards while being able to face and accept setbacks. We are willing and able to accept the consequences of the decisions we make."

"In one sense there is always a bit of a gamble when we innovate. A part of innovation is risk-taking and the results may not be what we envisioned or it may actually cause disappointment. On the other hand, what is achieved can drive future success and be very rewarding. Those rewards don't have to be monetary rewards such as earning or making more money, but they may well lead to that. How much more rewarding can it get than when one of your former students," Ben looked at the math teacher, "returns years after graduation to look you up so that he or she can thank you for the very positive impact you made on his or her life?"

"My parting comment on this folks is to urge you to expand your thinking of the word entrepreneurship beyond a description of just those who go out and start their own business. Every one of you, regardless of your occupation, can be an entrepreneur.

I also must say, if you happen to be engaged in homemaking as your occupation, never let anyone put you into a second class category. Your job of raising our leaders of tomorrow is paramount to defining what Mid America will look like in the future. This is by far the most important job there is and probably the most challenging. Believe me, I also know how innovative you can be as you engage in the roles of a wife, mother, domestic engineer, transportation manager, home school teacher and the list goes on."

"God bless you all and remember, be the person God intended you to be. Regardless of who you are, what the color of your skin is, whether you are tall or short, heavy or skinny, physically beautiful or physically not so beautiful as defined by society, who you are inside is how you will ultimately be measured and how you are defined by God."

It took Ben an hour to finally get out of the hall where the meeting was held. He always felt that some personal one-on-one interchange was really appreciated by the folks and so that is what he gave them.

CHAPTER EIGHTY-FOUR

Amber, as First Lady, had decided to spend most of her time championing the cause of women who found themselves in an abusive relationship. She wanted to use her influence, as First Lady, to support the efforts of those who escaped that abuse. At the moment, Amber was addressing a regional conference of administrators of local city abuse shelters in a four-state area. The governors of those four states were also present as a part of the program.

"As we all know," Amber was saying, "funding is always a big problem. In spite of that obstacle you have to be congratulated for the excellent job you are performing and for the outstanding service you and your staffs provide in your communities. Unfortunately, the need for your services is not diminishing but rather, is accelerating. The incidences of domestic violence in the form of physical assault, mental abuse and murder continue to be a staggering numbers. Statistics show that the large percentage of these abuses are committed by either current or past intimate partners, whether they are boyfriends, ex-boy friends, husbands or ex-husbands. That finding is a somber reminder that we have to keep hammering away at girls and women to really get to know who you are dating or marrying. Not to do this, is to put you in jeopardy."

"Stalking also continues to be a big problem for girls and women in our society and many times this stalking leads to rape, sexual assault, and even murder. The continued teachings starting in grade school, for girls to develop an awareness, a sixth sense if you will about their surroundings is essential. Also, we are recommending that a part of physical education classes should include physical defense for all girls." That brought a resounding applause from the group.

"It is now estimated that close to a million people a year are falling victims to trafficking, with approximately eighty percent of those being girls and women. It is hard to believe that such horrendous acts against mankind are taking place. When either through rescue or escape, these people come to you, the challenge is formidable to provide the kind of help and instilled determination they need to be able to successfully get on with their lives. As most of you probably know, the Vice President of Mid America was a victim of trafficking. You most likely have read her book about for those unbelievable years in a sex ring in Mexico."

"Among racial groups, we know that Native Americans, African Americans, and Hispanics have the highest incidence in terms of sexual abuse. In light of the statistics, it is little wonder you are staggering under the needs of so many who are seeking your help. Also, we must continue educating young American girls, on the potential calamity that could await them should they get involved with a Muslim man. They need to develop the understanding of the Muslim culture and how it perceives the role of women. They have to realize that the Islam culture regarding the relationship between men and women dates back to tribal days and generally, not always, there is a deep-seated disregard for the rights of women.

Over the last three weeks, I have been meeting with representatives of all the Villages that were established prior to Mid America being born. These meetings were to ascertain whether the Villages might be able to become an integral part of your operations. The Villages were born out of necessity. They continue to provide a place of sanctuary for the millions who have lost their jobs, their money and their dignity. They are a refuge for the many suffering religious prosecution."

"This effort was initiated and developed by your President and his brother along with myself and my sister-in-law. The thrust of this gigantic effort was handled through a corporation they established called A Mark of The Divine, Inc. It was conceived shortly after the famous trench in the sand was discovered out in the desert northwest of Las Vegas a few years ago.

The brothers retired from very successful jobs at a very early age and dove-head first into this monstrous challenge to overcome or offset the meltdown of principles, morality, jobs, assets, and an inconceivable National debt brought about by relentless and unbridled government spending and a complete disregard for their constituents. It was a debt that shamefully and embarrassingly was bound to have huge negative effects on the upcoming generations. "

"Now as thousands of these people who at one time were residents of one of these villages, have been able to get their lives back together and move on, we are in a position to work with you folks to help provide housing and security for many, if not all, of your clients who are in desperate need of this kind of help."

There was a collective gasp from the audience followed by a spontaneous standing ovation. Tears were streaming down the faces of many conference participants as they realized what this could mean. When things settled down Amber continued, "All the procedures you will need to know to get this worked into your own operational guidelines are included in your packet. These packets will be given out to you as you leave. May God bless each and every one of you in a very special way for your unselfish efforts and sacrifices to help your fellow human beings."

And so it went throughout Mid America as not only the O'Neil's but hundreds of representatives, governors, and federal and state staff fanned out spreading messages of the importance for everybody to work on developing their own individual strengths and encouraging feedback and ideas. What was being accomplished in the inaugural year for Mid America was phenomenal.

CHAPTER EIGHTY-FIVE
2017 – 2019

It was January 31st, 2017. Mid America had just recently celebrated its first birthday. One year ago today Ben and Erika were elected as President and Vice President of Mid America. Both were dressed in casual wear as they sat on either side of the blazing fire in the large fireplace. The fireplace was the centerpiece of the informal room which was located in the President's residence. After much discussion the new Capitol of Mid America was named after veracious Abe Lincoln, symbolizing honesty in Mid America's government, and was christened Lincoln Town.

Ben had decided that it would be quite fitting to revive what Franklin D. Roosevelt started in 1933 and continued during his Presidency, called the Fireside Chat. The basis of the Fireside Chat concept is exude a warm, casual mood and to use common and easy to understand language, while addressing serious matters in a broadcast to the people. Ben had also started a new tradition in Presidential addresses to the Nation in that they included the Vice President.

A Mark of the Divine

During Ben's opening remarks, the TV camera people started video recording at the entrance to the Capitol, showing the beautifully landscaped and sweeping boulevard that entered the Capitol grounds. "I would like to step away from the microphone temporarily, yielding it to Eric Smith, the commentator for this newscast.

"Along this two-mile-long boulevard as you can see," Eric stated, "are wonderful life-size sculptures of several of the previous Presidents of the old United States of America. There are also sculptures of great American heroes and heroines, including Lewis and Clark, Daniel Boone, Betsy Ross (Maker of the first American Flag), and several others. At each sculpture there is a small parking area large enough for a few tour buses and several more vehicles. People can drive into the area of the sculpture, park and then read the inscriptions and summarized history. At the end of the boulevard is a huge sculpture emblazoned in gold lettering with the Ten Commandments. Isn't that an awesome sight?" Then next to that is a breathtaking depiction of God in His entire splendor with the inscription that says 'In God We Trust'."

"You can see that at this point there is a junction that branches off into three separate directions. One street leads to the Administration building and the residences of the President and Vice President, along with houses that are used by the representatives and senators. This street also leads to the Senate building and the House of Representatives. Needless to say, the entrance to this street is gated and security is at the maximum twenty- four hours a day.

Another street leads to the buildings which house the various National agencies such as security, treasury, etc.. These buildings, although quite substantial in size, are by no means gigantic. Each agency is like a trimmed and manicured lawn, pardon the metaphor, but no weeds are allowed to grow inside or out. The third street leads to the residential areas that house staff members and other employees at the Capitol along with schools, a huge community chapel that is shared by all denominations of faith, a shopping mall and several forms of entertainment."

"In what was often referred to in the media as the Eighth Wonder of the World, the Capitol grounds, which measure exactly thirty-three miles square to allow plenty of room for expansion over the next decades, were ninety percent completed in just one year. Every building is finished in rustic brick and stone. They are a humble, but at the same time a magnificent sight.

Tens of thousands of workers were a part of accomplishing this unbelievable feat from the time the first engineers arrived on site followed by hundreds of giant earthmovers. Prior to beginning construction, Robert O'Neil and his team had determined that area -Washington County, in Kansas would meet needs of the new Capitol, because the criteria for location, population, county size and several other specifications were met here. They had many meetings with the County Commissioners, and had participated in informational meetings in practically every little town in the County. They also met with the larger farmers and ranchers in the County. They had laid out a fair proposal to substantially reimburse all property holders. When it came right down to the vote, 98 percent accepted the proposal. The team disliked the law of eminent domain which gives the government the right to seize private property for public use with compensation given to the owner. They didn't even hint of this as an alternative."

"The camera is now panning the Capitol from the air. Now we are focused on the airfield on the western edge of the site. This is a private airport used only by the National Government and its invited guests. The runways are long enough to accommodate a Boeing 747 jumbo jet that some visiting dignitaries might use. The airspace over the entire site and for thirty-three miles in each direction beyond those boundaries is classified as a restricted airspace. Interestingly, the President and his team all use a fleet of business jets for all travel. There is no distinction between jets, so that it is impossible to determine by sight if the President is flying in one of these jets and there is no so-called Air Force One. The savings to the taxpayers in just this one item is huge."

Now the camera returns to the room where President Ben and Vice President Erika are seated. "Thank you Eric for being our Capitol tour guide," Ben said. "At this time, Erika and I would like to briefly discuss with you some of the many highlights that have taken place over this first year. But before we do that, I would like to say a huge thank you to the thousands of men and women who so inexhaustibly gave of their time and talent so that our new Capitol could become reality in such a short time. I would also like to thank all the members of the House and Senate, who without complaint or whining, tackled this first year's challenge with all they could muster. They labored under extremely trying conditions in temporary and even quite makeshift facilities while construction was underway. You need to be proud of their efforts and accomplishments and be sure to thank them when you have a chance."

"Erika, would you like to bring the folks up to date on the other Herculean construction project that has also just been completed, and operations are about to begin?" "Sure Ben, I'd be glad to do that. A National Prison, including a huge medical facility that will also be available to the general public and a state-of-the-art psychological clinic which is considered to be the finest such facility in the world, is near completion. There is a capacity to greatly expand all facilities on this site as the need may dictate."

"In addition to the prison, medical facilities and the psychological facilities, the site has its own airport. A small town, where most of the staff will be housed, is situated in Carbon County, Wyoming. The site compromises an area that is approximately 30 miles wide and 60 miles long. Again, the same procedures for land acquisition were used by the legal staff as were used in acquiring the site for Lincoln Town."

"I'll give you an overview so that you have a feel for what we are doing and planning to accomplish. There will be four separate incarceration facilities which will be for adult males, juvenile males, adult females and juvenile females. Within each facility there are ceiling cameras that provide continuous taping of all activities except inside the cells themselves. No contact allowed between prisoners unless under strict supervision.

Robots are being used in as many places as possible. There are only female guards in the female facilities and male guards in the male facilities."

The highest of technology is incorporated in assuring that it will be impossible for any prisoner to escape. In addition to many safeguards, there is a ten mile barrier around the entire site that is loaded with high technology instruments and apparatuses of destruction. All prisoners will work a minimum forty-five hour week. Off-site work is limited to those judged competent enough and non-violent enough to risk guarded supervision in various jobs. These will be prisoners who have progressed far enough in their rehabilitation to warrant this kind of work.

A work program on site is being initiated between the prison and some manufacturers. This is incorporated into some tech school classes that are being taught on site. Should any prisoner refuse to work, he or she will be put into solitary confinement for as long as it takes for that person to change his or her attitude.

"Our goal is to attempt to rehabilitate all prisoners, even those who are serving lifetime sentences, so that in someway they all become productive at some level. Contrary to what is happening today in most prisons, which are now being replaced by the National Prison, rehabilitation of prisoners will be an on-going process. No prisoner will be released into society even if his or her sentence has been completed, if the Prison Physiological Board's revue deems the individual unfit for release. Compare that direction with what has been happening in the past under the old system of incarceration: overcrowding, no rehabilitation, and early release due to space and costs. Many people released are far worse criminals than they were when they entered prison."

"Just one more item regarding the National Prison, and then I will have to leave the rest of this story until a later time. There will be no physical workout facilities at the Prison. This is a previous prison luxury that we believe is pure nonsense. The big percentage of the work that the prisoners will be doing will be physical labor, thus providing them with plenty of exercise. We found it quite deplorable that under the old system, various kinds of gyms and gym equipment, including weight-lifting equipment, were made available to prisoners.

Recreation facilities such as movies, etc. will be available on a very limited basis and only available to those prisoners who have shown good progress towards rehabilitation. The idea that prisoners will be sitting around on their butts, lifting weights, and working on computers, or playing organized games is history in Mid America's National Prison.

Outside contact through the use of the Internet or any other device will not be available to any prisoner. Other outside contact will be very limited and guarded. I assure you there will be no gangs within the Prison. There will be no drugs, there will be no managing of criminal activities from the Prison to the outside world, and there will be absolutely no criminal or illegal activities inside the Prison walls. Any attempt by a prisoner to become involved with anything illegal will result in heavy suspension of desired activities along with solitary confinement."

"President Ben, do you have anything else you want to say before we sign off? I see we are getting a time signal from the producers. "Yes Erika, I would like to say that due to the efforts of its citizens, Mid America's economy is rocking, unemployment is practically non-existent, and we will actually have a budget surplus by the end of the year. Let me leave you with a big 'thank you' to each and every one of you for your bravery, prayers and good old American ingenuity." "All I can add to that," Erika said, "is may God Bless you and Mid America. Be safe."

CHAPTER EIGHTY-SIX

Amber had elected to work out of their home at the Ranch, because Ben travelled back and forth between the Capitol and the Ranch. He was only in the air for a couple hours and was able to attend to business during those travel hours. Amber also felt that since Suzanne wanted to stay at the Ranch and finish out her senior year there, she should be with her as much as possible. Sandy was also spending most of her time at the Ranch as Robert split his time between Lincoln Town and the Ranch. This was Maggie's senior year. Sandy knew how important it was for her to be available for Maggie as well as Jimmy, who was in tenth grade. His needs seemed endless. So, Sandy had also elected to spend most of her time at the Ranch.

After their meetings with the people from the abuse shelters, Sandy and Amber found their time was in demand constantly as they set about overseeing a smooth transition of this added dimension to the Villages. There were thousands of women and their children who would be taking advantage of this fantastic opportunity. These women were in desperate need of not only the housing that would be afforded to them, but also the safety, rehabilitation and opportunities to find jobs and start their lives anew.

With the help of a newly formed committee of abuse center managers, Sandy and Amber, with a lot input from Erika, were able to set up the formats for interviews and orientation. What really helped was the fact that so much of what this new undertaking required was already in place in all the Villages. Nobody could know what the total impact would be on these needy people nor how the communities and the Nation, would be affected, but it would be positive and staggering. Many news broadcasts had incorporated stories arising from this phenomenal movement.

Amber, as First Lady, did go to Lincoln Town on those occasions where Ben felt she should be in attendance for some function. Erika, who was trying to be involved with Sandy and Amber as much as possible on their new project for abused women, made it to the Ranch at least a couple of times a month to offer her insights and suggestions as this massive new program was born. She also made sure that she visited a number of the other Villages as she traveled about throughout the Nation.

CHAPTER EIGHTY-SEVEN

"Hey big brother, I need to have you put your thinking cap on," Ben said. "You won't believe two of the phone calls I got this morning. First, I got a call from President Schultz out in California. He wanted to know if there was any chance we would be amiable to developing a contract with West America to handle their prisoners. He really liked what we were doing and wanted to know if we had the capacity. He said if we could come to an agreement, he'd shut down their whole prison system and transfer all their prisoners to Wyoming."

"That is quite a turn of events," Robert said, "It actually could work out quite well for both Mid America and West America. It would provide extra income for Mid America and would undoubtedly save West America a considerable amount of money. I'll get my legal team on it right away. We'll figure out what problems we may have by collaborating on international basis and see if we can get a suitable contract drawn up. You mentioned two phone calls that sounded like stunning news. What was the second one?"

A Mark of the Divine

"Governor Michelle Buchman of Nevada called me. Maybe you better sit down while I tell you what her inquiry was. She and the governors of Idaho and Utah have been having been conducting several surveys over the last three months. She said the sentiment of the citizens in all three States is running extremely high for their States to secede from West America. In her words, 'We desperately want to become a part of Mid America. May we be allowed to do this?'"

Robert let out a long sigh and rubbed his temples. "Wow Ben, in one sense that is pretty exciting. It seems that it should be feasible. I'll get another team going on that right away and have them come up with the pros and cons. It's a little different than when Mid America was formed. All the States in Mid America filed notice of seceding all at one time. You really know how to mess up a guy's weekend."

"Robert, while your team is investigating this, you better take a look at additional states possibly following suit sometime in the future." Mostly talking to himself Ben said, "What if over a period of time most of the other States in the former U.S.A. felt the same way?"

"Ben said, "One of the major issues is what criteria do states wanting to become a part of Mid-America have to meet in order to be admitted and become a part of Mid America? I would hate for us to eventually slip back into the same old program that got us into all this trouble in the first place." "That's for sure Ben. I'll have the team address the criteria, as well as other very important issues."

"You're right Robert; setting up a separate team makes sense, as this is going to be a huge decision. Its different now as compared to when we all locked arms and formed

Mid-America, all the states involved were pretty much of one mind. I think we need some pretty stringent guidelines before accepting any more states into Mid America. We sure don't want to introduce a dilution factor. If we add states, their people must subscribe to our vision of a Country actually governed by its people." "I totally agree Robert, there will have to be a lot of discussion on this subject with the legislature and the governors before any decisions can be made. Just heap this project on your plate with all the other things you have going! Will you brother?"

Robert laughed and said, "Yah, thanks brother. I think I feel a headache coming on." They chatted briefly and decided, barring something of a catastrophic nature, they would hold a little family reunion at the Ranch the weekend after next.

CHAPTER EIGHTY-EIGHT

Ben looked out the window as he felt the jet ease off on power. They had started their initial decent into the Capitol city of West America. Looking down, he could see Lake Tahoe. He always marveled at the beauty of this area with its magnificent Alpine lake. Forty-five minutes later Ben was sitting with the President of West America going over Mid America's proposal. Paul Schultz was a big guy with a middle-age paunch. Ben found him to be a very affable leader. From Lincoln Town, Ben had faxed the proposal to President Schultz three days prior to his departing. This allowed Paul the opportunity to review the proposal before Ben's arrival.

"I've looked over your proposal and discussed this with both houses of Congress. Your bid of fifty-three dollars per day per prisoner will save us an estimated thirty-six hundred dollars a year per prisoner. That amounts to a savings of approximately three-quarters of a billion dollars. We are currently spending more money on incarceration of prisoners than we spend on education. This agreement will change that shameful practice."

A Mark of the Divine

"Our lower cost has a lot to do with the size of our National Prison. Sub-contracting many phases of operation to the private sector, is proving to be another significant saving. All prison sentences require each prisoner to work forty-five hours a week during incarceration; another big savings. All of this is helping to reduce our net costs per prisoner well below the cost of any prison in the any of the America's. Our National Prison is projected to have a very high percentage of rehabilitation. Our goal is to never see, in our prison, those people who get released.

Long term, we need to bring down the tremendous rate of incarceration that we have in the Americas. The Americas have a higher percentage of their populations incarcerated than any other country in the world. Another staggering statistic is that close to sixty percent of the people who are released from prison in the Americas, will be back in prison within three years. That has been our history. It is just plain disgraceful and certainly doesn't reflect twenty-first century thinking. Just imagine what we could do to incarceration costs if we could cut the number of returnees by fifty percent or more, which is our long-term goal. Think of the benefits that will accrue to society as we are able to move this plan along."

"Ben, our Congress has agreed to your proposal. We are ready to start transporting prisoners as soon as you can take them." We have twenty large transport planes that have been modified to transport prisoners. Each plane is capable of carrying one hundred prisoners. We will allocate half of our transports to your needs starting the first of next month if that is acceptable. This means we will be able to transport up to two thousand prisoners a day if each plane is able to complete two trips per day," Paul said. "Based on that assumption we should have our prisons empty within approximately one hundred days."

Ben said, "I checked with our construction people at the National Prison. The expansion we will need to accommodate your Country's prisoners is doable in that time frame."

"Converting all our empty prisons into something useful and revenue positive, is going to take some real ingenuity and work, but we think that we can achieve this over a period of time," Paul said. "I will put you in touch with a task force we have that is working on this very thing in our Country. I know they will be very glad to share their thoughts and tell you about the actions they are taking," Ben said.

As the two Presidents shook hands and Ben departed, he felt good about the approval of the contract between Mid America and West America. On the way to the airport Ben called Jan. Her company was primarily into heavy equipment operations and sales. She had taken the general contractor bid for the National Prison. He told her that the deal he had made with West America required a substantial expansion of the various incarceration units. He asked if she could be in a position to start immediately. She responded that she could.

Ben's next stop was Salt Lake City, Utah, where he was to meet with a joint session of the state legislative bodies and governors of Utah, Idaho and Nevada, tomorrow morning at ten. That would give him time to finalize his notes before the meeting. It seemed quite unreal that these three states wanted to become a part of Mid America and he wondered if President Schultz knew that his Country had the possibility of loosing three States at some time in the future.

A Mark of the Divine

After President Ben was introduced to this very unusual joint session of state legislatures and governors, he addressed the group. "First I want to say that we, the Country of Mid America would be more than happy to have Nevada, Utah and Idaho join our Union. However, having said that, I feel it is important for you to recognize and understand the differences between West America and Mid America. I am quite sure most of you are aware of the differences of which I speak. Perhaps these differences are a factor you considered in making your request."

"Approximately three-fourths of the people in Mid America now call themselves Conservatives. When our Country was formed we dropped the idea of having a Republican Party and a Democrat Party as it was our profound feeling the current system, as a prelude to and an influence on governing had run it course and was way overdue for an overhaul.

What all this boils down to is the fact that the big majority of citizens in Mid America are fiercely independent people, who want and demand as much freedom from Government as is possible. This translates to an extremely vigorous economy which in turn means extremely low unemployment and low taxation. But it requires of its people responsibility, innovation, and sometimes, sacrifices."

Ben continued to outline the differences between Mid America and West America. He was striving to get them to understand the importance of their people knowing what would be expected of them if they were to become a part of Mid America. He stated that this understanding was crucial before any vote to join Mid America takes place. "To be blunt, we have a major concern about any change which could dilute the efforts and accomplishments we have made as a new Country."

"We need to know that the big majority of your citizens want to become a part of what we represent and stand for in Mid America." Following President Ben's speech, there was about an hour of questions and answers. He was informed the three states would be broadcasting a lot of information on his concerns over the next month before the vote. If the vote was favorable, and then they were accepted by Mid America, quite conceivably Mid America would incorporate these three states before the year was out.

As Ben made his way back to Lincoln Town, he couldn't help but wonder about other states requesting to join their Country in the future. Both East America and West America leaned considerably in the direction of being much more on the Liberal side than on the Conservative side. It was estimated that their numbers were just the opposite of Mid America in that approximately 75% related to themselves as Liberals. It would be the leaders of Mid America who would have to make the determination of whether it was a good or a bad idea to accept more states into the Union of Mid America, should the formal request be made. Ben thought this was going to be real tough issue and highly debated.

Ben mentally switched gears to the meeting which he and Erika were scheduled to attend the day after tomorrow. It was billed as the Domestic Oil Production Summit Meeting for Mid America. Besides he and Erika, it would include all the governors of all the states. Even though some States were not directly involved in oil extraction, it was important that they had a voice in this conference. Also attending would be the leaders of both the Senate and House plus a few of the top environmental scientists from the Mid America Environmental agency. One of the keynote speakers will be Adam Marlinski, the Country's leading fossil fuels expert.

Mid America's oil reserves were of such a vast quantity that not only did they have the capability of eliminating foreign imports of oil but their production could actually make Mid America a larger exporter than OPEC. Ben was very excited about this conference as the significance and outcome of this get-together could be mind boggling.

Two days later the exhausting but electrifying conference had gone off just as Ben had hoped it would. Because the environmental scientists that were present had no political agenda and concentrated only on their giving and receiving factual information, eventually all environmental concerns had been laid to rest. They accepted the new technologies to be used in drilling and extraction and approved the extra precautions projected to be taken which would substantially minimize accidents. Mid America was a giant in the making with their fossil fuel resources. What a positive impact this would have on fuel prices for the Nation's citizens and businesses.

In addition to drilling, extraction, environmental issues, and transportation, security was a big topic at the conference. Ben and Erika promised the commitment of a Special Forces unit to protect all domestic drilling and pumping stations, pipelines, oil and gas refineries and all means of storage and transportation of fossil fuels.

EPISODE SIX

CHAPTER EIGHTY-NINE
COMING OF AGE

2019 – 2020

With just a little over a year left of the first four-year terms of Congress and the Administration, and only eleven months until the second National election would be held, the scramble was on for everybody to get their agendas completed. What this Congress and Administration had already accomplished was staggering. "It's amazing," Ben said, "when you look back at these first three years of our Country, I think more has been accomplished by our Legislators and Administration in that time frame than in any twenty years of the Congress and White House in the old America."

"When you realize that a fair number of those good-old-boy politicians probably spent seventy-five percent of their time campaigning in one form or another, it is no wonder that little was accomplished," Robert said. "And just think, from myself on through the Legislature, only a very few will be involved in trying to get re-elected. This in itself has and is providing tremendous benefits to the Country. We will be staying focused on our jobs that need completion. Our job performance will be in tact right up until the time all of our terms are completed. Then we'll be replaced by somebody else. This truly is a huge benefit to the people and the Country as a whole.

"I still don't understand how the people let our whole political process deteriorate to what it did," Erika said. "I suppose when the Constitution was developed nobody could have ever visualized politics becoming like a huge profitable business with the people's wishes coming in at a distant second. If people could have just concentrated and measured the politicians on results and not on all the rhetoric they spewed, the mess which brought the Country to it's knees would have never happened."

"What do you think will be the outcome," Ben asked, "of the first real challenge to the Freedom of Speech provisions in this Country's Constitution?" "I know it probably borders on the impossible," Erika said, "but perhaps eventually a separate court will have to be set up to handle these types of issues. One of the big differences is as it relates to Christianity and Judaism. Since this really defines our Country, the change that disallows any anti-Christianity or anti-Judaism defamation was a huge leap forward in putting some parameters on freedom of speech in Mid America. Another exemplary area of our Constitution, which is likely to be challenged, is the recognition of Christianity as the official religion of the land. But since this represents a big part of the very foundation upon which our new Country was formed, any challenge like that will fail.

"You are certainly right, Erika. In spite of the mammoth job the courts will have of trying to determine whether or not some issue is Constitutional or not, I totally applaud the changes we made to the old Country's Constitution's First Amendment. I think more damage was done to the old Country under the umbrella of freedom of speech than anyone could ever possibly imagine. I am going to be sitting on the edge of my seat when these issues come before our Supreme Court. To my way of thinking such challenges are purely and simply a nasty form of individual harassment. I don't think we have a place for that in Mid America."

"Well thank the good Lord," Erika said, "we have been given this fantastic opportunity to start over and correct a boatload of missteps that worked their way into the running of the previous Country. Lawyers had certainly been allowed, over a long period of time, to confuse and confound the interpretations of so many laws of the land. Is it any wonder why the court systems were inconsistent? The wide variance in interpretations overwhelmed the appeals courts."

Ben and Erika were an unusual President/Vice President team, at least if measured by previous Administrations in the 'old Country' as it was so often referred to now. They both shared the same vision, their communications were stellar, and although Ben lead the charge, he shared a lot of ideas, duties and responsibilities with Erika. They were sitting in Ben's large but very comfortable office. It resembled a combination office and great room which you would find in many homes across the Nation. They made it a point to spend at least a half-hour every day in Ben's office, going over high-priority items.

"When we are talking about our terms ending, we didn't discuss your plans Erika," Ben said. "You know of course that under our Mid America's Constitution, you can only serve one term in a given office. However, you are one of the few who are eligible to advance to a higher office for one term if you so desire and can get elected to that office," Ben said with a smile. "I believe there is a large percentage of the voters who would very much like you to consider running for President, Erika."

Erika knew that she was being touted as the Country's next President. She and Luc and the children had held a family round table discussion about the effect it would have on all of them. "It's true; you and I haven't discussed this possibility Ben. Tell me what you think I should do." Without hesitation Ben said, "Erika, in all honesty I think you would make the finest President our new Country could possibly ever have."

The job you have done as Vice President has been exemplary and the people know it. Frankly, deep in my heart I had hoped that during the four-year term, I have groomed you for assuming the Presidency. There is nothing that would make me happier." "Ben, although I have appreciated the many opportunities for leadership you have made available to me, I didn't realize you felt that way. Thank you for the grooming and such a wonderful vote of confidence." The subject was left on the table for the time being as they moved on to more pressing issues.

CHAPTER NINETY

"Hi Luc, come in and have a seat," Ben said. "Before we get started on why I asked you to come in, I just want to tell you that Erika and I had a short conversation about her giving very serious consideration of running in the upcoming election to be our Country's second President. I know what a strain this would be on the family but for the good of our Country I hope that you both will arrive at a positive conclusion on this matter."

Not really giving Luc a chance to respond, Ben jumped right into why he had asked Luc to join him. He brought him up to speed on the big oil summit they just had and then got right into the meat of their conversation: Security for oil production, refinement and transportation.

For over an hour they went back and forth drafting the fundamentals of these security issues. Luc said, "I think we should utilize the very best, most secure communication technology we have available to us. We will need a national communications control center that monitors all activities from every single drill site, be it on water or land, to all transportation, be it by pipeline, truck, rail, ship or air. We will need this to include oil refineries and storage depots in the communications network. Within the Special Forces Group, we will need response teams stationed at strategic geographical sites, be they in the Gulf or clear up at ANWR. There will need to be two missions for the teams within this group, one to deal with accidents and one to deal with covert actions attempting to take out any part of our operations."

Ben sat back and looked at Luc. "Tell me you didn't just put this together as we have been talking," Ben said. Luc grinned and said, "I wish I was that smart, but actually Erika and I had a confab on this subject, so I have had time to start putting this whole thing together."

"What you have said makes a lot of sense. Once you have a security plan fine tuned, we'll present it to all the attendees of the summit conference. It is vitally important for everybody to be assured that we have taken every foreseeable precaution to protect our fossil fuels industries. This would certainly include using the best of technologies and having military response teams ready to deal with any potential enemy on very short notice. An enemy might send in special force teams of their own to disrupt our production, transportation or storage. Good job, Luc and I'll look forward to seeing your report in what, two weeks?" "Yes, Ben. My strategic development teams and I will have the plan together within that time frame; I'll keep you aware of our progress."

CHAPTER NINTEY-ONE

The gate buzzer sounded in the office at the O'Neil Ranch. Amber engaged the speaker, "This must be the transportation company that is bringing out Leah and her daughter?" The driver responded in the positive. The gate swung open and Amber told them to take the road all the way to big log house. Amber greeted Leah as she and her five-year-old daughter emerged from the car and bid the driver farewell. Introductions were made and then Amber said, "Leah, Stephanie please come into the house." Both carried small satchels that possessed all their earthly belongings.

After getting some tea and some cookies and some milk for Stephanie, they all went into the family room. Sandy had joined them and been introduced. The topics of conversation began with the weather and the Ranch. Sandy kept it pretty light to take away the nervousness Leah was so obviously struggling with. "Leah, would you mind just giving Sandy and myself a brief summary of the events that have led up to your seeking refuge here at the Village?"

Tentatively, but appearing more confident then what she felt Leah said, "First, Sandy and Amber, I want to thank you from the bottom of my heart for providing us this wonderful opportunity to get our lives back together. About six years ago, I married a guy that I had absolutely fallen head over heals for. I was only twenty years of age. Although we had been going together for only a short time, I thought it didn't matter because we were the perfect match. "

"A year later Stephanie was born and it was shortly after that when my husband began to change. He became more demanding and seemed almost jealous of our baby. Perhaps he thought I was spending too much time with her and not enough with him. Over the next four years, he became a control freak and abuser. At first the changes were almost imperceptible, but at long last I came to the realization that I was a prisoner."

"It started out very subtly, with his always wanting to hear about every single thing that I did while he was at work. Then, under the guise of limited income, he started controlling the number of miles I could drive in a week and the places I could go. From there it went to his taking away my cell phone, again the pretense of not having enough money.

From that point his control continued to escalate. He sold my car, and we moved to the outskirts of the town we lived in. I was virtually stranded and prevented from going anywhere without him. Then he cut up all my credit cards. I was instructed that I would have to pay cash for everything, but I had no money. He would dole out a little cash from time to time, when I told him how it would be used. Then, the physical violence began. On top of all that was the continued mental abuse as he always belittled and mocked everything I did. Life for me became a living hell."

"I don't have any family, but I had a close friend before we moved. She became concerned that she never saw me and never talked to me on the phone anymore. Through some investigative work on her own she found out where we lived. She had the intuition that things were not the way they should be with me. One day she parked near our apartment. She saw my husband leave and place a padlock on the door when he left. She came to the apartment and we talked through the closed door. To make a long story short, she convinced me that I had to leave forever. She called the fire chief and the police chief, informing them of the padlocked door. Her call triggered an immediate response."

"The fire department arrived quickly and broke down the door. My friend took us to the abuse shelter where she did voluntary work. I have been going through therapy at the shelter as has Stephanie and I think we are finally, at least mentally, going to make it. My husband was convicted and sent to prison, but unbelievably, for only a year. That year is just about up, and I fear he will have revenge at the top of his list when he gets out. I just know he will leave no stone unturned to find out where I am. I am sure he plans to punish me severely."

"What a sad story and a sad testimony to how inhumane some people can be," Sandy said, "and how screwed up the justice system is in the 'Old Country'. Has there been any indication at this time through some kind of communications that your husband will try to find you?" "The shelter helped me secure a divorce. After that we know that he has made a couple of attempts to find me through some buddies of his. Frankly I am scared out of my wits."

A Mark of the Divine

"I know that Judy went over everything about our operation with you before you left the abuse shelter to come out here, but I just want to reemphasize that you and your daughter will be completely safe here at the Village. You don't need to worry about that jerk anymore." Sandy said. "We have your house ready for you. You'll have a few days of orientation. Otherwise you can just get settled in and acquainted with your neighbors. You are starting a brand new life, Leah, and we will do everything we can to see to it that you and your daughter will develop a life that is fulfilling, fun and safe."

"Also, as a part of our indoctrination program, every able-bodied person over the age of fifteen that comes into the Village is required to complete a course in gun safety along with shooting lessons. I know that might sound a little scary, but on the other hand we as a community have been very glad this was a part of our policy. It pretty much ensures the safety of our Village." Sandy went on to explain the alarm system and all the precautions that were taken as far as security.

Leah and Stephanie stood up as did Amber and Sandy. They all hugged. Amber said, "Leah, here is a Kleenex to mop up those tears." They all laughed and it was the first time in years that Leah felt loved and safe. "There is just no way that I can express my gratitude. My daughter and I are so blessed to have been invited into your home and Village."

So another new venture for the O'Neil's was underway. They anticipated that from this point forward they would allocate up to approximately twenty-five percent of their available space to taking in families from the various abuse shelters. Erika had suggested that if the Village could afford it, they should hire a doctor of psychiatry to be on staff. They should be sure he or she had experience working with abused women and children.

From the statistics they were able to gather, the kind of occupancy ratio the O'Neil's were planning on for the abused folks, if carried out by all the Villages, should come close to accommodating the needs of all the abuse shelters in Mid America. The positive impact of this was priceless.

CHAPTER NINETY-TWO

It was just four years ago on this date that a big group sat around the large family room at the O'Neil Ranch, glued to the television, awaiting the Presidential elections' result. Now two huge community centers were once again packed with a large percentage of the Village watching the various TV's which were placed around the facilities. There was a tension and electricity flowing and ebbing through the crowds as they awaited the election results.

The Big Ben clock in the corner of the family room chimed nine and at the same time Eric Smith came on and said it wasn't too early to make the call that Erika McCannon was our Country's next President. Everybody jumped and screamed, laughed and cried and hugged and congratulated Erika. The noise from the two community centers must have been heard halfway across the State. When things settled down a bit Ben said, "well Luc, how does it feel to be First Man?!" That got a huge burst of laughter and some hoots. "The only thing I can say is somebody had to be first First Man!"

A Mark of the Divine

The celebrating went on into the wee hours. It was hard to imagine that the first two presidents of the new Country had come from the O'Neil Ranch. They all figured it must be a confirmation of some kind that the development of A Mark of the Divine, Inc. was pleasing to God.

CHAPTER NINETY-THREE
2020

All the new Legislature and the President and Vice President would be sworn in on March first, just one month from now. A month that would be hectic as all the old members would help the incoming group transition to their new job. For Ben and Erika, it was a no-brainer. She was well-groomed for her new job already. But Ben, after consulting with Erika last November, had convinced his long-time friend and State Senator Jim Peterson to run for Vice President. Jim and Erika had several meetings and Erika had told Jim that she wanted to continue the direction and tradition Ben had established as far as the working arrangement between the President and Vice President.

Now over the next thirty days, Ben, Erika and Jim would develop a lot of strategies for their upcoming term. The trio was very enthusiastic and Erika and Jim were looking forward to working together to build upon what she and Ben had accomplished in their first term.

A Mark of the Divine

When March 1st came around Ben and all the first-term legislators moved out and the new team was ready to go. "Ben, Erika and Jim were in Ben's favorite room in the President's quarters in Lincoln Town. "Well," Ben said, "I am going to say my goodbyes. I know in my heart that you two will be a fantastic team and I wish you both the very best. Ben gave Erika a big hug and said, I'll be seeing you back at the Ranch from time to time and feel free to consult with me anytime you feel the need." "I will Ben and thank...", she couldn't finish the sentence as emotions completely overwhelmed her. Then she laughed as she swiped away the tears and said, "Some President I am going to be!" Ben said, "I told you this before, and I will tell you again. In my humble opinion, you will go down in history as one of this Country's greatest Presidents. Now get to work!"

Ben turned to Jim, "You take good care of both yourself and Erika. You have no idea how excited I am that you are in the Vice President's slot." After a quick hug and a slap on the back, Ben wheeled and left. As he exited the area he couldn't help but feel both elation and a little sadness. This had been his life for the last four years. But now he was excited to get back to the Ranch and Amber and Suzanne. He had a lot of make-up work to do in a lot of different areas of his and Amber's life. He was ready to start working with the same energy as he had when he served as President of Mid America.

He had decided to drive back to the Ranch rather than fly. As anxious as he was to get back, he needed some quiet time and driving back would give it to him. He hit the button on the dash and speed-dialed Robert. "I am on my way to the Ranch and I should be in late tonight. I was thinking, all of us have not had a real vacation in about six years. What do say we pack up the families and fly down to a resort in the San Diego area for a solid week of just plain fun?" "That sounds like a great idea Ben. The kids will be ecstatic. They have never seen the ocean before. This is probably one of the best ideas you have ever had!"

CHAPTER NINETY-FOUR

"I think I could get used to this," Amber said to Ben as they lounged in their chairs on the sand beach and watching the kids have an absolute ball. "I think you have the right idea Amber," Sandy said. "What do you guys think? Should we just sell the Ranch and stay here on the beach?" Everybody laughed and got right into the swing of things as they enjoyed their first day of what would be a glorious, relaxing and well-deserved vacation. Even the kids, needed some rest and recreation pretty badly. "Thanks Ben for coming up with this great idea," Robert said.

"Hey kids," Ben said, "we probably should do some sightseeing. What do you think?" Everybody else thought this was a good idea as did the kids. "Alright, they are going to be feeding the alligators just down the beach in a about a half-hour. How about we go there? Then as a special treat, I'll take you to the marina where the neatest thing in the whole world happens," Ben said. "What is that Uncle Ben?" Jimmy asked. "Everyday, right at three o'clock in the afternoon, two huge whales swim into the marina and come right up to the big dock. Then all the kids that are there jump on their backs. The whales take them all for a long ride out into the ocean and back. So what do you think? Would you like to do the alligators and the whales?"

Jimmy, Maggie and Suzanne all stood there looking at Uncle Ben. Jimmy's one eyebrow went up, and he thought, *is this for real, I wonder if he is pulling our leg again.* The girls were thinking the same thing, but nobody was saying anything. No longer able to hold it, a smile started to spread across Ben's face as he looked at the facial expressions on the kids. Then he busted out laughing. The kids hollered and launched themselves at Ben, tipping him backwards into the sand. They all were laughing and rolling around in the sand really giving their Uncle Ben a friendly pounding. Ben thought, *I think the kids are getting to old to appreciate a good story anymore!*

As the sun was starting to set, the ocean had calmed and life just couldn't get any better. They were all making their way up to the lodge from the beach when Suzanne started singing God Bless America, and all of the rest joined in. As they sang, the adults in particular were thinking that the song was written for old America, which they had left behind, yet the new America—Mid America—was indeed blessed by God. It was truly their home sweet home, land that they loved.

CHAPTER NINETY-FIVE

The O'Neal's were relaxing in their water-front cottage, listening to soft music on Mid America radio, a powerful station whose broadcast reached all three of the Americas. The music was suddenly interrupted. "This is Eric Smith with a late-breaking news bulletin. An Unidentified Flying Object was sighted today, over the Amargosa Desert, northwest of Las Vegas. It emitted a brilliant golden light which was painful to the eyes of observers. Although it was a very dark, cloudy day, with minimal light from the sun, no artificial light was necessary to perform even the minutest task, once the UFO appeared. Than, it vanished after a very brief interval."

"Now, here is Page 2. The Line in the Sand has disappeared! According to a high-ranking military source, there are no clues as to the identity of the UFO, nor to the disappearance of the thirty-three mile long trench which has existed for eight years in the desert. The trench just simply disappeared.

This is truly a heart-stopping phenomenon or, we are witness to another miracle and message from God. Listen carefully to the next part of this stunning announcement. A trench emitting a golden glow of the same dimensions as The Line in the Sand, has been discovered today in the Chihuahuan desert of Mexico. The trench was discovered this morning by a private pilot flying over the desert twenty miles west of the town of Chihuahuan."

"You can certainly draw you own conclusions, but for my money, its more than just a coincidence that this trench is discovered in Mexico on exactly the same day The Line in the Sand disappears in West America."

"The Lord works in mysterious and wondrous ways.... We'll keep you up to date on further developments. This is Eric Smith wishing you a great day.

*****

Authors note: Although this is a work of fiction, it is my sincere hope it will give you pause, thinking of political and judicial decisions affecting our way of life. We need to realize how fragile life really is and how precious our freedom of religion, of speech, and the freedom to pursue happiness really are.

We also need to recall that freedom hasn't come easily. Hundred's of thousands of American men and women have given their lives, most at a very young age, so that Americans can be free. The sacrifices of so many who have gone before us, not only on the battlefield but in our schools, our businesses, our churches, and our families should not be squandered. Those sacrifices should be as torches to light the way for our continually building a better America for all Americans.

Securing and maintaining freedom is the responsibility of every citizen and in my humble opinion. You do not inherit freedom; you earn it and those who would mock that stance ought to find a different Country to call home. When we come to believe that being a citizen involves a larger dimension than our personal lives, own families, and our jobs, the time will have arrived when we no longer need government to dictate the type of life our political leaders think is in our best interests.

Russ Brown

About Russ Brown

I am a retired CEO of an Upper Midwestern company whose primary activities encompassed retailing, wholesaling, distribution and light manufacturing.

<u>Some</u> of my experiences that I can draw on include:
- Truck driving, construction, administration, advertising, sales and executive management
- Served in the Armed Forces
- Attended the University of Idaho and University of North Dakota
- Served on many boards including several industry trade association boards
- Served as the president of a national trade association board with offices in Washington, D.C.
- Served on a bank board for several years
- Was awarded the SBA's Small Business Person of the Year award for the State of North Dakota
- Was awarded the State's Innovator of the Year award
- Served as President and CEO of the company I worked for

A Mark of the Divine

Father of six children, thirteen grandchildren and ten great grandchildren
Married fifty four years.
In my humble opinion, this all relates to having achieved a Doctorate in Life.
Relative to the novel, that portion of my career that I was in Sales and Sales Management, I called on farmers and ranchers from North Dakota to Texas, crisscrossing the Plains and putting on hundreds of meetings.
I did self publish a novel approximately ten years ago to gain some experience

PROMO FOR 'TURNING THE STAMPEDE'

Dear Reader,

Here is a novel you just do not want to miss out on reading!

This is a multi-layered futuristic adventure that offers solutions to many of our current dilemmas, many of which would be entirely plausible with some modest advancement in technology. Bold and innovative, this tale is based on a mandate from God issued to four gifted and extraordinary men who are charged with implementing four very basic changes to America as we now know it.

In concert with the governors of all fifty states and their chosen representatives, the Four, as they are called, go about reversing crime and poverty, establishing government accountability and regaining control over the media. With an underlying theme of Christian commitment, the four visionaries eventually create a utopian community that serves as a headquarters for this momentous undertaking.

Exciting, uplifting and provocative; Turning the Stampede will challenge all readers to think more seriously about our contemporary predicament and our own positions within the family of man.

Made in the USA
Charleston, SC
30 July 2011